Readers Love Rebecca Raisin

'Absolutely loved this book!'

'A lovely feel-good story'

'A real gem of a story, loved it'

'Enjoyable holiday read'

'Full of anticipation, a real page turner'

REBECCA RAISIN is the author of several novels, including the beloved Little Paris series and the Gingerbread Café trilogy, and her short stories have been published in various anthologies and fiction magazines. You can follow Rebecca on Facebook, and at www.rebeccaraisin.com

Also by Rebecca Raisin

Christmas at the Gingerbread Café
Chocolate Dreams at the Gingerbread Café
Christmas Wedding at the Gingerbread Café

The Bookshop on the Corner
Secrets at Maple Syrup Farm

The Little Bookshop on the Seine
The Little Antique Shop under the Eiffel Tower

Celebrations and Confetti at Cedarwood
Brides and Bouquets at Cedarwood Lodge
Midnight and Mistletoe at Cedarwood Lodge
Christmas at Cedarwood Lodge

Rosie's Travelling Tea Shop
Aria's Travelling Book Shop

The Little Perfume Shop off the Champs-Élysées

REBECCA RAISIN

ONE PLACE. MANY STORIES

HQ
An imprint of HarperCollins*Publishers* Ltd
1 London Bridge Street
London SE1 9GF

This paperback edition 2020

1

First published in Great Britain by
HQ, an imprint of HarperCollins*Publishers* Ltd 2020

ISBN: 9780008389161

Printed and bound in Great Britain by
CPI Group (UK) Ltd, Melksham, SN12 6TR

For Jeff. Like Del in this book we'll always wish for just one more day …

Chapter One

Sunlight blistered the window of the car, shooting in bright prisms of light as I unfurled, shaking the grogginess of travel fatigue. The chauffeur came to a slow stop at the entrance of an apartment just off the Avenue des Champs-Élysées. Goggle-eyed, I stared at my new lodgings, awed at the grandeur, from the wrought iron balconies to the elaborate stone work surrounding the windows whose white shutters were thrown open to receive the breeze. Planter boxes housed a riot of red flowers which spilled over in search of the sun.

I was going to live *here*? A place so wildly different from the family ranch in Michigan, it may as well have been on another planet. I thanked my lucky stars once more.

'*Mademoiselle*,' the driver said smoothly. 'Aurelie will meet you at the entrance.'

'Thank you, *Monsieur*.' With brisk efficiency he exited the car and opened my door, took my bag, and led me to the grand entrance.

'Do you need anything else?' he asked in heavily accented English.

I shook my head and smiled. 'No, I'm all right. Thanks for the lift.' I waved him goodbye as he sped off, blasting his horn at unsuspecting pedestrians. From what I'd seen so far, the French drove like they were competing in Le Mans, hair-raisingly fast, beeping and cornering like they had someplace special to be.

I checked my watch and glanced up. A second story curtain shivered as if someone stood just behind it. Aurelie? I clutched my small suitcase close and waited while doubt grabbed a stranglehold.

What if I was out of my depth here? What if the other contestants all knew more than me with their formal training and chemistry degrees? What if … I gave myself a stern talking to – no more *what ifs*. I was just as good as anyone else, if not better! So I'd struggled a little without Nan when it came to composing new formulas; I was sure it was just a stage and I'd soon be back to my best with my secret weapon, Nan's trusty perfumery bible. And I had passion, enthusiasm, *and* the desire to win.

Honestly, it could have been Mars and I'd have been happy to escape the gossipy confines of aptly named Whispering Lakes and everything I'd left behind.

The application process for the *Leclére Parfumerie* competition had been interminable, with rigorous testing in every facet of perfumery. I'd made videos, sent perfume samples, been grilled by the *Leclére* management team over Skype about perfume regions, produce, blending, extraction techniques, ageing, and marketing strategies. They'd frowned at first when I explained I used perfumery almost like a tonic for all that ails, so I soon stopped mentioning that and focused on wowing them with secret formulas I'd developed with Nan. Thankfully, she'd left me them as a legacy, but I knew I needed to step out from the shadows and make my own again soon. It felt so wrong without her, that's all. Like part of me was missing.

It had taken months to get to the last round of the application process; so many times I thought I'd bomb out, so when I got *The Call* I felt like I'd earned my place. And the timing couldn't have been better. This was my chance to escape small town living, and take my perfumery to the next level.

The grand prize was an impressive amount of money, and the chance to design a perfume range which would open a lot of doors in the notoriously cliquey world of fragrance.

So here I was, in the most romantic of cities. The *Leclére Parfumerie* store was just down the street; I couldn't quite make it out but the alluring scents of jasmine, cedar, and French vanilla drifted into the summer day, beckoning to me like some kind of fragrant Pied Piper. Could I resist the urge to follow my nose? The mélange of aromas was intoxicating and warranted further investigation …

As I dithered about taking a quick peek, my scarf disentangled itself and flew across the street, the delicate silk undulating in the wind. Without thinking I stepped off the curb to grab it, just as a car whooshed past perilously close, sending me sprawling backwards to the pavement. With an *oomph* I landed hard, hurting both my *derrière* and my pride.

Taking a shuddery breath, I caught the eye of an attractive stranger across the road. His face was etched with concern, his deep green eyes clouded with worry. Red-faced, I shrugged in apology to the man, the witness of my near miss. Our gazes locked for fraction of a second. Time stopped and my lonely heart skipped a beat. That feeling was quickly replaced by mortification, so I closed my eyes and counted to ten, trying to steady my heart. When I looked up again, he gave me a brief nod and continued on, striding down the Champs-Élysées, hands in his jean pockets, black hair ruffled and windswept.

Whew! I reminded myself I wasn't in Whispering Lakes anymore and couldn't just blithely step out on the road like I could back home. I took some comfort in the man whose concern had given me pause. And a little zap of longing too.

Standing up, I patted myself down and straightened my skirt just as Aurelie appeared. With immaculately coiffed hair and make-up she walked surefootedly in high heels and came to greet me, smelling of Indian rose, a scent I adored. She had the posture of a dancer, and was lithe and graceful, a trait it seemed many French women shared. Was that glamour something they were all born with? Or was it something they were taught? I envied it. My newly purchased clothes suddenly seemed gauche, so obviously chain-store bought.

'Welcome, Del.' She smiled graciously and ushered me into a luxurious foyer, all gilt and dark wood, velvet draperies, the scent of polish and whispers from the past. It was grand and sumptuous, and I had to work hard not to stand there slack-jawed with wonder.

Aurelie smiled as if she knew what I was thinking. 'Welcome to Paris,' she said in thickly accented English. 'I'll to take you to your room so you can settle in. Hopefully Seb will be along later to greet you.'

Hopefully? Sebastien had been promoted to head of *Leclére Parfumerie* after his father's death, but so far I'd had no contact with him despite the myriad of calls that had gone back and forth between me and the management team in the lead up to the competition. Truth be told, I itched to meet the enigmatic man because there was so little known about him. All my internet searches had come up blank.

'I'm looking forward to meeting him,' I said as a yawn got the better of me. Damn! It smacked of bad manners and my nan would have told me so in no uncertain terms.

'You must be tired from all that travel?' Aurelie said with a smile.

'Yes,' I laughed. 'I binge-watched TV shows on the flight when I probably should have tried to sleep.' Who knew air travel was so fun? From the little bags of peanuts to the plastic flutes of champagne, I'd said yes to everything offered, delighting in it all. And now I was too wound up to feel anything other than excitement and a new level of jitters.

'Enjoy every moment, I say. Life is for living.'

There was a real warmth in the French woman; she wasn't the least bit standoffish like I'd presumed the Lecléres would be. They'd shunned the press for years claiming their perfumes told their own stories and they refused to muddy those with their own, so I expected her to be more contained, less friendly.

After the death of their patriarch, Vincent, things were changing. It was out of character for the family to open their doors and let strangers in. Was son and heir Sebastien going to make his own mark on the world of perfumery? Were they going to expand the business? Were they secretly holding the competition to find another head perfumer? So many questions remained unanswered.

Sebastien was a master at eluding the paparazzi and after many years they'd eventually given up, so what the man looked like was a mystery. I imagined the stereotypical perfumery nerd; the typical pinched-face, thin-lipped, starved-of-sun type. Sad as it was, I could've used a good dose of vitamin D myself.

'Come this way. I want to show you something,' she said and led me back outside.

I followed Aurelie's brisk pace, and then came to a sudden stop. Before me stood the wondrous *Leclére Parfumerie*. At the sight of the legendary boutique my pulse raced. I'd dreamed of stepping into this fragrant nirvana for years! Any good perfumer revered *Leclére* and its heritage; it was famous the world over because Vincent had turned the art of making fragrance on its head and revolutionized scent, but the store resembled an old apothecary, and was even more breathtaking in person. 'Oh, Aurelie, this is like something out of a dream!'

'Our little version of Wonderland …'

The dark stone façade of the store was weather beaten and grey with age. Thick teal-blue velvet ruched draperies graced the edges of the window. Inside, antique chairs in hues of royal blue sat solemnly in front of golden display cabinets. Knotty and scarred cabinetry lined the walls, and housed a range of lotions and potions. A black and white portrait of the master himself, Vincent Leclére, hung centre stage. The eccentric man with kind eyes and a secretive smile.

Perfume bottles glowed under soft spotlights. They were unique to each other; some were fringed with delicate gold beading, others had sparkling crystal stoppers. What magical scent did they contain? It was all I could do not to step inside and test them all on the soft skin on the inside of my wrist. Just as I pulled myself from the window I caught sight of a woman who looked so much like that red-haired, powerhouse singer from the UK. When that famous bawdy cackle of hers rang out I was certain it was her.

If rumors were true, *Leclére* perfumed the biggest names in showbusiness, but of course the family never uttered a word about their famous clients. 'Is that …?' Today was no different; Aurelie gave me the ghost of a smile and just lifted a brow.

Aurelie pointed out this and that of special significance through the window – a pretty pink high-back chair that had once belonged to a princess long gone from this world, and was gifted to Vincent, along with her antique dressing table where customers now sat and stared at their reflections. Did the princess visit the store late at night, the mirror a portal from another world? As farfetched as the idea was, the perfumery gave you that kind of impression, that it was a place where magic abounded.

And it was so French, I felt as though I'd stepped into a vintage postcard. Even though Jen wasn't here, I could hear her voice. *Would you look at that,* she'd say, or *aren't you a lucky thing getting to visit Paris?* If only my twin sister Jennifer could see the perfumery! She'd be clutching my arm and exclaiming at everything like a child.

There was a dull ache in my heart when I thought of her, a quiet thump that reminded me we were under different patches of sky for the first time ever. She was the girl who mirrored my movements, finished my sentences and was identical to me in every way except she was born with no sense of smell. Incredible really, when I lived, breathed and dreamed fragrance. Still, we had planned on opening our own business. The perfumery boutique we envisaged, our empire, the thing that would take us from small town Michigan and catapult us into the stratosphere, was on hold. *Indefinitely*. It still smarted, to be honest, the way she just gave up on me. Never in a million years did I see that coming – not from my twin, the girl who wanted the same things as me. Or so I'd thought.

But I was here now, fresh start and all that.

'You'll have more time to explore the perfumery,' Aurelie said, bringing me back to the present. 'But for now, let me show you to your home for the next little while.'

Back at the apartment, Aurelie glided noiselessly upstairs while I clomped behind her, hefting my suitcase and trying not to huff and puff like I was out of shape. The space was rich with the scent of French cooking; buttery garlic, white wine, fresh thyme, and something delectable slowly simmering, its intoxicating flavors wafting through the walls.

'Down the hall to the left is a sitting room and there's a shared kitchen and dining room just past that. If you want anything in particular, let me know. You have a mini kitchenette in your room, but any proper cooking will have to be done in the shared kitchen. I trust you'll enjoy it here.'

I nodded my thanks.

'This is where you'll stay with your roommate, our Parisian entrant Clementine. If you need me there's an information pack on the bedside table with my contact details. The afternoon is yours, though there's not much left of it. Dinner is at eight o'clock at our apartment. Sebastien will be there to welcome you.'

'*Merci*, Aurelie,' I said mustering a smile. There'd be plenty of time to size up the other contestants at dinner, to find out where they were from and most importantly about their perfumery. I was eager to make friends with people who didn't know every last detail about me the way they did back home.

Here I'd just be me, not Jen's twin, not the daughter of wandering hippies. It could be a reinvention, of sorts. Alone, I would learn about myself in a way I hadn't before. Out of the fishbowl, and into one of the most beautiful cities in the world. Who would I be?

Chapter Two

Inside my new abode, I slung my handbag on one of the beds and gazed around. While it was economically sized, it was immaculate. Two double beds took up the majority of the space and were dressed in fine white linen with plump European pillows. The room was light and bright and utterly Parisian with little touches here and there to make it homely. A vase of fresh peony blooms sat on a chest of antique drawers and perfumed the space. There was a small bathroom with plush white towels, and by the balcony was the kitchenette, which was really only an island bench with coffee and tea supplies and a small bar fridge underneath. I resisted the urge to call my sister, as I'd normally have done. I had to prove I could live without her; I didn't need to check in every five minutes anymore. Did I?

Outside from the balcony, I caught a glimpse of the Arc de Triomphe standing elegantly as it had done for hundreds of years. The Avenue des Champs-Élysées was abuzz with tourists, cameras slung around necks, and maps held aloft, ice creams melting down hands. Cars zoomed up and down and a world of accents bounced towards me. It was so damn hectic!

A commotion rang out down the hall, and I turned to the sound, straining to make out what was being said.

A loud French voice carried, along with the rolling of a suitcase or two.

'*Excusez-moi*, out of the way, please. *Ooh la la*, these are heavy.'

I could smell the woman before I could see her. Her perfume was an intense mélange of sultry fig bursting with the intense sweetness that comes with ripe fruit.

'*Bonjour, bonjour*, coming through.' It sounded like she was barreling people out of the way as she stomped noisily down the hall looking for her room, *our* room. I held my breath for a moment. Did she always make such a loud entrance?

A few moments later the door flew open and there she stood.

'Del!' she said, launching at me, hugging me to her as if we were long-lost friends, squishing the breath from my lungs. 'I'm Clementine, and I've 'eard all about you. The American girl with the best nose in the business.' When she freed me, I gulped for air, before taking in my roommate. She was exquisite with her voluptuous figure, form-fitting dress and heavily rouged cheeks. Next to her curvaceous body, I felt suddenly boyish with my straight up-and-down physique.

My mousy-brown waves and more naturally made-up face were no match for her cascading blonde curls, bright blue doe eyes, and bee-stung scarlet lips. Her style was quite incredible, almost burlesque in its extravagance. I was no slouch in the fashion department; I followed trends just like the next girl, but Clementine was something else. It took guts to dress so outrageously, *and* pull it off.

'*Bonjour*! I love your outfit,' I said, giving her a wide smile.

She paid no heed to the compliment, instead shaking her head and sighing theatrically. 'This?' She pointed to her hourglass figure, swathed in ruby-red velvet. 'I have a little … 'ow you say, addiction to the cherry *clafoutis*. Nothing can cure me of it except another bite of the sweetness itself.' She tutted. 'French women don't get fat …? That's what is said, *non*? Pah! French women can do whatever the 'ell they like! Fat, skinny, square, triangle, I don't care! No one shall dictate to me! You know my *maman*?'

Of course I didn't, but that had no bearing on the story as she continued. 'Well, she says I'll *never* get married if I eat the way I do. Says I'm not a real Parisian with my appetites! I should show *restraint.*' She reeled back as if it was a dirty word. 'But why? Why should I deny myself pleasure? A man will surely love *all* of me, if he's the right man.' She patted the soft swell of her belly. 'And until then I'll eat whatever I please, whenever I please.'

Another girl, with vivid red hair straightened to a shine sashayed past, stopping to lean on the door jamb. 'It's not a matter of depriving oneself, Clementine, it's simply a matter of balance.' The redhead conveyed in one long look that she thought Clementine was on a slippery slope to *im*balance. The pair obviously knew each other, but the girl had an English accent.

'Pah,' Clementine said. 'That's why these girls are always so *misérable.*' She waved her French-polished nails at the redhead. 'They're hungry.'

My mind had to work overtime to make sense of Clementine's hastily delivered, emphatic *and* heavily accented monologue – and to keep my laughter in check. She was so dramatic and more overt than the Parisian women I'd come into contact with so far.

The English girl rolled her eyes and stuck out her hand to me. 'I'm Kathryn, from London. You'll get used to Clementine – she behaves as if all the world is a stage, that's all.'

I laughed, liking both women on sight. 'How do you two know each other?'

Clementine gave an airy shrug. 'Kathryn lived in Paris when she took a perfumery class here a million years ago. Back then she ate the cherry *clafoutis* and she was a lot 'appier, I can tell you that.'

'I studied here a few years back, but Clem would have you believe I'm in my twilight years or something. I might have imbibed more back then but people mature, they grow up. Well *some* of us do.' She gave Clementine a pointed stare.

You could sense their comradery even though they mocked

one another, something that was more for my benefit.

'I'm Del, from Michigan, America.' Not Del 'n' Jen. Jen 'n' Del. Gosh, that felt weird.

'We know,' Kathryn said, her eyes twinkling. 'And rumor has it, you're one to watch out for.'

I cocked my head, debating how to answer. 'I don't know about that.' Better to downplay any skills they thought I had. I didn't want them ganging up against me when the challenges began.

Kathryn folded her arms. 'Don't be so modest,' she said, and flicked her hair. 'We know all about you, your beloved nan taught you perfumery ...' The sentence was left hanging.

How did they know about me and Nan? We came from nowheresville ...

'Who told you?'

'It's not hard to find out information if you know where to look,' Kathryn said. 'Social media is a marvellous thing.'

'*Oui*,' Clementine cut in. 'And so what if you 'ave ambition for eyeballs and a nose that could rival Anais Laurent ...'

I laughed at her transparent attempt to get me to admit I was one of the main contenders. No chance I'd be that easily fooled. While it was clear they'd done some digging, they really didn't know much in the scheme of things.

'I think comparing me to Anais Laurent is stretching it a little.' Anais Laurent had paved the way for female perfumers in what was once a man's world. Her nose was legendary, and her perfumes still sold well despite being designed half a century ago. Every perfumer desired a formula so popular it lived on long after you'd left this mortal coil, just like Anais.

Clementine narrowed her heavily made-up eyes. 'There's no room for humble 'ere, Del. Better that you admit you're in contention for the prize and then we can all play fair, *non*?'

Straight-shooting Clementine fascinated me, but I kept my game face on. 'Of course! And I hope we can all be the best of friends.'

'We already are.' Clementine tossed her bag on the double bed closest to the balcony, the bed I'd already laid claim to. 'So tell us,' she said. 'How did you find the selection process? Wasn't it *intense*?'

I laughed. 'You can say that again! Towards the end I didn't think I'd make the cut. There were so many tests! And taking them on the fly on a video call …'

She rolled her eyes. 'Right? My 'ands shook so bad on those video calls, it was lucky I didn't drop my *parfum* and smash it to a million pieces. But look, we're here! What made you enter, Del?'

I folded my arms, considering. 'So many reasons: meeting the mysterious Lecléres, adventure, wanderlust …' And the desire to win. 'Perfumery has always been my happy place.' Without Nan, I'd struggled to find the joy in creating, struggled to find the joy in anything, and Jen figured this competition might help me find my way back … Or had she orchestrated this so I'd be out of the way?

'I see,' said Clementine, drawing me back. 'From what we 'eard, you had plans to open a perfumery boutique in New York, but your sister got cold feet. That must have been tough for you, especially as you're so close. And she gave it all up for the love of a man …?'

I stood there dumbstruck, wondering how she could know such a thing. I wasn't one to overshare, and I most certainly didn't pour my sorrows out over social media. 'How could you possibly know that, Clementine?' I tried to sound relaxed, but the words came out clipped.

'I 'appen to know a few people in Manhattan and they mentioned that you'd forfeited your bond for your cute little pop-up shop before you'd even set foot in New York. *Tragique, non?*'

I swallowed back sudden tears and turned away, pretending to hunt for something in my bag. What a stroke of fate that she'd known that part of my past. Giving up the pop-up shop had

13

cut me to the quick but I couldn't go to New York alone and without Jen's half of the investment. Basically, the decision was all down to money – without her I just plain couldn't afford it. And it hurt, knowing that prime piece of real estate would probably never be available again, not in my budget. Jen would have loaned me what she'd saved but I just couldn't ask her. Not if she wasn't joining me there.

'Now 'ave I upset you?' Clementine asked.

I pasted on a smile. 'Not at all. I'm still going to New York, but first I wanted to see Paris.' *And win the money to go to New York … Did desperation shine in my eyes?*

'Right, well, we have to keep an eye on Anastacia, apparently she's a little bit of a wizard when it comes to perfumes. I hear she's notoriously egotistical though,' Kathryn said, I think sensing a subject change was in order.

Quick as the click of fingers exhaustion hit me. Was it Clementine and her digging or the memories it conjured? I pulled my shoulders back – I was here to win, damn it, and win I would.

The girls were competitive but at least they weren't shy about revealing it. They didn't hide the fact they wanted to win the high stakes game and it was brave to show their hand so openly. Alliances aside, at least I knew what I was in for. Didn't I?

Paris suddenly felt like a long way from Whispering Lakes …

Chapter Three

'I'm going to meet a friend before dinner,' Clementine said, giving me a bawdy wink that helped ascertain the friend was of the male persuasion. 'Back soon!' She air kissed me and left, swinging her hips like a diva.

My phone buzzed and Jen's name flashed. *'Bonjour, Mademoiselle,'* I said, adopting a woefully bad French accent to mask the fact I didn't quite know how to act with my sister any more. Such a foreign feeling, and one I hoped would fade.

'Look at you, all Frenchified already!' she said. I'd never been away from Jen before and now we were on entirely different continents. 'So fill me in. How was the journey? Is Paris as beautiful as they say?'

Falling back on the bed, I launched into story mode as if nothing had changed and I wasn't disappointed in her. I told her every little thing *except* the part about stepping into oncoming traffic and the gorgeous stranger I'd locked eyes with for the briefest moment. No need for her to worry about me in the big bad world.

'So no hot men? The pilot, the driver, the *Leclére* staff? I bet they're all gorgeous in that broody French way?'

I tutted, 'I'm not here for love, Jen. As you well know.' And it was a bit of a sore point considering …

She huffed. 'Surely there's time for a little romance in the city of love?'

'City of *light*,' I corrected. She knew how important this competition was and what I'd given up to do it. Namely my own dead-end job and financial security. If I didn't win, I'd return home to unemployment, and I had no intention of letting that happen. Especially now.

'*But* French men are hot, like throw-caution-to-the-wind hot, right?' Jen's latest project was pushing me to find a soulmate. But only because she'd fallen in love, mind you. Suddenly she was all, *oh look at that guy, he's got marriage material written all over him*, or *knock me down that guy looks like he'd make adorable babies, why don't you ask for his number?* Like I was some kind of desperado, champing at the bit to get married when I clearly was not.

The dreamy romantic in her was new, and I wished she'd get over it already. Sure, I wanted the fairytale too, love, marriage, babies, but first I needed my career to take off. Love would have to wait. Besides, I was so overwhelmingly bad at dating. My previous relationships had all fizzled out because when I got lost making perfume all else faded to black, and that wasn't conducive to a healthy relationship. Turning up to a dinner date a day late one too many times had put paid to any chance of love; besides, no one had made my heart sing. Depressing, really, since my thirties were creeping up.

Whoever I met had to be as important to me as perfumery, and when you come from a town as small as I did, it wasn't hard to find yourself single. The dating pool was more of a puddle really.

Perfumery was the key to a decent future. Security. As much as I loved my folks, I didn't want to end up like them, unemployed drifters with no ambition, relying on us to care for them.

'Well?' she said again. 'You've met someone, haven't you?'

'What? No. I've been here for all of five minutes!' I said

exasperated. 'Look, I'm sure there's plenty of princes among the frogs, but who cares? That's the last thing I'll be worrying about.' With the proverbial rug pulled from under me, I had to plow ahead and chase a different future or else I'd end up back home, a failure, my five-year plan now just words on parchment. Things seemed more precarious than ever before. Sure, I'd still go to New York, but it wouldn't be until I had the funds, and so many obstacles stood in my way.

'It would seriously be a waste to go all the way to Paris and not kiss a Parisian ...' she said dreamily, caught up in the romance of Paris, and not thinking sensibly.

'And lose the competition and come home and beg for my job back? The job where I *sell* perfume, not make it? Nope. Not going to happen! New York is calling ...' The past was the past, and there was nothing I could do to change it, but still, that feeling of abandonment lingered just under the surface and bubbled up and out.

We lapsed into silence, which was becoming a new habit. This strange shift in our lives provoked these sorts of awkward moments and I was at a loss how to fix them or what to say. Normally we'd be chatting at a hundred miles an hour, never running out of steam.

Eventually with a half sigh she murmured, 'Nan would be so proud of you, Del, living in the perfume capital of the world, chasing those dreams.'

Our dreams had become only *my* dreams. How could she give it all up for a guy?

I put a hand to my heart, feeling the same ache as I always did when I thought of my nan. 'As crazy as it sounds,' I said, 'sometimes I think Nan orchestrated this adventure.'

I'd loved perfume since I was a child when my nan had discovered that I had the 'nose' for it – a highly tuned ability for olfactory compositions. Since then Nan and I had been conspirators and I still missed her so much it hurt.

She'd been more than my nan, she'd been my best friend, conspirator and stand-in mom when my own was braying at the sky, or off on one of her adventures, her responsibilities scattered like the fuzz of a dandelion flower on the wind.

Jen spoke softly. 'If anyone could pull strings from the afterlife it would be Nan, but this was all you, Del. This is your chance to learn from the masters, and I hope you'll forget all about me and everyone in Whispering Lakes, and focus on perfumery.'

She spoke as though she was giving me permission to let her go. We'd always shared everything, and I didn't see why things should change, even if she was head over heels in love. But the days of mirroring each other, and finishing each other's sentences were clearly over.

They were all on my mind though; my beatnik parents, Pop with his melancholy eyes. And Jen who'd broken my heart the way only sisters can do.

'As if I'd forget about you, Jen. Jeez.'

I didn't quite know where I fit in the world without my twin. In the past, any decisions were made with both of us in mind. A sort of seasickness crept up on me. I felt untethered and adrift without her, knowing I had to go forward on my own and wondering if life would be the same, if I'd ever truly be happy again, alone.

'Del, live in the moment, soak up as much as you can. This will be the making of you. Make some new friends. Be brave, fearless, and flirt!'

'Yes, Ma'am,' I said, wishing the worry would float on past.

With laughter in her voice she said, 'You're saluting, aren't you?'

I dropped my hand. 'Maybe.'

'What are the other contestants like?'

I told her all about Clementine, the OTT Parisian, and about Kathryn, the soft-spoken Londoner. 'Sebastien will be there tonight, so I'll finally get to meet the enigma himself. We're all having dinner with the *Leclére* team. A sort of welcoming party,

18

I guess. And I can finally see who I'm up against.'

She picked up my nervousness in the nuances of my voice. 'They might have had proper perfumery training, Del,' she began in a pep talk tone. 'But they didn't learn from Nan! Textbooks and chemistry teachers can't compare to Nan's lessons at the perfumery organ. No one can compete with that. *No one.*'

I'd spent years with Nan at our perfumery organ, a semi-circle desk with tiered shelves that held all the aroma oils in neat rows and in order from top notes, heart notes, down to base notes. Our knees used to bump as we mixed essences as assiduously as if we were making love potions for strangers. Which in spirit we had been. Bespoke perfumes created for customers who wanted a fragrance unique to them.

Nan had taught me every aspect of the art of perfumery. She'd been a daydreaming avant-garde type, way ahead of her time. Days were spent creating perfume and getting lost in the world of scent, only coming up for air when Grandpop asked politely if he was to have toast for dinner again. He always said it with a rueful half-grin, knowing her other great love was perfume itself, and how could he be jealous of that? He'd shuffle off and soon the smell of buttery toast would waft back to us.

Nan was taken from me a few years ago, and nothing had been quite the same since. One day she was there, and then she wasn't. Our time together suddenly felt as ephemeral as a spritz of perfume.

'Thanks, Jen. I'll remember that.'

At the memory of Nan, I gave my handbag a reassuring tap, feeling the outline of her trusty perfumery notebook: a fat and swollen tome filled with formulas, complex perfume equations, and her scribbles and drawings. It was my bible; I cherished it.

'You've got this. Text us when you can, so I can tell Grandpop how it's going. Mom and Dad say hi.'

'Give them a hug from me will you? Tell Pop I'll write him.' We said our goodbyes and I hung up, feeling a twinge of guilt that

I was grateful to end the call, just as Clementine returned, her lipstick smudged. 'I need a nap!' she announced and flung herself on the bed. I hadn't met anyone quite as dynamic as Clementine before. She took up all the space with her big personality.

Chapter Four

After unpacking, and eventually convincing a drowsy Clementine that half the wardrobe was in fact mine, I went downstairs and headed back to *Leclére Parfumerie* hoping to visit before it closed. No such luck. Instead I peeked through the window and ogled the beautiful cut glass bottles of perfumes which blinked like gems under the lights. Scent radiated through the window pane; lily, ambergris, rose, and vanilla …

With an hour until I had to dress for dinner, I continued on, eyes wide with awe at the sights and sounds before me. I came from a place the size of a postage stamp, a small lakeside village in Michigan where everyone knew everyone and nothing ever changed. A suffocating place to live when the whole village knew your business.

The main street back home would have a dozen cars parked down its length on a busy day, and maybe a handful of people window shopping, or dillydallying about which loaf of bread to buy at the bakery. Here, groups queued in ores, others had noses pressed to windows, and some rode bicycles and dodged traffic. It was like someone had turned the volume of life all the way up.

It would take some getting used to. The noise level was incredible but I couldn't help feeling energized by the big city vibe.

Paris pulsed with life! This is what I wanted, to be thrust into a big city, to live and work among so many people, opportunities galore, unlike back home.

I wandered on, delighting in the warmth of the Parisian evening. Around the corner I found a little café with bright red shutters and lots of people milling nearby. I took a table out the front and tried to decipher the French menu, counting back in my mind to when I'd eaten last and on which time zone. Not wanting to spoil my appetite for dinner, I settled on a *café au lait*, but promised myself I'd return for the bevvy of mouthwatering food on offer. *Croque monsieur. Chouquettes. Soufflé fromage.* The list went on and I shut the menu with a decisive bang, as my stomach rumbled in protest.

The café was a hive of activity but I couldn't grab the attention of the bustling staff so I made my way inside and got to the front of the queue and ordered my coffee.

A waitress wearing a bored expression said, 'We'll bring it to you.' Her voice brooked no further conversation, and any reply died on my lips, unsaid. Her attitude was wildly different to back home, where any stranger would be grilled about their lives, why they were in town and for how long, and within minutes, they'd find themselves sharing far too much information on account of the barrage.

Here I was faceless and nameless. Wasn't that what I wanted?

Hurrying back to my table, I was lost in these thoughts when I tripped over a shopping bag. There was no time to react, instead I flew towards the back of a stranger and tried to strangle the shriek that rose from deep within me. Soaring through the air at a ridiculous speed, I tried to break my fall, by latching onto the man in front like a koala bear. We fell to the floor with a resounding thud.

Way to blend in, Del!

We were a tangle of arms and legs, as he groaned and turned from his front to his back, pinning my ankle, and I sat half-straddled atop him. Not the best position to be in; quite personal, really.

'So, *so* sorry,' I said and struggled to disentangle myself from his limbs, my face aflame. One of my legs was skewed so far to the left I wondered if I'd broken it. With that in mind, it took me a moment to recognize him. My breath hitched at the sight of those intense green eyes. *Of all people!* I straddled the guy who'd witnessed my near-miss on the Champs-Élysées and who I'd now taken down in front of a café full of elegant French people, some laughing behind their hands, some frowning at the disruption to their meals. But all looking square at me. Goddammit.

'It's not my fault,' I said a little more haughtily. 'I tripped.' I jerked a thumb at the businessman at the table above us whose seemingly twenty-seven-meter-long baguette had been the cause of all this fuss. 'Over his baguette, which clearly was not tucked away in a safe manner.'

He didn't utter a single word. We competed in a stare-a-thon until I gave in.

'Well?' I said. Perhaps he didn't speak English? 'Would you mind moving? I can't get up until you do.'

With a bit of effort, I managed to wrench my leg from under him, hoping the numbness wasn't anything serious. Imagine if I had to limp from here? Or drag my dead limb behind me like some kind of peg-legged pirate. Not exactly the fast getaway I was hoping for.

Once upright I held out a hand and helped him up, when realization shone in his eyes. 'It's you.' His eyes widened. 'The girl who stepped *into* the path of oncoming traffic.'

Jeez. 'Well, yes, but I was …'

'You're a walking disaster.'

I lifted my chin. 'The traffic thing was an accident. And *this* could have happened to anyone.'

'Are you hurt?' He frowned.

'No.' Yes. My pride withered and died on the spot.

'Are you sure?'

'Quite,' I said primly. If my leg was broken in eight places there was no way I was going to confess to him. I'd damn well walk out of here if it killed me! But his sudden concern was touching and lightened the mood. Our audience went back to their meals and their chatter grew loud once more.

His lips twitched as if he found me amusing. Did he find this funny? Why of all the millions of people in Paris did I have to make a scene in front of this guy? *Twice*. I wanted to slap my forehead.

'I'm sure we'll meet again,' he said, his green eyes unfathomable in the dim light of the bistro.

'Perhaps.' I walked away, heart hammering.

***

After a quick shower, I read some texts that Jen had sent. It was hard to break the habit of a lifetime, or maybe guilt was driving her. We'd only spoken on the phone an hour ago! I didn't want to feel as though I was relying on her here. If she could live this shiny new life, then, damn it, so could I.

In my reply to her I left out all the whole falling-for-the-Frenchman thing or she'd start planning the wedding. And it wasn't like I was falling *for* him, more like, *on* him. Instead I told her more about Clementine, and her sidekick Kathryn, who'd both been scheming when I'd returned.

A reply beeped back instantly.

Oh, they sound like fun girls! What's a little competition between friends, hey?

I shook my head. I could've told Jen the girls made me stand on my head for five minutes and she would have said, 'Aww look at you making friends!'

24

Nan would have told me to keep my guard up, but be open to any possibilities, so I kept that thought in my heart.

I replied: *Fun, maybe, but I wouldn't call them friends just yet. What's up with you?*

In truth I wanted to say, are you missing me, have you changed your mind about moving to New York? Are you joining me in Paris? Any of those things … But I didn't.

She replied: *Mom has chanting group here (how long will this last?!) and Dad is busy in the shed (whittling) and me and Pops are making popcorn and about to watch a French film in honor of your adventure. He says hi and wants you to get off that dang piece of machinery and enjoy yourself. Gotta love him. xxx*

I smiled picturing my grandpop admonishing me from afar. He was always on about that *dang piece of machinery* we used to communicate. To him, cell phones were the devil, no matter how much easier they made our lives, especially now I was so far away. When I showed him I could read a book on my cell phone he almost keeled over. *But why*, he'd cried, *when there's plenty of books right here?* And any mindless games, forget it, he was actually offended by them.

Tell him I love him and I'm putting the dang thing away for the night. Xxx

We sent a few more texts before I shut off the phone, shaking my head at Mom's latest pastime. She saw no reason to live in the real world, and instead spent her time on the periphery. Dad was much the same, and it often struck me how normal Jen and I were, considering. I could have announced I was going to live my life naked in a commune that worshipped sunflowers and

25

they would have applauded us for following our dreams. They had good hearts, but were just that little bit *too* away with the fairies …

Growing up hadn't been easy when they were M.I.A. for yet another school play, or at exam time when we needed some semblance of stability. They were often the laughing stock of Whispering Lakes, their behavior always fodder for local gossip, which was tough when you were a kid. Even now, there was still that same whispering behind hands when I walked past, laughter following me down the long road to home, and I'd wonder what they'd done this time. They lived life on their terms though and as unreliable as they were, you had to give them a grudging amount of respect for it. They didn't care one iota what people thought about them. There was a freedom in that.

That freedom came at a cost though. Nan and Pop raised us, Mom and Dad were more like errant siblings than parents. I gave myself a few minutes to grieve again for the woman I'd lost and the one who was left behind.

Don't give into it, Del. Grief was a strange thing. Even after all these years it crept up when you least expected it.

I heard Nan's voice, like I sometimes did: *Come on, Del. Pull those shoulders back and go wow those people!*

OK, OK! I smiled at the memory as I dithered about which perfume to wear. It had to be perfect because it would set the tone for who they perceived me as. The Madagascar rose was too soft, too dreamy for a group setting. The citrus blast was a daytime fragrance. Oriental flare, maybe? It was spicy and sultry, a balmy evening scent and had enough *oomph* to stand out in what would be a very fragrant group. Although, I also had my special remedy cache – aromatherapy oils made for certain situations: to calm, to endear, to love, laugh – but tonight I would need to show them what I was capable of …

I spritzed the perfume on my pulse points and grabbed my handbag on the way out. Clementine had left earlier and hadn't returned so I locked the room and wandered down the hallway. A few doors down, a rail-thin guy wearing an ill-fitted suit swore as he tried to lock his door.

'Can I help?' I asked. His hands shook and when he turned to me I smelled the sourness of stale alcohol on his breath. The whites of his eyes were bloodshot but he smiled, making his features impish, which contrasted to his scruffy appearance that even a suit couldn't disguise.

'This blasted key won't fit.'

Another contestant, but who? His accent was American but with almost an English inflection. 'Let me try,' I said, taking the key and slipping it easily into the lock.

'Must've needed a woman's touch,' he laughed. 'I'm Lex,' he said.

'From …?' I asked as I held out a hand to shake.

'World citizen,' he said swaying slightly on his feet. 'But I've just flown in from Thailand. And you?'

There was something amiable about the guy despite his scruffy appearance and hollowed features. With his rheumy eyes, and wrinkled brow I put him at around fifty, maybe fifty-five years old. His fragrance was marred by the stale smell of cheap wine, with the undercurrent of mint as though he'd tried to mask it.

'I'm Del from America.'

'Shall we, America?' He extended an elbow so I looped my arm through, feeling strangely at ease with him, like I would an uncle or someone harmless.

'So tell me,' he continued, 'what are they like? They're not all chemistry nerds, are they?' While he slurred his words slightly, he still had a sparkle in his eye that led me to believe the alcohol he'd consumed didn't affect his thought process at all. Maybe he hated flying and had imbibed? Who was I to judge? Though a simple oil blend of basil, clary sage, palmarosa and ylang ylang could have helped alleviate his fear of flying if that was the indeed the case …

'I've only met Clementine and Kathryn properly, and they seem …', I grappled with words to describe the crafty duo, '… well studied about their opposition.'

'Internet stalkers, you mean?'

I laughed, liking that he played it down, as if it was nothing to be concerned about. 'Pretty much. They seem to think Anastacia is the one to watch.'

'Ah, it's always the Russians who get cast as the bad girls. And how did they rate you?'

I shrugged, not wanting to share their summation of me because I didn't want him purposely pitting against me if he thought I was a threat. I kept reminding myself to watch what I said, and not give too much away.

'They didn't say much at all,' I lied, smiling up at my new friend. 'No fancy chemistry degrees for me. I was taught by my nan at home …' So my nan had one of the best noses in the business; there was no need to share that piece of information.

'Ah,' he said. 'So you *are* one to watch then. You home-taught perfumers always want it more for some reason. A point to prove and all that.'

Lex had an innate skill at reading between the lines. Perhaps *he* was the one to watch. 'I wish,' I said, making my voice light. 'I've never been to Paris. It's about the experience for me.'

He grinned as if he wasn't going to pull me up on the lie. 'The world of perfumery is much smaller than you think; everyone has secrets which aren't so hard to uncover, so tread carefully, and don't trust anyone.'

'Including you?'

He threw his head back and laughed. 'Especially me.'

I returned his smile but I didn't believe a word of it. What was the worst any of them could do? Hunt for one of my formulas? Gossip about me? Big deal. It would all hinge on our perfumery skills.

Generally speaking, perfumers were quiet, studious types who found comfort in numbers, formulas, the magic of chemistry. I doubted they'd be devious, or play unfairly. But I didn't really know that for certain, and with the prize on offer it could potentially turn a quiet wallflower into someone else entirely, so I'd just tread carefully until I got to them know them all.

We walked out into the starlit evening. 'So let me guess, your nan was some kind of cloistered genius and she's passed on her gift to you?'

I laughed. 'Yes, you could say that. Though she was fond of making perfume almost like an elixir.'

'A cure-all? Why not!'

I smiled. Most people never understood that. Nan believed the right scent could cure anything from heartbreak to the common cold. She was way ahead of her time. Aromatherapy was huge these days, but she'd taken it further, and decades before it was in fashion too. It was where I saw my own niche in the world of fragrance, making not just a scent, but bottling a perfume that could lift a mood, throw sunshine on cloudy days …

'Is she in Paris, along for the ride?'

'If only,' I said. 'She died a few years ago.'

'I'm sorry.'

'Don't be. She's here with me in spirit.'

And she was, or at least I'd convinced myself of the fact so I could function without her. Still, I knew I'd never forget the day she died. It'd been memorable for so many reasons. We'd almost perfected a heritage rose perfume based upon the bloom of first love. I'd railed that you couldn't bottle love – how could you? We'd been missing a key ingredient to balance the perfume but we couldn't figure it out.

Nan had joked it was because I hadn't fallen in love before; I hadn't explored the world and learned how to say the words *I love you* in three different languages. She was always on about that; fall in love, tell the man you love him in French, in German, in the language of love itself … whatever that meant! God, I missed my whimsical nan.

I'd scoffed that day, rolled my eyes and gone back to trying to capture the elements we were missing but falling short.

It was the closest we'd come to capturing something as tangible as love in a bottle. It was a concoction of rose, cashmere wood, raspberry leaf, patchouli, freesia and blackcurrant, but lacked an element, an aroma we just couldn't pinpoint.

That antique rose perfume remained there still, unfinished. I couldn't bring myself to touch it without Nan.

Those early days were grey and full of the scent of rain without her.

'Let's meet this motley group then,' I said, smiling and shrugging off the cloak of memory so it didn't bring me down.

Chapter Five

We arrived at the Lecléres and were shown to an enormous and elegant dining room by an elderly man in a suit that fit much better than Lex's did. The chatter stopped immediately and all eyes landed on us like laser beams. Some gave us slow onceovers, others cocked heads and smiled, a few narrowed their eyes summing us up with one long stare. Contestants and the *Leclére* management team mingled as I tried to put faces to names from our various video calls.

A trio broke from their circle and came over to introduce themselves. Someone handed me some champagne which I guzzled to settle my nerves. My roommate sauntered over, a faux fur stole over her shoulders despite the warm weather.

'Clementine,' I said, relieved to see a familiar face. 'This is Lex. Lex, this is my roommate, Clem.'

Introductions were made and more bubbles quaffed. Clementine barely let anyone get a word in, so most of us slowly edged away from her, clustering in couples making polite if not stilted conversation. Kathryn called me over and I excused myself from Lex.

'So where is Sebastien, then?' she asked, casting her eye around the room.

I surveyed the men present and recalled their faces from

innumerable video chats, so none of them were the great man himself. He'd be tall, and wiry, and have intense eyes that darted about. Or would he be more masculine and suave, letting his famous name carry him?

'I don't think he's here or surely he'd have introduced himself,' I said with a sigh. No wonder no one could snap a picture of him, he never turned up. 'Is he even real?'

'Makes you wonder,' Kathryn said. 'Aurelie's not here either. Some welcome party.' She toyed with her napkin. 'It's all a little strange, this whole competition. Why *would* they suddenly open their doors to strangers, when they've been so reclusive?'

I'd asked myself the same question too. 'And now they're not here. Do you think they're regretting it?'

She frowned. 'I hope not.'

'They're probably running fashionably late to make a grand entrance once we've all broken the ice and got to know each other a bit.'

'You're probably right,' she said. 'I suppose we should mingle then.'

Normally I'd hang back and let people come to me, that small town reserve always just below the surface, but no one knew me here, and I could be whoever I wanted. So I made the effort to approach a tall girl who scrolled mindlessly on her phone. I'd done the same thing myself to look busy when I felt like the odd one out, so I introduced myself, only to have her nod as if dismissing me on sight. So much for feeling emboldened.

'And you are …?' I pressed on, not ready to give up, on pride alone.

'Anastacia.'

'From?'

'Moscow.'

It was like talking to a rock. And she was the one they were worried about? Boredom shone from her half-lidded eyes, as if she couldn't wait to get out of here.

Part of me wanted to walk away, but another part told me to persevere. Maybe Anastacia felt wildly out of place and her silence was all an act.

'I'm from Michigan,' I said.

Again, the brief nod.

Clementine chose that moment to wander over; she must have sensed my unease. 'Del, come and try the canapés, they're divine.'

At the sound of Clementine's voice Anastacia's head snapped up, and the pair stared each other down, a bitterness charging the air. I had the distinct impression Clementine was envious of the girl, or felt threatened by her, and that's why she was telling anyone who listened to watch out for her.

With one last withering stare, Clementine grabbed my elbow and steered me away. 'Isn't she icy cold?' she said in a stage whisper loud enough to bounce around the room.

'She's probably out of her comfort zone.'

'*Non, non,* don't be fooled. You have to remember this is a competition.'

I shrugged. Clementine would have had you believe we were contestants on *Survivor* the way she acted, and it dawned on me that I'd have to be careful around the beautiful Parisian girl, and keep her onside so I wasn't suddenly offside.

Before long we were huddled with the management team who were intent on grilling us all over again. We'd answered their questions enough, hadn't we? Couldn't we let our perfumery talk for us here? One of them, Luc, a tall blonde man with a pinched face, took me by the elbow. 'Del,' he said, in a deep voice. 'How do you think you'll cope here, without the comforts of home?'

'Great,' I said, trying to make the lie sound genuine. 'I'm ready to forge ahead now, step away from what I know.' Truth be told, I worried I'd freeze up. Forget everything Nan taught me. Be so far out of my depth I'd drown. But I had to keep my game face on for now, and hope it all came together.

'So would you say you're ready to break the rules?'

'My nan never followed the rules, she made her own, and I am very much the same.' I lifted my chin. Luc smiled. 'Good, very good. You are our wildcard. The one who could go either way.' He drifted off and I was glad he couldn't see the hurt on my face.

The wildcard? Did that mean I wasn't as talented as the rest but they'd been prepared to take a risk on me? Whatever confidence I'd had vanished, taking the breath from my lungs. Despite my bluffing, they'd picked up on the fact I'd struggled with perfumery since my nan died. It just wasn't the same without her. I could mix oil blends, and simple scent remedies but the more complex perfumes eluded me. Without her it was like working with my eyes closed; I'd lost that vision. Had my sister noticed that too? And was that why she hadn't wanted to risk the money she'd been saving for years? Suddenly I felt impossibly alone, and close to tears.

As the night wore on my feet ached and my eyes grew heavy. I longed for escape. When dinner was finished and the Lecléres still hadn't arrived, I made my excuses and left them all gossiping heatedly about where the Lecléres were and why they hadn't shown up to host their own welcoming party. No two ways about it, it was strange, but gossip wasn't my thing, and the answer would arrive eventually whether we clustered around guessing or not.

My heels bit into my feet as I walked, making my hobble from earlier more pronounced, so when I came to a wine bar right near my apartment, I stopped and peered in. Only a handful of people dotted the place, so I ventured in and took a stool at the far end of the bar. I wasn't one to drown my sorrows at the bottom of a wine glass, but tonight it seemed the tonic. One glass of wine and then bed. It wouldn't do to start the first challenge fuzzy headed.

The barman took my order and poured me a glass of white wine and placed a small bowl of peanuts next to it. I took a handful, and munched away, mind spinning at all that had happened, and grateful for the space to think without the contestants nearby.

Part of me wanted to relish this new persona, this girl who sat in wine bars late at night in exotic locales. Why not? Just hearing French accents spring about the room was intoxicating. I could have listened to them all night and it stopped me from worrying as I got lost among their musical accents.

'Are you following me?'

I turned to a velvety French voice. Oh, jeez. If Jen was here she'd be harping on about fate and divine intervention. The fact that I'd run into this guy three times in one day! 'I was here first, so you must be following me.'

He smiled, and this time it reached his eyes, as though he'd shrugged off the stresses of his day and was relaxed and amiable, different to the stiff-shouldered, smoldering-eyed guy in the daylight. 'I promise I'm not,' he said. 'I live around the corner.'

'I'm close by too,' I said, feeling a little buzz that I could say I lived in Paris. 'Have you just finished work?' Despite the hour he wore a dark suit, his tie loosened off a notch as if it had been strangling him and he was finally free of it.

'Not quite,' he sighed and scrubbed at his face. Just then his phone buzzed but he ignored it. 'I have a few more things to do when I get back. I needed a break, to step away from it all.'

'I know how you feel,' I said. 'I've just come from this dinner, and suddenly it was all too much.'

'Why?' He sipped his red wine. His phone buzzed again and this time he switched it off.

How to tell him? We weren't supposed to advertise the fact we were working with *Leclére Parfumerie*, as per the competition rules. The team didn't want rogue reporters getting any inside information. 'Well, it was just a little overwhelming. I'm not used to being among such competitive people. I'll have to learn how to handle that.' Oh, god I sounded like some backwater hillbilly.

'Paris is a good place to discover who you are. And competitive people usually show their hand early on and then fizzle out.'

'I hope so,' I said. 'I need to be one step ahead of them. My whole future depends on it.'

'Why's that?' he asked, his fingers worrying the stem of his glass.

I told him all about my sister, and our doomed plans, leaving out any talk of perfumery itself. How I had to make a go of it here, or else there was nothing left for me. It sounded dire, so I tried to laugh it off as if it was nothing.

'Why can't you go alone to New York if that's your dream?' The wildcard thing flashed in my mind. Maybe I wasn't as gifted as I thought, and everyone but me knew that. I pushed that anxiety down once more. Nan wouldn't have boosted me up all these years if I was mediocre, would she?

I realized I hadn't answered him. 'It's complicated.'

'I see,' he said, but clearly didn't.

He'd never understand, he was probably born with a trust fund by the looks of him and probably dabbled in the stock market or something equally high flying. Still, it was nice to chat with someone who didn't know me but listened intently as if he cared.

Usually I'd never confide in a stranger, but Paris made me bold. There was a freedom in sharing, an almost cathartic quality about it. 'What about you? You said you've got more work ahead of you tonight?'

He nodded, and stared into his wine glass, his demeanor changing at the mention of his work. An uplifting blend of basil, lime and mandarin would lift his mood and galvanize him, but again I didn't dare mention perfumery because of the rules in my contract, plus the fact he'd probably baulk at the suggestion that a blend of oils could ease his angst. 'I was supposed to do a lot of things today, but they didn't happen for various reasons, and I know it'll make tomorrow so much harder.'

'Why didn't you do them? Ran out of time?'

He sighed, and gave me the type of rueful grin that was more a grimace. 'Some days I find it impossible to do what's expected of me; today was one of those days. It's like I'm walking through mud, and I wonder why I'm bothering.'

I nodded, watching as the green of his eyes clouded, his mood sobered and I got the feeling it was more than just a hectic work day. Like me, he wasn't giving away much detail and I respected that.

'Perhaps tomorrow will be better for both of us. Aren't we woeful sitting here, slumped over a bar when we're in Paris?' Although I didn't feel particularly woeful. I felt alive in a way I hadn't in years. Maybe it was the fact he was a good listener, or that we were both having a challenging day and yet we'd found some common ground. Or maybe it was the amount of alcohol I'd consumed.

'We can only hope.'

I finished my drink, and jumped when I checked the time. It was past midnight! Contestants were supposed to be back in our rooms well before then. A curfew had been set so that we gave the competition our all, and here I was breaking a rule already.

'Thanks for the chat,' I said, holding out a hand to shake, feeling a distinct spark when he squeezed back softly.

'Thanks, Del. It was lovely to meet you without incident this time.' His eyes sparkled with mirth.

I shook my head, he just *had* to mention it. 'Au revoir,' I said smiling and walking into the balmy night. If only I'd met him at some other time, when I didn't have my whole future hanging in the balance. It was only later, I realized I hadn't caught his name, but he'd known mine. Too much champagne, I groaned, had turned me into an over sharer of the worst kind …

Chapter Six

Brilliant sunlight broke through fluffy clouds while I waited impatiently for the day to begin. Challenge one was here, and I was raring to go, albeit with a slight headache. Still, no one seemed any the wiser that I'd crept in past curfew. My secret was safe and I vowed never to do it again.

I showered and dressed as quietly as possible so as not to wake Clementine who slept like she lived – loudly – her snores and random burst of sleep-talking punctuating the space.

'Del, stop with that thing you are doing. It's driving me crazy!' she said, and held a pillow tight to her face.

'What thing?' I said, as I sat quietly on the edge of my bed, waiting for the right time to go down to breakfast. I'd already flicked through my nan's perfume bible and re-made up my face, going from matte red lipstick to nude in an effort to appear barely made up and carefree.

I'd googled the best way to tie scarves (French women are born knowing such a skill and I didn't want any more roadside scares while I chased an errant piece of fabric!). I'd also settled on wearing a beret for all of three minutes until I realized I was trying too hard. Being a morning person had its fallbacks. And I was not under any circumstances thinking of the guy the universe had flung in my path three times, because I *wasn't* here for love. Those deep unfathomable green eyes of his though …

'Stop that clink, clink, *clink!*'

'What clink?'

'Your bracelets!'

'Oh! Sorry. Nervous habit. Well you're awake now. It's time to rise and shine, Clem.'

'I'm not awake!' she hollered. It was evident Clementine only had one volume. Loud.

'Clem, we have to go soon.' It wasn't my place to babysit her, but I didn't want her to miss the first day.

I opened the curtains and sunshine brightened the room. She tunneled further under the blanket, swearing at me in French.

'*Non, non, non!* Shut them!'

'OK, fine,' I said, breezily. 'I'll be the first one at breakfast and I'm sure I can find out what the challenge is today. I'll be one step ahead! I'll probably win this week …' I let the words hang in the air as she sat bolt upright, her once heat-styled curls a bird's nest atop her head, smudges of mascara in panda rings around her eyes.

Raking her fingers through her hair and wincing, she said, 'Argh. You're right. Give me an hour.'

'An hour? It's already seven-thirty. We're supposed to be at breakfast by eight and be assembled out front of *Leclére Parfumerie* at nine.'

'*Mon dieu*, OK, thirty minutes!' With a groan she dragged herself from bed and surveyed herself in the mirror, gasping at the sight of her semi-dreadlocked tresses. I shuddered to think how much time Clementine spent on her morning *toilette*: intensive hair dressing, the over-the-top outfits, make-up application including dramatic fake lashes, and color-coordinated nail polish.

I let out a long sigh, more for effect than anything. 'Don't fuss with your hair, just put it in a ponytail.'

She reeled back as if I'd suggested she go running through the streets naked. 'I don't think so, *ma cherie*. Run the iron over my pink dress.' She hopped into the shower, steam filtering out the open door and filling up the small space.

'No, Clementine!' I yelled over the hissing water. 'I'm not your parlor maid! Just wear something casual.' Still, I flicked through Clementine's clothes out of curiosity, each of her dresses more outlandish than the last, but stunning in their extravagance. I envied her confidence to wear such fabulous clothing.

'Pah! I don't *do* casual, Del! Did you see a pair of jeans or a sweater in my collection? *Non*, because I am French and …'

Before she could start on one of her monologues, I pulled the pink dress from its hanger, and laid it on her bed. 'All right, relax, it doesn't need ironing. Just hurry up.' Honestly, she acted as though she was used to having hired help at her beck and call.

Miraculously she showered in under five minutes and, wrapped in a towel, sauntered back into the room, bare-faced and beautiful. Without all the make-up and the thick ebony eyelash extensions, she was lovely, like something out of a Botticelli painting.

'*Merci*, Del,' she said quietly. 'Without you, I might have missed the first morning.' She gave me a grateful smile.

As she pulled the curling iron through her hair, she sung softly to herself. There was no sign of the previous evening's abundance of *vin rouge* and lack of sleep, and she looked every inch the bright-eyed sunny Parisian once more. Life was so unfair. If I didn't sleep well, the next day I resembled the walking dead no matter how much make-up I applied, and today was no better. My eyes resembled a puffer fish in protect mode that no amount of concealer could fix. But I reasoned the French probably grew up quaffing wine so it had no adverse effects on their complexions.

'We're roommates so we have to stick together, right?' I said, knowing I had to be careful of Clementine and keep friendly.

She broke off her song. '*Oui*. You're *mon amie*, and I am yours.'

Friends? Perhaps we would be. Once the shutters came down and Clementine wasn't on show, she was calmer, more real. In front of others she was a caricature; a big, bold woman of the world. Was it a ploy, that drama, to get noticed in the competition, to stand out in the group of perfumers? Hard to tell at this early stage.

Outside, birds chirped; their mellifluous musical chatter drifted in, as they gossiped among themselves and we joined in too. Clementine gave me the low-down on everyone in her overzealous way. She thought Lex was too old to be a threat (he wasn't that old, and he most certainly was a contender) and Lila was too timid. And Clementine believed that Anastacia was the danger. She'd studied under some formidable perfumers and didn't give much away about technique or skillset, so she thought we should freeze her out.

'Freeze her out? Clem, that's school yard behavior.'

She frowned. 'Oh, Del, you'll never get anywhere with an attitude like that! Don't come crying to me when she wins, then.'

I shook my head. She was clearly put out that I wouldn't consider such a thing.

'Trust me, I won't.'

Thirty-four minutes later we were downstairs and ready to greet the day.

Breakfast was a noisy affair. We ate slowly and had long enough to down a couple of strong black coffees and munch on some fresh flaky croissants before assembling out front as instructed. The mood was ebullient; we all wore wide smiles, and fidgeted and jittered in anticipation. What would the day bring?

Lex wandered over, his face grey in the light of morning as if he hadn't slept well, but his lopsided smile firmly in place. What kind of perfume would fix that malady, that sleeplessness that plagued him? Maybe a lavender and bergamot blend?

'Hey, America. Ready to battle it out for the lead?'

'Ready as I'll ever be,' I said. The air was electric with the unknown and I couldn't wait to get started.

Maybe Lex would be an ally? The chat with Clementine and the whole freeze-her-out conversation left me a little dubious about her motivations. There seemed to be two sides to Clementine. I told myself to be careful, and not trust so easily. It was a game, after all, and the desire to win hung heavy in the air, though we all tried to downplay it. But with affable Lex, I felt as though he had the potential to be a real friend, and that I wouldn't have to pretend around him.

'What about you?' I asked.

'I was born ready,' he said, laughing, the deep lines near his eyes crinkling like stars.

We huddled together, awaiting the Lecléres. Would there be an explanation as to where they'd been the evening before?

The group hushed as Aurelie appeared, a tight smile in place. Just behind her stood a man, his back to us as he spoke in rapid-fire French on his cell phone. Would this be the elusive Sebastien, finally?

I waited impatiently for him to turn, excited to finally see the man in the flesh! He wasn't tall like I'd imagined, but he filled out his suit in all the right places, and even from behind, he had a presence you couldn't miss. He finally pivoted to us with his brow knitted. And those brows were glorious as far as men's brows went. Black as midnight, and arched just so, framing those luminous green eyes of his. And then it struck me, a realization so chilling I gasped. Please god, he was *not* the elusive Sebastien Leclére!

Not him! My stomach flipped – of all the luck!

Chapter Seven

'And so we meet again,' he said, his expression unreadable.

Oh god, had he known who I was all along? My own smile felt a little more wooden, but I forced my lips to curve, goddammit. With his face inches from mine, I could smell the passionfruit note of tea on his breath, the peppermint of his shampoo on his hair, and his perfume, a fresh slightly tangy oceana. But my anger flashed through me, making it hard to think. If he'd known who I was, surely he should have told me? Not sat there listening to me complain! Why would he do such a thing?

'So we do,' I said, trying to mask the hostility creeping into my voice but failing. Kathryn must have sensed I had the upper hand because Sebastien was giving me his full attention, so she moved to stand just in front of me, partially blocking my view. Probably a good thing, in the circumstances. My mind scrambled to think about what I'd confided in him the night before. Had I mentioned anything about the Lecléres? My heart pounded with worry. No, I'd been careful, but I'd also quaffed wine like it was water! This was not the start I'd envisaged!

'It's such a pleasure to meet you,' Kathryn said, holding out her delicate hand. I willed myself not to roll my eyes at the sudden change in the English rose, as her complexion pinked, and her voice honeyed. Seriously. This is what I was up against? Were they all going to swoon in his presence? So, he was good-looking, but at least his presence took the attention away from me. I slid away, subtle as anything, when he took my elbow, and steered me back. Dang it.

I willed myself to look at him with a glare. Up close I could see he had the same kind eyes as his father. The same secretive smile. How could I have missed that? *Holy moly …*

Why did he hide who he was the night before? I suddenly felt like I couldn't trust him, either. Maybe they'd set me up on purpose to see how I'd react … No, surely not. He'd missed the welcoming party, and that was obviously what he was alluding to when we'd met the evening before. It was just unlucky I'd kept walking into his path. But he'd known my name when I was *sure* I hadn't given it to him! That was clearly no accident; the guy knew I was a contestant and played dumb and for what reason? He searched my face once more, a frown marring his features. 'Are you OK?' he asked.

'Yes,' Kathryn zoomed in on me, all sweetness and light, 'you look a little peaked, Del.'

I narrowed my eyes. Peaked, yeah right. 'I'm fine, thank you,' curtness spilled out.

When he took my arm again, his touch sent a volt of longing through me. Had my heart not caught the memo that I was angry? And so what if he was good-looking? So were millions of men. Big deal. Urgh, but my heart had other ideas and tangoed inside my chest like this was some sort of celebration, when it clearly was not. It was his scent, I decided, that was making me cuckoo. I'd never met a man who intrigued me so and I told myself it wasn't him, it was simply his *eau de parfum* making him desirable, proof that everyone should invest in quality fragrance.

'I need water …' Isn't that what they did in the movies? Honestly how did water help at a moment like this? But it bought me some time to gather my thoughts, which were more like my twin sister's thoughts, and for an insane moment I wondered if she'd figured out a way to control my mind. I wouldn't have put it past her, the minx.

For one lonely minute I understood my nan's advice about falling in love in a different language. And all her nonsensical chats about the language of love! What was French for falling in love … How did you say I love you?

Je t'aime. Je t'ai …

He placed a hand on my head. Was that some kind of French thing? I struggled with my confusion and anger, and the fact it was suddenly so damn hot. What was happening to me?

'You're *tres* hot, Del.' The compliment took me by surprise. He was pretty damn hot too. 'I … uh, appreciate you saying so, but isn't it sort of a conflict of interest?'

He frowned, two lines marring the perfect symmetry of his features. '*Pardon*?'

'Well you do *own* the perfumery, and I am here to win …'

With narrowed eyes, he cut me off. 'And what has that got to do with your sudden … fever?'

Fever? *Oh, god!*

I wanted to die. He didn't mean hot as in attractive, he meant hot as in feverish! I had to backtrack, and quickly. 'My mistake,' I said haughtily. 'It's the fever talking and I am confused.'

A smile played at the corner of his lips, as though he understood *exactly* what I'd implied. I would have liked to smack myself upside the head but settled for silently berating whatever part of me was dropping the ball so spectacularly. Was this some sort of travel sickness and it had only just caught me?

'Kathryn, would you mind getting Del a bottle of water please?' His silky accent rolled off his tongue like he was reciting poetry and again I pushed any thought of him aside. Millions of French men spoke exactly the same. *Millions.*

'Of course,' she said, but saved her mouth-full-of-marbles expression for me. Yikes, I was not making friends.

He was relaxed and efficient as if he'd met me a hundred times. I, on the other hand, felt wildly uncomfortable, and like I couldn't trust myself to speak anymore. What if I blurted out some other *faux pas*? Suddenly he wasn't just the gorgeous guy I'd run into (literally) – he was Sebastien Leclére, and it changed things.

'Shall I call a doctor, just in case?'

'A doctor?'

'For your … fever.' The wry smile was back and he placed his palm on my forehead to test my temperature. I shrunk under his touch, my mind spinning in a hundred different directions, and finally landing on … him. Damn it. I was suffering some kind of malady, the symptoms being a butterfly belly, jelly-leggedness, and a strange desire to run for the hills.

'No, thank you.'

'You're still very hot.' He winked, he bloody well winked!

I folded my arms, and took a step back. Was he teasing me? I ignored the god damn alluring sparkle in his eyes and said, 'Cured with a couple of painkillers and some … space.'

He raised his brows. '*Oui*. If you're sure.'

I lifted my chin. 'I'm sure.'

With a nod, Sebastien moved to the front of the group, leaving only faint traces of the spicy scent of his perfume. The sillage, which came from the French word for wake, and was one of many magic moments in the lifecycle of a spritz of fragrance. If the perfume was balanced properly, the sillage was an aromatic whisper, a goodbye just tangible enough to make you want more …

Damn it.

All chatter quietened as Sebastien called for attention. There was a sudden tightness to his jaw, implying what? He didn't like public speaking? Us? The whole thing smacked of mystery. I guess that's what they did best, those reclusive Lecléres … Just like last night when he should have been upfront with me.

With us gathered together and the competition about to start in earnest, perhaps he was thinking of his late father, who was lovingly referred to as *le savant fou* – the mad scientist – by his fans. If that was the case, then I understood Sebastien's sorrow. It had only been a year since he'd lost him; a drop in the ocean for bereavement, like only yesterday. No one knew what their relationship entailed but I suspected it was grief playing on his features and that made me soften slightly toward him. Even though he was the biggest jerk for pretending he didn't know who I was!

With sunshine on his face Sebastien gave us a smile. Everyone stared, mesmerized by his presence. Still, his smile didn't seem genuine to me. Almost as if he were acting. I only recognized it because I did the very same thing whenever anyone asked me how my parents were doing. *Heard your folks were up to mischief again, everyone's talkin' about them!* And I'd want to dissolve into the pavement, but instead I'd laugh it off. *You know my folks, crazy as coyotes, but hearts of gold*, I'd say, time and again.

Even still, there was something magnetic about Sebastien, and it wasn't only me who felt it, going by the open-mouthed, wide-eyed ogling going on around me from men and women alike. Under the soft sun he had magic in his eyes, just like his father.

Then Aurelie linked an arm through her son's, giving us all a wave.

'Welcome, friends,' she said. 'Our deepest apologies for missing the welcoming party.' She shot a look at Sebastien. 'An unforeseen circumstance cropped up, we promise it won't happen again.' Passers-by stopped and stared, some snapped pictures commemorating the moment in case we were noteworthy, but Sebastien held up a hand and dodged the photographer. '*Non*,' he said. 'No photos.'

Why did he hate the limelight so much? Those tourists were just being tourists. But I guessed he wasn't going to let anyone catch him unawares – oh the irony! And what exactly was so unforeseen about their absence? I got the feeling Aurelie was fighting a silent battle with her son, but why?

Sebastien spoke up, 'Today is a monumental day for *Leclére Parfumerie*. I hope being in Paris will take you and your *parfumerie* to new heights.' While his words were measured, they came out stiff as if he'd memorized them and spoke by rote.

No one else seemed to notice; they grinned, and pleasure bloomed on their faces. My own face was dark, I bet. I couldn't seem to let it go. Now he knew I was struggling here already, what a terrible start! Would he have reported back that the wildcard's knees were knocking already?

'You're probably wondering, as is most of the perfume world, why we decided to invite you, virtual strangers, and offer such a prize as we have.' He paused, dropped his gaze.

'*Oui*, everyone wants to know,' said Clementine, huskily. So she too was affected by the man. There was no hope.

He gestured for us to come closer, and we each took a big step forward. My proximity to Sebastien made me anxious. My ego and my *derrière* were still a little bruised from the previous day. Best not to think of it.

As we crowded around him, he said, 'This competition was my papa's idea, but sadly he didn't get time see it come to fruition.' When he spoke about his father his face pinched and his voice tightened; it must've been very raw for him. Jen always told me I read too much into things, but I couldn't help it. I'd always been that way.

My emotions were yo-yoing all over the place, I couldn't work out if I liked or loathed the guy …

'So in the spirit of keeping his legacy alive, we decided to go ahead with the competition as per his wishes. He wanted to give someone a chance to make their name in the perfume world. A person with daring, an adventurous spirit, the type who'd think outside usual *parfumerie* parameters. The winner of the competition will get a chance to read through his notes, and make a range for Leclére.'

What! My heart hammered so loud I was sure everyone could

hear it. The winner would get to read through Vincent's notes! I was light-headed with the thought of it. That hadn't been mentioned before and it wasn't expected since the Lecléres were so private …

If I'd wanted to win before, it was now amplified a hundredfold. Vincent Leclére had granted one interview in his lifetime – only *one* – where he talked about his love for perfumery and how he'd wanted to make a spritz of a perfume take you somewhere, somewhere *more* than just a memory, an evocation of time and place. What he'd wanted to do was heady, audacious, and I wasn't sure it was possible, but how enlightening would it have been to see him try? To be able to read through his notes, to get an intimate look at what he believed was heady stuff.

I stole a quick look at the other contestants but I needn't have bothered; the tangible bouquet of desire was heavy in the air. Everyone wanted to win such an honor.

Was that regret in the summer breeze? Sebastien's fragrance salty and sandy, like a receding tide, changed with his mood. Perhaps it wasn't his choice to share his father's work? If it were me, I doubt I'd want to let a stranger into that private world either.

But it could further my own perfumery journey … I'd managed to create perfumes that were like potions, a bridge to help clients cross to feel better about themselves – but I'd never managed to bottle an emotion, a tangible feeling.

Could it be done? Vincent thought so, my nan had too …

'Does anyone have any questions before we begin?' Aurelie asked.

Hands shot up, including mine.

She pointed to me. '*Oui?*'

'What will the days consist of?' Just how prepared did we need to be? What if I made one mistake and lost this once in a lifetime chance? The stakes were even higher now and my thoughts scrambled like eggs. Should I have prepared more? Studied chemistry books? Memorized perfume combinations? Packed more practical shoes? Taken more vitamin B? My anger at Sebastien disappeared as all thought turned to winning.

Aurelie laced her fingers. 'Each day will be different. On some you'll face challenges like we'll have today, specifically organized in such a way that you must think on your feet. You'll make perfume to submit to the judging panel, and be marked on originality, daring, risk-taking, but of course the final product must still be desirable. You'll partake of classes with masters in the world of perfumery. You'll each be mentored exclusively by one of the *Leclére* staff. There'll be excursions too; you can choose to come along or not. But we don't want your time in Paris to be all about perfume – we are French after all. We invented long lunches and champagne made from stars. Life is about balance, just like perfume. So while you're here, *se hâter lentement*; hurry slowly.'

Cheers rang out among the group. Knowing we'd be able to sightsee in the city of light was a bonus. I turned the phrase over: hurry slowly. It was so apt for the French and the way they stretched the hours to suit their lifestyle.

After a nudge from his *maman*, Sebastien said, 'And weekends you'll have free. We hope you'll use that time to explore our beautiful city and partake in all sorts of pleasurable activities.' With that he gazed straight at me, we locked eyes, and I willed myself not to look away as a shiver of longing raced through me.

'An incredible opportunity,' I managed, my voice too high. Damn it! I coughed for effect, hoping they'd think it was just my *faux* flu affecting me, and not the laser beam of Sebastien's eyes seeing into the depths of my soul. Why did he have to zone in on me?

'Sadly, at the end of each week the contestant with the lowest score will be sent home.'

Please not me. I had to win; everything depended on it.

'Who is my mentor?' Clementine asked.

Aurelie took a sheet of paper from her pocket and matched the contestants with their mentors. When she came to my name, she said, 'Del, you have Sebastien. Mentoring, however, will not begin officially until after you've submitted your first perfume. We believe this will give your mentors time to see what you can do alone and under pressure and then they'll be more able to guide you. You can, however, meet with them at any time if you need support.'

That announcement gained Clementine's attention and she glowered at me. 'Well, aren't you *lucky*?'

I pulled my shoulders back. 'He's not making my perfume, Clementine, he's only mentoring me, so it's not as if I've got the golden ticket.' My pulse raced in spite of it all. Was it an advantage having Sebastien? What if he was too busy to spend time with me? What if he wore that same look of disinterest I kept catching crossing his features? I had the feeling Sebastien's heart wasn't in it. Still, I kept my face neutral and wouldn't let Clementine bully me, or there'd be no end to it.

'We'll see,' she said. 'It doesn't seem fair to me that you have one of the Leclére family, and we have their employees. Next minute you win, because you've spent all that time flirting with him!'

I shot her a despairing look. 'Don't be so ridiculous! I'm here to win on merit alone, Clementine. Unlike *some* people.' Two could play at that game.

They might have been invisible to the eye but I sensed battle lines had been drawn.

With one last withering glare she turned away and whispered to Kathryn. *Oh boy*. Did they give me Sebastien because I was the wildcard and therefore expected to need more help? I wished that self-doubt would disappear!

Aurelie clapped to get our attention once more. 'So, that brings us to the challenge today. Behind you are backpacks filled with supplies you might need like Metro tickets, maps, euros, snacks and water. It's up to you what you use.'

Lex grinned at me. 'I wonder if there's any *vin blanc* in the bag?'

'We *are* in Paris,' I winked.

'Your first challenge is a fun one, designed so you get to see a bit of our beautiful city,' Sebastien said. 'At one of our landmarks, or places of significance, there's an envelope. In it is a key. This key unlocks my papa's private studio and whoever finds it can use it exclusively for the week. For the rest, you will use the *Leclére* lab to make a perfume that shows us who you are, your style. The judges are looking for originality, something they wouldn't expect. Surprise them. After that you'll work closely with your mentors for the rest of the competition.'

I had to find that key! I so badly wanted to see Vincent's perfumery studio, to sit where he did, to concoct perfume there …

I'd studied maps of Paris, and all the landmarks, but put on the spot all I could think of was the obvious ones: the Eiffel Tower, the Arc de Triomphe, Notre-Dame … Surely they'd choose something a little left of centre? Or was that what they expected we'd all think, in which case wouldn't they hide the envelope in plain sight?

Before I could ponder any more, Aurelie spoke again. 'In your backpacks are directions to the *Leclére Parfumerie* laboratory, which is just behind us here near the *parfumerie*. Inside the lab you'll see a workspace with your name on it and everything you could possibly need to formulate a perfume. Of course, we know your perfumes won't have time to age, but we can still get a sense of who you are as a perfumer.'

I crossed my fingers, praying to the perfume gods that I wouldn't be sent home after the first challenge.

Once again, the contestants directed a barrage of questions at Aurelie. I had one ear pricked at her answers as I visualized my guidebook, and which attraction I thought the key would most likely be at. A *jardin* of some sort where flowers abounded? Roses, lavender, lilies, tulips … Should I make a floral perfume?

Or was that thinking outmoded? When they said be daring, just exactly how daring did they mean? Was a floral scent too sedate? I didn't want to play it safe, but I also didn't want to make something too odoriferous that would have their noses wrinkling in disgust. It had to have the right balance of daring and sensuality; an ode to the nomadic and their wandering heart.

When everyone's questions were answered Aurelie held up a hand. 'Let challenge one commence!'

With that there was a scrum for the backpacks. Only Lex hung back, cigarette dangling from his lip, his mouth curved in a wry smile, seemingly in no rush to move.

As the contestants scattered like marbles, I froze, already one step behind as they took off as if their lives depended on it. Which they practically did! Their perfume lives! I rushed for my bag but Lex caught my elbow.

'America, chill. You've got this, but don't waste the day rushing all over Paris without a plan. It's a huge city, absolutely massive. Plan your route before you get lost.'

He was right, I knew it. I had to decide on which landmarks to visit and try to avoid wasting time zigzagging back and forth across the ginormous city. Logistics were never my strong suit, but I desperately wanted to find the key before anyone else. But really, without a plan what chance of that did I have?

'Thanks, Lex.' I gave him a daughterly peck on the cheek and tore away, but not before I caught a look of surprise on Sebastien's face. Was I going the wrong way? I didn't have time to translate his expression as my mind flew just as fast as my legs. I got to the nearest *jardin* and sat down to formulate a plan and consult the maps.

Chapter Eight

If I was thinking outside the box, then landmarks or places of significance didn't necessarily mean anything. A famous bistro could be a landmark, an indistinct patch of pavement where Edith Piaf once sang could be the spot. Who else made Paris famous? Would it have a perfume connection?

Moms with strollers milled around as tiny tots chased birds, and a couple of elderly tourists sipped coffee from takeaway cups, and consulted guidebooks. The day had grown warm, and I hurried to rifle through the backpack before I had to search for more shade as the sunlight turned my skin pink.

With map in one hand and phone in the other, I searched the internet for tourist attractions, but all that I found were the usual suspects. Think, think! There had to be some kind of message, something that if not directly connected with perfume, was related to it.

It was like looking for a single blade of grass in a field, impossible to narrow it down. Instead, I decided to make a list of the places I'd go and mark them out on the map, hoping along the way something would come to me.

The Ritz Paris: the most iconic and luxurious of all Paris hotels. All the greats had clinked champagne glasses and told tall stories there from Hemingway, to Anais Nin, F. Scott and Zelda, but more importantly Coco Chanel herself, who made the Ritz her home for over thirty years! It had to be a contender – in its illustrious past there'd been many a scandal amid the celebrations. I'd heard that Coco Chanel designed the shape of the Chanel No. 5 perfume bottle in ode to the square out front of the Place Vendôme. And Sebastien's father had once worked for Coco, or so the rumors went.

And if the key wasn't there, it was close to the Jardin des Tuileries, the Musée de l'Orangerie, and the Place de la Concorde with its eighteenth century Egyptian Obelisk. I could cross the oldest standing bridge in Paris, the Pont Neuf, to the Île de la Cité, one of two small islands in the middle of the Seine that housed the Notre-Dame. I could make my way around all the little hidey-holes in the *arrondissements* I'd yet to explore.

On the left bank sat the famous bookshop Once Upon a Time. It was well known in bookish circles from readers to writers, and anyone who wanted to feel welcome in a city that sometimes made them feel lonely. Could I make a scent that explored the notion of reading bringing people together? How words on parchment were more than just words, they were ladders to another realm. The challenge would open my mind to new perfumery possibilities. It would help me to master the skill of bottling a tangible *feeling*.

Or should I stick to the heart and soul of Paris, somehow conjuring romance in a bottle? Roses, bergamot, pink peppercorn, musk, wisteria. What Nan and I had tried to do and failed – our first bloom of love perfume was missing one key ingredient, and I just couldn't pinpoint what it could be. Nan would approve of me trying to create something that bold in the city of light …

City of love, I heard my sister whisper in my ear.

It was something to consider if I didn't find the key. Time was ticking so I shoved everything back into the backpack and made my way to the Ritz Paris, wondering how I'd sway them to allow me to wander freely through the sumptuous hotel on my hunt for a key! If Sebastien hadn't hidden it there they'd think I was insane. The thought made me giggle as I pictured all of us on this great big scavenger hunt all over Paris, sneaking into places, or grabbing handfuls of inspiration; petals from lavish gardens, sprigs of rosemary, or twigs, or bottling air itself to sniff later and hoping no one would think we were strange.

As I made my way to the Place Vendôme my heart skipped a beat at the beauty before me. I'd never seen such majesty, from the gothic buildings to the wrought iron lamp posts, and a thousand tiny markers of time, which had really stood still for Paris in terms of its architecture.

As I rounded the corner I caught sight of Anastacia running in a half crouch, trying to what – be covert? She was more conspicuous because of her odd manner, and I held my breath hoping she'd go straight past the Ritz, but no such luck. She stopped out front, consulted a notebook and charmed the top-hat-and-tail-wearing door men with big smiles as they ushered her in.

Damn it!

With quick steps, I adopted a haughty expression as if I visited the Ritz Paris every day and nodded to the men. They greeted me politely and asked if I needed any directions inside the hotel. I declined and told them in halting high-school level French that I was meeting my lover, to which one of them frowned. Why? Did I look so unlovable? Or perhaps no one used the term lover these days? I was so out of the loop with the whole romance thing.

There was no time to rue my language skills. From what I could see, Anastacia was chatting to someone about Bar Hemingway which was closed during the day. She was trying to cajole him to let her peek in. She was fluttering her eyelashes, touching his arm and speaking breathily, but was met with stony silence. I suppressed a giggle, lifting my backpack to my face to edge past, hoping she wouldn't see me. Salon Marcel Proust was on my list, and Spa Chanel too. Bar Hemingway was a possibility but it didn't open until much later, and I could always come back.

Obviously Anastacia and I were thinking along the same lines: greats who'd made names for themselves in Paris and had ties with perfumers, either professionally or romantically.

I found the Spa Chanel first, and a beautiful French woman with the most luminous skin I'd ever seen welcomed me.

Before I could say anything Anastacia crept up behind me. I sensed malice in the air but didn't have time to react.

She spoke in fluent French to the woman, so fast I couldn't take a word of it in. Something about an appointment. The woman nodded and, taking a gold monogrammed fluffy bathrobe from a hook, she indicated *I* should undress and slip into the robe. Anastacia pushed me in the back and said, 'Don't waste time, the key could be in that robe!'

I didn't trust her one bit, if the key was in the robe Anastacia would have nabbed it, that much I knew. She was setting me up, but in the glamourous spa I suddenly didn't know what to do to extricate myself.

The spa was scented by essential oils burning unseen somewhere. Orange and patchouli, a reinvigorating blend that relaxed me with every inhalation, despite Anastacia's attempts at sabotage.

'*Au revoir,*' Anastacia said as a parting shot.

'Anastacia, wait! Tell her …' But she was gone.

Soft music played overhead, some kind of relaxation soundtrack with lots of rain, or waterfalls, and light cymbals. The more I tried to relax the stiffer I became.

'Please change.' She left me to undress, and I took the time to quickly search the room for the envelope. Nothing, no key, no clues. The drawers only held linen, face washers and hand towels. The shelves had various tubs of creams, bottles of hair and skin products, I reached a hand behind them and they jiggled like bowling pins but still no key, as I righted them as best I could.

As footsteps approached I wrapped the gown over my clothes and jumped on the bed, not wanting to be caught snooping. Grimacing, I tried to steady my heart, and thought for one lonely second how utterly beguiling the Ritz was. I felt like a princess about to be thoroughly spoiled. Until reality set in. I couldn't stay here! I wasn't a guest, and I most certainly didn't have time for this.

Before I could act the woman came back with a champagne menu (a champagne menu!) which I waved away politely.

'I have to ...'

'Shh,' she said softly, pushing my shoulders gently down, and securing a towelled headband to hold back my hair. Shoot. I shouldn't have laid on the dang bed!

Before I could protest she was washing my face, toning my skin and applying some kind of mint scented moisturizer. It felt good, damn it!

'Now concentrate on your breathing, and I'll be right back.' She threw me a look that implied she expected me to relax, but it was the small folder she'd left on the desk that caught my eye.

I'd just grabbed it when a familiar voice hissed, 'What the hell are you doing, America?'

Lex! 'Oh god, I don't know! How did you get in here?' The spa was private, each room a sumptuous oasis, and not one anyone could just lope in to.

'I bribed the security guard! But look, I think you should leave ... I saw Anastacia follow you!"

I groaned. 'I know! I came in here to look for the key and then Anastacia came in behind me and spoke in rapid-fire French to the woman.' I spat the words, frantically looking over my shoulder in case she came back and caught us. I opened the folder, hoping to see a key but instead saw an eye-wateringly sky-high bill. Jesus, was she calculating her commission before the treatment had even finished? Oh lord, how was I going to pay? I'd have to sell my first child ... I didn't have a child, first or otherwise!

'Why would the key be in here?'

'It's the Chanel Spa! *Coco* Chanel of Chanel No. 5 fame! Synonymous with *perfume*!' I hissed. 'She mentored Vincent Leclére ...'

He tutted. 'America, you have to get out of here. There's no time for …' He gesticulated at my face. '… For whatever that is, now get going!'

'I know, god! I didn't expect …' The click clack of high heels rang out. Shoot!

'Get up and go!' he said frantically once more and made himself scarce.

'I'm so sorry,' I said as the woman walked regally back into the room. 'I have to go, an urgent business matter has cropped up.' I tugged off the robe and gave her an apologetic smile, internally reeling at the thought of the unpaid bill. I didn't even have a MasterCard with that much money on it let alone enough euros in the backpack. Anastacia would answer for this!

The woman frowned, her perfect eyebrows pulling together. 'You have to go … now?'

'*Oui!*'

'But I have applied moisturizing …'

I cut her off. 'That's great, I'll leave it on for extra hydration. I promise I'll come back.' *Never.*

'But …'

Fingers around the door handle, there was only her confusion peppering the air.

Eyes narrowing, she said, 'What suite are you staying in?'

Suite? I didn't have a suite! This was a disaster. 'Erm … four, seven, one, four.'

She frowned. Wait, weren't the suites named after famous people? Too late!

'*Au revoir!*'

I walked as fast as my legs could carry me without actually breaking into a run. As I passed people they edged backwards, and I wondered why I was so out of place here. Could they sense I was a foreigner? Perhaps I was walking too fast, tourists sort of meandered here.

Out front, with hands on hips, I took great big gulps of air, adrenaline pulsing through me with the craziness of it all. I had not handled that well! Really, I hadn't banked on a contestant sabotaging me quite so openly.

'Oh my god, what happened?'

I glanced up sharply at Lila, a shy contestant I hadn't spoken to yet, who was staring at me, her eyes wide. 'What do you mean?'

'Your face.'

All these strange looks were starting to hammer at my confidence a little and now this? Everyone was a critic. 'I'm just a little out of breath, my cheeks go red when I run.'

'They're green.'

'Green? What!' I tentatively touched my face and my fingers came away a defiant mint colour.

'You look like the Hulk,' she said helpfully.

She must've put a face mask on! So much for the moisturizer or whatever the hell she was going on about.

'Have you got any tissues?' I asked, trying to keep the desperation from my voice. I calmed myself; it was only Lila, no one bar her need see this next level of mortification – well, aside from all the people I'd rushed by inside the Ritz and everyone in the square out front. Also the people on the hop on/hop off tour buses driving past. And those with zoom lenses. Argh!

As I tried to formulate an explanation, a car pulled up directly in front of us, and out got Sebastien himself. *Why universe, WHY!!* I debated whether to run, but I could tell by the barely suppressed smile on his face he'd already noticed me. Damn it!

Come to Paris, they said, you'll learn the art of sophistication, they said! You'll learn why French women are so graceful, so poised, you'll learn all of that and more, UNLESS YOU'RE DEL! I hadn't even been here twenty-four hours, and I'd managed to draw his attention for all the wrong reasons.

'Hey,' I said to him as if my face was *not* distinctly green. As if I was just your average American girl, enjoying the French summer day.

'*Bonjour*, Del, Lila. Erm, Del, you have a little …' He tapped his cheek, his nose, his forehead, his chin. Would I ever live this down?

I folded my arms, trying not to look defensive. 'Sun block on, I know. I don't cook for looks, no matter if I'm in Paris, fashion capital of the world, or hell itself. I take my skincare *very* seriously.'

'I see,' he said, pinching his chin. 'And you don't like the regular sun block? The one you can't see?'

'No, not strong enough. UV is *everywhere*,' I said seriously. 'And this is top of the range, expensive stuff.'

Lila guffawed but I shot her down with a look that conveyed how very close to the edge I was. Golly, Paris was really pushing my buttons and this wasn't helping. I could see the day slipping away from me.

'If there's nothing else?' I said, my voice tart.

Sebastien shook his head. 'Nothing else. I'm late for my appointment so I'll leave you to it.'

I gulped. 'An appointment?' Mouse-like. 'Here?'

His lips curved into a half-smile. '*Oui*, here.'

Heat rushed my face. It would be a million to one that his appointment was in the Chanel Spa. He didn't look like the type of man who got manicures, but really what did I know about men? Most likely he was meeting a friend for a *tête-à-tête* in one of the lavish restaurants. A business meeting. Or a game of racquetball? Slugging whisky and telling tall tales, more like.

But how to find out for sure? 'I've heard the food here is excellent.'

'Of course, it's the Ritz. But I'm not here to eat, I'm getting my weekly remedial massage.'

'A massage … in the Chanel Spa?' Holy mother of god.

'*Oui*. I have an old tennis injury, the massages help.'

Do not panic, I told myself, panicking. I'd skipped out on the bill! Would they discuss the girl with the green face who went running from the Ritz? What would Sebastien think of me? As some kind of thief who runs out on her bills? I wanted to cup my green face and wail.

'Well, enjoy!' I trilled. I had to get away. I had to put as much distance between myself and this place as humanly possible. Again, he had that same bemused look on his face as I rushed away. Aware I was scaring people, I ran to find a bathroom and make myself presentable again. Eventually I found one that had a monstrous queue which gave me plenty of time to berate myself and fill my sister in by text.

Her reply came back within minutes and once I scrolled past the crying laughing emojis, it read:

OMG, Del! Send me a pic before you wash it off! I am rolling laughing. It sounds like you're having a great time! xxx

A great time? Did she not read my text? In my haste to leave I'd managed to walk close to the Seine, so next on the list was the famous bookshop, Once Upon a Time.

Chapter 9

With a freshly scrubbed face, I surveyed the façade of the famous bookshop. I'd be mortified later, right now I was back into hunt mode, though god knew what Sebastien would think of me. A weathered Once Upon a Time sign creaked backwards and forwards in the breeze, like it was beckoning me to enter. The wooden step, bowed with age and the surefooted tread of thousands, sighed as more footsteps graced it. The briny scent of the Seine filled the air, and the cherry blossom trees with their fragrant pink flowers stood proud like ladies in waiting.

Inside, it was like something from a fairytale, like stepping into another world. The scent was evocative, timeless, the perfume of second-hand books, dusty mustiness ... but also a thousand nuances from the people who'd once leafed through their pages leaving fragrant fingerprints, perfuming the parchment. They left an indelible trail; a memory of those who once found comfort between the covers.

The dim bookshop was a wonderland and I wanted to explore every nook and cranny of the dark wooden shelves which climbed up to the ceiling and were filled with double-stacked books, a few edging out as if they were about to land in my outstretched arms. I couldn't get past that perfume – old and new, and the smell of words and worlds was heady. Instead of sniffing everything like I so desperately wanted to do, I hunted for the key, promising myself I'd come back later and peruse the perfumery books. This was the kind of place that fired up my imagination for perfumery ...

I followed an exposed well-trodden pathway, books stacked

haphazardly along each side, and found myself in a room with a baby grand piano. I tentatively touched the ivory, a haunting C note filling the space.

'It's gorgeous, *non*?' a woman with cropped blonde hair said, as she leaned against the door jamb.

'Beautiful. The whole shop is. It must be amazing working here.' I didn't dare start talking about the way it smelled or she'd think I was mad. Even the piano had absorbed fragrant memories in its ivory and ebony, right down to the brass foot pedals. But it was more than that – it held the wishes and dreams of all who'd sat before it and poured their desires into the keys and were rewarded by the music that drifted into the ether. Like perfume, those notes evoked varying emotions unique to us all.

The bookshop cast its magic over me, making me dream about strangers' lives whether fictional or not. It was the loveliest little place.

'*Oui*, it's my dream job, even with the tourists,' she laughed, her china-blue eyes lighting up. She was so chic and French, as though she'd got the style brief like the rest of them, immaculate hair and make-up, all effortlessly elegant. It was only after a minute or two I realized she was pregnant under the layers of her clothing.

'I'm Del,' I said.

'Pleased to meet you, Del. I'm Oceane. And you're the third contestant in here today.'

My face fell. 'How did you know I was a contestant?'

'You've all drifted towards this room. It's where we keep our perfumery books and, without knowing it, you somehow all made your way to it.'

I looked back into the main area, and realized she was right. I could have chosen a few other paths, including one leading up a rickety staircase.

'Perfumers,' she said, grinning. 'You can't hide anything from them.'

I smiled. 'So I take it the key isn't here?'

'*Non. Je suis désolé*. It's not here. I rang Sebastien to find out after the second contestant came in. I must admit, my interest is piqued. But, secretive man he is, he wouldn't tell me anything.'

'You know him?'

'Of course. Everyone knows the Lecléres. Parisians are proud Sebastien is continuing his papa's legacy. He's a closed book for the most part, though. I wondered if he'd escape Paris and we'd never see him again … but here he is, back and opening up the doors of *Leclére* no less.'

When Nan died, perfumery was so hollow without her and seemed pointless. I lost the joy in creating it for a time. And for Sebastien, whose father was arguably the greatest perfumer the world had ever seen, it must've been the same. Not to mention the added pressure of having a world-famous name and the demands that went along with that.

Sebastien was a mystery all right. But how *could* he escape, when he had the Leclére empire to run out of the little store off the Champs-Élysées? He had to be here, to run the place. Already I'd noticed his phone rang incessantly, like the most annoying buzz that seemed neverending.

'It's only been a year since he lost his father,' I mused, thinking back to my nan and how raw it still had felt at twelve months. Still, being busy definitely helped and perhaps Sebastien would heal himself this way too. Step from the shadows of his famous father, and cement his own place in the world of perfume …
'Perhaps he just wants space?'

'He has always craved a quiet life. When Vincent died, well, for Parisians it was like losing one of the greats like Piaf, Coco, Voltaire, but the world keeps turning, people marry, babies are made, and …' She let out a laugh and patted her the swell of her belly. 'Perhaps I'm just baby mad, but the days march on and I only hope Sebastien settles soon into life *sans* Papa. He's a wonderful guy … So many admirers and yet, he doesn't socialize much.'

I didn't care, truly I didn't. But out of courtesy I said, 'He doesn't have a girlfriend?'

She guffawed. '*Non, non, non, non.* Not since Giselle, a steely-hearted lawyer who was *so* unsuitable. Can you imagine them as a couple? The frosty contractual attorney, and the perfumer? It was never going to last.'

I raised a brow. 'What happened?'

With a tut, Oceane said, 'Sebastien took her to live in a little Provençal village and before long Giselle was back and he was not. Perhaps they were opposites, she the analytical type and he more a dreamer. Since they split up, he's been resolutely single. A waste, *non*?'

'Maybe she broke his heart?'

Oceane tilted her head, contemplating. 'You can never really tell with men.'

I nodded as if in agreement, but men were a curious unfathomable lot to me. And since Whispering Lakes hadn't been exactly swarming with bachelors, I hadn't dated as much as a city girl probably would have. Well, that was the excuse I used anyway. I guess I'd never met anyone that made my pulse race enough to compromise my future. Because that's what happened, wasn't it? You always had to give up something in return for that love. Case in point: Jen. She'd let our dreams roll on by the minute a guy confessed his love for her.

'So does Sebastien live here now, or not?'

She shrugged. 'He comes and goes. I think he'd prefer to hide away forever but his *maman* can be quite formidable when she needs to be. The business would not work without him, and I guess that is all there is to it.'

'It must be hard if his heart is elsewhere.' It struck me he craved small town life and I was seeking the opposite.

'And you …?' She narrowed her eyes.

'What about me?'

'Single?'

'Did you give all the contestants the same inquisition?' I said, playfully.

'I didn't get the same vibe from them, so *non*.'

'And what vibe is that?'

'Loneliness.'

Was it so obvious? 'I'm missing my twin sister, we were … are … very close.' I stumbled on the words. 'And this is my first time away from her.'

'And is she wearing the same long face?'

From her funny, lovey-dovey texts about James, I'd hazard a guess. 'No, probably not. She's in love, you see, so everything is sweet and the world is a wonderful place.'

'Ah, new love, the best drug in the world, aside from a new book, of course.'

'I guess,' I said. We chatted about our favourite novels – having similar tastes, we both loved quirky romance novels and exotic settings – before I noted the time.

'I better let you get back to it,' I said as the doorbell chimed and a group of tourists wandered in, their faces lighting up as if they'd discovered Narnia.

'Visit me again, sometime.'

'Thanks,' I said, kissing both cheeks in the French custom. 'I will.'

I gave Oceane a wave as I left the lovely little bookshop on the left bank and went in search of the key elsewhere, ruminating about what I'd heard about Sebastien. He was certainly a paradox. But really what did I know? He hadn't exactly been truthful with me.

Map aloft, I continued the search.

My feet ached as I found the Salvador Dalí sundial, still no key. Before I pressed on I took a quick photo of the dial and the shadows that played on the rendered wall, knowing Jen would get a kick out of it. She loved Dalí's surrealist artwork, and I'd thought it might be the spot because like Vincent, Dalí was an eccentric, highly imaginative man who made his mark on the world on his own terms. I found some sprigs of wild thyme and shoved them into my bag for inspiration later.

Next, I went upstairs at Sainte-Chapelle – a breathtaking thirteenth-century chapel with the most amazing stained glass windows that funneled in kaleidoscopic light. It was so heavenly you'd believe in God if you didn't already. Without drawing undue attention to myself, I coughed and dropped to the floor, looking determinedly for an envelope with the key inside and feeling ridiculous as people stepped around me, frowning. Not under any of the benches, not behind the security guard, who asked me what the heck I was doing. 'Lost an earring,' I mumbled and off I went.

Because I was close, and a huge fan of Gertrude Stein and Alice Toklas, I jogged to 27 rue de Fleurus, where the couple lived until 1946, but was disappointed to find no envelope, not even a garden from which I could pilfer a few flowers to remind me of the day.

Still, I stopped for a moment, and tried to envisage the many visitors to the Saturday night salons that Stein and Alice hosted, from Picasso, James Joyce, poet Ezra Pound and F. Scott Fitzgerald. They'd all stood here once, too, and I wondered how I could capture that in a perfume – master painters and literary greats, creative types made famous and sometimes *in*famous by their crafts …

There was no time to waste, so I snapped a photo of the plaque and the apartment itself and headed to Luxembourg gardens. In a shady corner a bee keeper waved me over, and I told him about my mission. He smiled, displaying tobacco stained teeth and gave me some honeycomb, expounding on the many health benefits, all the while with a smoking stub of a roll-your-own cigarette stuck to his bottom lip, another example of Paris and its contradictions. We chatted about the hives and the history while I marvelled at such magnificence in a park that everyone could enjoy.

A few hours later I still had no key but had a backpack full of this and that to awaken my olfactory receptors when I needed inspiration making perfume. Along the way I darted through various Parisian attractions, including Cinéma Pagode, an Asian temple that had been shipped over from Japan in the late 1800s and later became a cinema. It was so remarkable for its old-world charm with oriental East meets West style.

With increasingly slower steps, I made my way to Hôtel de Ville where the famous Kiss photograph by Robert Doisneau had been shot. Possibly one of the most well-known locations in Paris, I had an inkling the key would be in a place of significance like this. It was hard to picture the iconic couple captured in the black and white photograph with the world around me in technicolor, but still I felt a little rush of excitement at the thought. Paris was steeped in history and it was intoxicating walking in the footsteps of so many before who'd left their mark. I searched high and low, drawing suspicious glances from people when I dropped to my knees to inspect a place of interest, but came up short. I didn't bother to lie, I just laughed and shrugged and hoped they'd forget my face if I bumped into them again.

I'd covered more of Paris in a day than people did in a week! With leaden legs, I passed the Centre Georges Pompidou library and museum, whose architecture was high tech post-modern but to me it looked like it was still under construction with its exposed piping and strange framework. It seemed so incongruous against the beauty of Paris. But then I remembered reading that, when first erected, the Eiffel Tower was thought by Parisians to be the ugliest of eyesores and had almost been pulled down twenty years after it was built for the World's Fair. Perhaps in a couple of decades I'd come to like the strange architecture of the Pompidou.

Feet screaming, I found a small bistro and plonked myself down, desperate for a dose of caffeine or six in the hopes it would reinvigorate me. So much hinged on this very first challenge. The day had been interminable. And yet I still had no clear plan. A few fuzzy ideas about the scent I wanted to capture, but nothing definite.

I'd only just ordered a *café noir* when Kathryn raced in, her eyes wide.

Chapter Ten

'Del,' she said, breathlessly, holding a hand up to the waiter at the same time. 'Have you heard?'

'I haven't, but I have a feeling I know what you're going to say.'

Breathing heavily, she said, 'Anastacia found the envelope with the key.'

Anastacia! Was I on track at the Ritz? I silently berated myself for being flustered by her and then later, Sebastien. What if I'd let the perfect opportunity pass me by all for the sake of escaping with my green face? It jarred a bit too, that she'd set me up in Chanel Spa and then found the key.

'Where?'

Kathryn flicked her mane of red hair back, and sighed. 'Point Zero.'

'Point Zero? What's that?'

She moved the checked cane chair to face me, and before I blinked a waiter appeared, telling her gruffly to move her chair back to face the street. Kathryn complied with an exaggerated rolling of her eyes, and ordered a *café au lait* in perfect French.

Why were we to face the street? I found it odd that all the chairs faced the road and not your companion, another French quirk to add to the list. I didn't dare ask the man why, after his huffy puffy performance, as though we'd upset the order of things by being so clueless. It was quite comical without knowing why.

'Elbows in, *mademoiselle*,' he muttered as he walked off. Other patrons gave us the side eye, and it was all I could do not to laugh. It managed to distract me from the matter at hand for a moment or two.

'Legs bent at the knee,' Kathryn admonished with a laugh.

'What?'

'Terrace etiquette in Paris. There are unwritten rules for seating. If you have an outward facing terrace position then you must keep your elbows in and legs bent at the knee. Also, you've sat at a table with cutlery yet you're only having a coffee, and that's a big no no too.'

'I had no idea.' What other rules had I broken without being aware? 'Why do they face the street though?'

'Why not? Isn't it nicer to watch the world go by?'

'I suppose so.'

'It's a French thing.' She sighed and lit up a cigarette, taking a deep drag before blowing out smoke rings. So she hadn't given up all her vices when she left Paris all those years ago. Every second person smoked here. There was seemingly no concern for those eating; people inhaled slowly, and then blew their smoke all over the place. It didn't really concern me, it was all part of the perfume of Paris.

While I waited impatiently for an answer, Kathryn's fragrance shivered in the afternoon breeze. She wore a bold, herbaceous scent; it suited her.

She stubbed her cigarette out, and puckered her lips. 'I shouldn't smoke. Don't let me smoke. It tastes disgusting, I really can't understand why I crave them so much. It's the pressure that's doing it.'

'Try making a blend of black pepper, cedar and patchouli, and put it on your pulse points. That will stop the nicotine cravings,' I said. I'd helped a number of people to quit smoking, a simple fix if you balanced the blend well with the right notes.

She titled her head. 'Really?'

'Really. So, the key. Point Zero?'

'Oh, yes, so Point Zero is the *exact* centre of Paris, where all distances are measured from. Out the front of the Notre-Dame a small octagonal brass plate is embedded in the pavement. You probably stepped over it if you dashed past.'

I slapped a hand to my forehead. I'd been so close! Just around the corner – this proved it was time to switch on and start playing the game better. I had a deeper understanding of what lengths the others would go to win, so I had to up my strategy, or risk losing out like this again. Damn it to hell and back, I had been so close.

'It's not what I expected them to choose,' I said, sipping my coffee and willing my legs not to ache, so I could walk back to my room once I'd finished my drink.

'You don't understand the significance, do you?'

'Not really.' Measurement didn't seem very auspicious to me.

'To some it might be a marker which distances are measured from, but for others it's something much more significant. It's a *wishing* place.'

'What do they wish for?'

'For true love! You're supposed to spin in a circle on one foot, make a wish and then *voila*, very soon your heart's desire will appear. A man – a perfect specimen of man – tall, dark and handsome … if you're into that.'

I laughed nervously, as Sebastien's green-eyed gaze popped into my mind and I silently berated myself once more. Didn't I just give myself a talking to about focus? I could've sworn my sister had inhabited my body and was running things. It just wasn't like me to worry about anything other than perfume, but the idea of love kept swirling and I couldn't think why. I had a clear five-year plan (OK, so it needed tweaking after Jen's bombshell) and men didn't figure into that. Especially broody French men who lied about who they were …

I cleared my throat, shrugging off my inner turmoil. 'I'm not really into men.'

She did the duck-lip face and said, 'Well, petite, fair and pretty then.'

'What …?' Oh! I slapped my face. 'No, no, I meant, I'm not into men *right now*. I'm more worried about my future. You know being almost thirty and all that.'

She gave me a dubious look. 'No need to justify anything to me.'

Great, she didn't believe me. The situation was suddenly hysterical; once again we'd got off track, so I tried to bring it back to the matter at hand.

'Point Zero is a romantic spot, as whimsical as it might be. Goes to show, we really don't have any idea what we're up against with these challenges. We'll be on our toes that's for sure.'

'Especially if they're going to be so …' she folded her arms '… random. Like how does that place equate to perfume?'

I contemplated the link too. It would help if we knew why they chose such a place. Surely it wasn't just by chance. It had to be significant for a reason. 'I get it!' I said, holding up a finger. 'It's *symbolic*. Our journey should start at the very centre of Paris … Add some romance into the mix by choosing a location where lovers kiss, or people wish? It's perfect. Perfume *is* romance, after all.' Nan's whole mantra about the language of love sprang to mind. Perfume was love, love was perfume; it was how you translated it that mattered.

'Of course, you're totally right,' she sighed. 'How could I miss that? I can see it now in hindsight, but I went straight for the Musée du Parfum. It wasn't there – too obvious, right? Like Sebastien said earlier, we have to think outside the usual parameters of perfume, and this just proves it. You can't count on anything! It's going to be a hell of a ride.'

I nodded, grateful that I had someone to chat to after the whirlwind day.

She continued: 'I have to think faster; today was a complete write-off in terms of the competition. I can't even summon up the energy to move but I know I need to.' Her face twisted, and the lemony scent of worry perfumed the air.

It was my turn to sigh, I felt the same, zapped of energy and down about not finding the key. Outside the day cooled as the sun dropped. 'It's getting late,' Kathryn said morosely, her enthusiasm vanished.

This had been the girl alongside Clementine who'd been hell bent on studying everyone's social media profiles, finding out every tidbit of information about us all and the first day had leached her confidence.

I raised my hand for the bill, and paid for Kathryn's coffee, hoping she'd appreciate the small gesture of friendship.

'Come on, Kathryn, it's not the end of the world. Get yourself together and get back out there. Wow them with your perfume and forget about the key. It's over and we've just got to press on.' If anyone had to worry, it was me, the wildcard of the group.

'Yes, darling, I'll think perky thoughts – or intravenous coffee might help,' she said through half-slitted eyes.

I left her cupping her head in hands, and collected my things and wandered into the softly falling twilight.

***

Hours later, as moonlight cast gauzy fingers onto the Avenue des Champs-Élysées, I turned into our little side street and trudged upstairs to our apartment, fatigue making my mind fuzzy. Every muscle ached and I was ready for bed. The thought of taking off my boots and freeing my poor blistered and bruised feet was all I was focused on.

My bed had been freshly made and I was seconds away from slipping beneath the covers for a power nap until Clementine came noisily down the hall, and all thought of peace quickly disappeared.

'There you are, Del! What an exciting day, *non*?' Somehow her make-up was still as perfect as it had been in the morning – was it really only this morning that we'd set off? It felt like aeons ago – and an eager smile lit up her face. How had she remained so fresh? Perhaps being Parisian helped. There was no studying up on tourist attractions or Metro maps, she'd have known them all, but still she hadn't found the key.

'Yeah, exciting,' I said, weariness tinging my voice, as I noted Clementine could go from foe to friend as swiftly as the blink of an eye.

'Ooh la la, you're tired. You look a sight with your wind ravaged 'air, and …' She leaned in to survey me. 'Did you go swimming?'

'Swimming? No. Where would I swim in Paris for god's sake?' Not in the Seine that's for sure.

'You'd swim on the barge, 'aven't you seen it?'

'No?'

'*Piscine Josephine Baker*, a swimming pool built on a barge in the Seine. You 'aven't been there swimming, are you sure?'

'There's a swimming pool on a barge?' Paris really had it all. How long would it take to hunt out all the hidden gems in the huge city with its twenty *arrondissements*, curling around one another like a snail shell.

'*Oui*. We swim laps there, my *maman* says I must because of the cherry *clafoutis*, but for me it's more about the men. They wear the little trunks, those teeny tiny …'

I interrupted in case I spent the next hour listening to her wax lyrical about men's nether regions. 'I get it,' I said. 'But no, I haven't been swimming, Clem, as nice as the *piscine* sounds. I've been running madly all over town.'

She scrunched her nose. 'You are 'ow you say, fresh faced. *Sans* make-up. To be quite honest you look a little *misérable*.'

'Oh,' I said, her question making sense. '*That!* Well, Anastacia tried to sabotage me and I ended up with a green face mask on and had to run out of the Ritz in the middle of a treatment without paying. And of course I ran into Sebastien when I resembled the Hulk. And to hear *she* found the key, well if I had a voodoo doll …'

'I know a place we can get such a doll.' She held her finger up to her lips as if it was a secret. 'You just say the word, *non*?'

'Erm, thanks, Clem. I'll keep it in mind.'

She arched a brow. 'You think I'm joking? *Non*, you must take extreme measures or she'll always pick on you. Cunning as a box she is.'

'A fox, you mean?' I shrugged. 'I think pretty much *everyone* is cunning, Clementine. I don't trust anyone.' Who knew what they really wanted? Kathryn's arrival at the café might not have been innocent. Even Sebastien kept his real identity secret when he had so many chances to tell me. They were all suspicious.

'*Oui*, you're correct,' she said as she took off her earrings. 'But you're still not playing the game right, Del. You may as well wear a flashing sign saying NICE GIRL. Your perfume skills might be *fantastique*, but you're too nice. Nice never wins. You have to start thinking like they do. And they'll do anything to win, so don't let them.'

I flopped back onto the bed. 'Yeah, well, that's easier said than done.'

'Not really. Strike before they do. Or stay the 'ell away from them all.'

'Aren't you a little disappointed though, Clem? Like I was expecting we'd all be friends, and this would be some life-affirming competition and despite the prize on offer, we'd make these everlasting friendships, and have lunch when we were in whoever's town. I didn't expect sabotage.' And really, Clementine was up there with Anastacia, shady as hell too.

She harrumphed. '*Non*, I did not think it would be like that, that is for TV, that kind of fairytale,' Clementine said with a shrug. 'Who knows what will 'appen. Just focus on fragrance, we're not here to make friends.'

'You said we were friends.' I couldn't help but tease her, but

I sensed Clementine picked and chose her friends on whatever whim she felt at the time.

Her features softened. '*Oui*, of course we're friends! What's the nice girl going to do to me? Nothing, that's what! She's too nice!'

I lobbed a pillow at her for good measure. She ducked and it sailed over her head. 'That's more like it, Del!' she said proudly. I could only shake my head; she really had no idea who I was and had pegged me for a sucker but that was probably a good thing. Better if I was no threat to her.

She kicked off her heels (how did she spend all day in heels!?) and sat at the end of my bed. 'You know, I helped Lila out with directions? Silly girl must have misheard me and got on the wrong train. She ended up visiting Versailles …' Her eyes twinkled mischievously. 'Whoops.'

My mouth fell open. Lila must've run into Clementine after she left Place Vendôme. 'You didn't!'

'I did. One less person to worry about. But now we have Anastacia with the advantage.'

Poor Lila! Out of the group, she was the one hanging back, eyes darting nervously around. For Clementine to do such a thing was plain mean. 'Clem, that wasn't cool. Lila is young, and this is probably her first time away …' (Mine too!) 'How could you be so mean?'

She shrugged, and blithely went to the balcony and flung open the doors, letting in the balmy evening breeze. 'Pah! It's part of the game! You'd do well to learn from me.'

It took all of my might to swallow the scoff that bubbled up.

She continued unabashed. '*I'm* not worried about Anastacia finding the key and 'aving the advantage of using Vincent's personal studio, because she's not the best perfumer.'

'What makes you think that?' Anastacia was here, and that meant she was a threat as far as I was concerned. Everyone had been subject to the same rigorous selection process as we had.

Clementine unwound her colourful scarf, and scrutinized

herself in the mirror, puckering her lips and batting her eyelashes before turning to me. 'I've done some digging on Anastacia and, well, her style is pared back. Minimal. She believes you don't need to complicate fragrance. A handful of aromas and that's all she uses; she doesn't layer the scent. Lazy, *non*?'

Dragging myself vertical once more, I took off my boots, wiggled my toes, relishing in the freedom. By the sound of it, Clementine had spent an inordinate amount of time internet stalking the contestants when she could have spent that time perfecting her own style. It made me wonder if her own perfumery lacked a little *je ne sais quoi* …

'We don't know if Anastacia's style is lazy or genius, Clem. Maybe she's on to something, *we* could be muddling perfume by adding unnecessary elements, and how could we know unless we try?'

Like writers, or artists, perfumers each had their own style, their own voice, and their perfumes reflected that. Anastacia's style was understated and I was interested to see how it worked. 'Less is more' appealed to me; I often made herbal tinctures with only a handful of ingredients and they turned out just fine. Perfume was more complex, but I could envisage it working as long as the scent was perfectly balanced. Anastacia's style had piqued my interest and reminded me that I was here to learn, and soak up as much as I could while I had the chance.

'Pah!' Clementine said again, a word that for her brooked no argument. 'I may as well rub a sprig of rosemary on my wrist and be done with it! And why are you standing up for 'ér? Didn't she do the wrong thing by you today, Del? You should be planning revenge not 'aving that doe-eyed deer look in your eyes.'

I laughed. 'Oh, Clementine, you speak of me like I'm this timid little bird! I *was* plotting revenge for a good few hours as I raced over Paris, but you know what? It distracted me, it stopped me thinking about perfume and this week's challenge. I'll let the rest of you sabotage each other, while I dream about fragrance and what I'm going to do when I win.'

In Clementine's perfume was the scent of wind and rain, and zephyr of challenge. She wasn't intimidated by anyone and part of me thought it would be her downfall. But what the heck did I know really, except Paris wasn't all rainbows and butterflies and neither were the contestants.

'I'm going to shower,' she said. 'And then we are to attend dinner.'

At the mention of food my stomach rumbled but after the long day, and the memory of them clustering around gossiping the night before, I was put off. I'd grab dinner in one of the cheaper bistros in the 5th instead. And truthfully, I didn't want to have to stare at Sebastien all night. 'I'll pass,' I said. 'I'm so tired, I just want to eat as fast as possible and sleep.'

She tutted. 'I thought you Americans were a little more fun!'

'My feet are about to fall off.'

'Pah!' she said.

Chapter Eleven

The next day was mayhem in the lab. Emotions were high. Stress, and grim and gritty determination, shone on my competitors' faces. We were being judged purely on our mettle and how we coped working in a new environment on a strict timeframe.

As the day wore on, nerves turned from taut to frazzled and the noise level increased. Someone would push past someone else and foreign curses would ring out. It was interesting that I could always translate a profanity even if I didn't speak the language.

For some reason, Anastacia kept coming in and yammering on that the prize of working alone in Vincent's studio bored her. I'd have given anything to take her place! Working amid this chaos took a toll; I couldn't think straight with all the noise. Clementine played some bawdy burlesque music, and warbled away operatically and it was all I could do not to scream.

Anastacia goaded Clementine but I got the feeling Clem relished the drama, going by the back and forth between them. After the third argument in as many minutes, I grabbed Clementine's phone and shut off her music. 'Are you purposely riling her up?'

The Parisian giggled behind her hand. '*Oui*! Isn't it great? Look at her, you can almost see fire coming out of her nose!'

I risked a quick glance at Anastacia, who gave me a death stare so fierce my legs wobbled. '*You* are playing with fire,' I admonished Clementine, and concentrated at glancing anywhere but in Anastacia's direction.

'Pah!' she said. 'If she's concerned about me, then she's not concentrating! She should be in Vincent's studio working!'

'But you're not concentrating either!'

She did that thing, a sort of head loll and tongue cluck that implied I was obtuse. 'I *obviously* don't need as much time as everyone else, Del. I am French!' she said, as if that explained it all.

'So?' I failed to see her reasoning.

'So we *invented* perfume!'

That wasn't actually the way history remembered it but for the sake of saving everyone from another thirty-minute monologue I let her have the point. 'Right-e-o, Clem. *I* have to concentrate but just be careful.' I left the two women to battle it out.

Kathryn with her lovely sleek red locks just shook her head and mouthed, 'She's a nightmare.' I wasn't sure if she meant Clementine or Anastacia, but I had a feeling it was her Parisian friend.

Sebastien wandered in, and all talk ceased. I watched him from the corner of my eye as I continued to work. With each contestant he hurried to answer their questions, as though he was in a rush to leave. When he came to Clementine's bench he deflected her flirtatious banter easily so her pride wasn't hurt. Golly, I could hear her overt attempts from where I stood, and internally rolled my eyes. Nothing was off limits to her. Would it be her downfall, not taking anything seriously and relying on other methods to get ahead?

The fragrance in the room swirled and shimmied, heightening as he continued to visit each contestant. I wasn't sure if it was his magnetism that they were attracted to or the fact he was a Leclére; either way it was interesting to watch them flirt, bumble, or mumble alongside him. When he got close to my bench the room was abuzz.

Sebastien stepped towards me, a question in his eyes. I averted my gaze, and moved around him, brushing his hand as I did, feeling that same sizzle race through me.

'Sorry,' I said, snatching my hand back as if it had been burned. *Do not act like a fool, Del!* 'Have you come to save me?' The words spilled out before I could stop them. Save me?

'Do you need saving?' A smile played at his lips. Gosh, they were lovely lips, if you were into lips.

'No, not really.' I squirmed. 'But I will definitely be having your larger than average glass of *vin blanc* tonight.'

He tilted his head. 'Why?'

The room fell silent, I could almost hear them breathing, and they were hanging on to every word we spoke. Best not to rile them up by complaining about them! 'I'm sure you know, since I poured my heart out to you in the bar that night, not realizing you in fact knew exactly who I was.' No need to act the *ingénue* either, better he understood I was still annoyed at his double cross.

'I'm so sorry, Del. I was grappling with so many things that day, and I didn't actually recognize you until you jumped on my back and attached yourself to me.'

I gave him a hard stare. 'I tripped over a baguette.'

'If you say so.'

I scoffed. 'You know so.'

He gave an airy shrug, but I could tell he was just playing with me.

'If you're free later, I thought we could have coffee?'

'Maybe. I'm fairly busy so I couldn't possibly confirm.'

'I'll meet you at the café with the red shutters at six.'

I pursed my lips and he smiled and left the room.

Once he'd gone, Clementine dashed over. 'Aren't you the flavor of the month?'

'Don't start,' I said, glaring at her. Could she even make perfume? All she seemed to care about was having the upper hand and intimidating everyone. Well, I wouldn't put up with that! 'He's my mentor, remember?' That's all it was, a mentoring session so he could say he'd done his job and walk off into the sunset …

She shook her head and flounced off. Next, she'd be sabotaging *me*. When I calmed down, I thought of the green-eyed Frenchman. He'd actually seemed pained having to stand around and answer questions. I'd have pegged him as the opposite, like his father, a dreamer who loved talking about fragrance, the type who got lost in conversation, their passion radiating from every pore, but he wasn't like that at all. Why?

Out of the window I caught a glimpse of Sebastien striding down the Champs-Élysées, hands in pockets, wind in his hair, head down as though he had the weight of the world on his shoulders. There was a real sense of desolation about him at times when he thought no one was watching. As though he was lost, his moods shifting like the tides.

I spent a moment watching him, just for the sheer loveliness of the fine figure he cut walking against the wind and felt a pull in that direction. A sense of understanding.

***

At the café with the red shutters, I took a seat out the front, the fresh air like a balm after all day inside with so many aromas. The summer breeze blew away the tension I'd been holding and I flopped back in my chair, and waited for Sebastien. He was late, damn it.

A few minutes later, he arrived with a mouthful of apologies. A waiter fussed over him, and then pointed to me. I blushed, feeling caught out, staring so openly. I made a show of checking my cell phone as if I had something wildly important that needed doing, while Sebastien answered his phone too.

How's Pop? I miss him. I sent the text to Jen as he ended his call and sat down.

'Have you ordered?'

'Not yet, I didn't get quite the welcome you did,' I said with a smile.

He gave a half shrug. 'Let's remedy that.'

The waiter fell over himself to serve Sebastien, returning with two small black coffees and a plate of icing-dusted madeleines.

'So,' he said, taking a sip. 'I noticed the mood was fraught in the lab today. How did you cope?'

I took a deep breath, and debated with what to say. 'It's certainly different to what I'm used to. But isn't that what this is for? To push us out of our comfort zones and apply pressure?'

He sighed. 'Yes, a commercially viable perfumer would naturally work in a lab, like you're all doing. So it was thought by the management team that you'd be tested under the same conditions. More for your benefit, than for ours. If any of you do go on to work for a large perfume house, you'll have experience. You'll know what is expected of you in a professional capacity.'

'I get the feeling you don't agree?'

The green of his eyes flashed. 'Not really. This was supposed to be about helping perfumers find their voice, their style, not some apprenticeship … My papa never worked in a lab, he always worked alone. I work alone.'

'But you're in charge, aren't you? Why don't you say no?'

He waited a beat. 'It's complicated. But I made a promise and I'm sticking to it, even if it's not what I agree with for the most part.'

'You made a promise to your father?'

When no answer was forthcoming I continued. 'It surprised me, that *Leclére* would open the doors to us so soon after …' I left the sentence hanging.

'He asked me to.' His voice grew thick. 'Just before he died, he made me promise him that I'd do this one thing.'

'Why? Why did he suddenly want you to help a group of strangers?'

He exhaled. 'I don't know, but he was adamant about it. And I figured it was the least I could do; listen to a dying man's wishes.'

I shivered at the sadness in his voice, and pictured a frail, old Vincent beseeching his son to do this one thing. The question remained though, why did he want to escape when he had the world at his feet?

'But …'

He cut me off, the subject clearly closed. 'How are you finding Paris?'

'I love it,' I said. 'I've always wanted to live in a big city. Now I've had a taste of it, I know it's in my future.'

He gave a tiny nod and I continued, 'It's the noise, the early morning trucks unloading their wares, the traffic, the beeping of horns, a signal it's a new day, the busy *boulangeries*, *patisseries*, *fromageries*, the clatter of cutlery and conversation …'

This time he just shook his head and laughed. 'It's everything I dislike,' he said. 'Paris can swallow a person whole.'

How could he not love Paris?

Chapter Twelve

A few days later Lex shuffled over to my bench and folded his arms. 'How goes it, America?' He radiated calm, his mouth curved into a wide smile, exposing his crooked teeth. I sensed Lex had nailed his perfume and was happy with what he'd made. All week he'd had his headphones plugged in and wasn't bothered by the rest of the group. I got the feeling nomadic Lex could work anywhere.

I scraped back my hair, not sharing his zen but happy for him. 'It's not going great, Lex. I'm struggling a little at the moment ...'

'It's hard, isn't it?'

'Making perfume like this?'

He nodded. 'Yeah, I'm used to playing around on my own, at my own leisure, music cranked up, not a soul in sight. Not like this, like we're re-enacting *Lord of the Flies*.'

I laughed. 'But you managed here amidst the chaos. That's the sign of a great perfumer.'

'I still have a bit of work to do with it,' he said, pulling his lips to one side to imply it wasn't that great a perfume, though I was sure it was. 'But I wanted to let it go for the day, see if I still like it as much tomorrow.'

'You will, and I'm happy for you, Lex. I really am.' I truly hoped he came back tomorrow and his perfume was everything and more than he expected. Back home, some days I'd rush back to my perfume organ and find the previous day's work a disappointment, like overnight the compounds had decided they wouldn't play nice and split, the perfume producing a bitter odd note. But then there were other days, where I breezed back and there it was, a little shining beacon of hope and beauty, the sweet smell of success.

Leaning in, he whispered, 'They're getting to you, and you can't let them.'

How did he know? I wasn't the only flustered one in the room. Again, I had that sense that Lex was more self-aware than most. 'I know, it's just the air is thick with so many aromas, it makes it hard to know what I'm smelling.'

'Keep taking sensory breaks, and do the tricky stuff when you're alone.'

'Yes, I will. Let's hope they leave soon, eh?'

'Let's grab a drink, and you can breathe a little.'

Perfumers took sensory breaks to ward off olfactory fatigue. Some believed in the old notion of sniffing coffee beans, others sniffed the unperfumed skin in the crook of their elbow but to me they were more old wives' tales and the best thing for it was fresh air and some time away from your work in progress.

'OK,' I said, tidying my bench. 'A break might be just the thing.'

We found a small café and I made sure to keep my chair facing outwards and my elbows tucked in and legs bent at the knee …! Lex on the other hand had his fingers laced behind his forehead, elbows distinctly out and splayed his legs. The rebel.

We ordered two cups of *café au lait* while Lex studiously ignored the waiter's pursed lips and warning frown.

'Did you hear the latest?' Lex asked, lazily.

'Latest what?'

'Apparently one of the contestants is considering withdrawing from the competition. All too much for them apparently.'

I gaped. 'Who?'

He gave a one-shouldered shrug. 'No idea. But I think Anastacia and Clementine have a lot to answer for.'

Lila? Had to be. Being sent on a goose chase to Versailles when she'd asked the only Parisian among us, Clementine, for directions.

Our coffees arrived and Lex thanked the waiter, managing to draw a small smile from the man. 'Be a shame to give up this kind of opportunity. Makes me wonder why, you know. Were they intimidated or bullied by another contestant, or was it just the pressure, or being away from home?'

'Yeah, perhaps it's a bit of everything.'

'It's not you is it, America?' There was a worried edge to his voice which lifted my heart a little. It *was* a daunting situation, being thrown into a pressurized environment away from the comfort of home, surrounded by big egos and with sabotage going on behind the scenes. I was heartened to know Lex cared enough to hope it wasn't me. Especially when one less contestant meant everyone else, including him, were closer to the prize.

'It's not me,' I said, taking a sip of coffee. 'But thanks for asking.'

He feigned nonchalance but his open-book face made it impossible.

'You're a big softie at heart, aren't you, Lex?'

'Let's not be ridiculous,' he said, but grinned. 'You'll ruin my reputation.'

'Your secret is safe with me.'

As we sat sharing a quiet moment, I wondered if Aurelie had truly managed to convince the runaway contestant to stay. I'd find Lila later and see if she was OK.

When I returned to the lab everyone was still hard at it and the arguments had shifted from hissed profanities to hands on hips belligerence. Sebastien sure had chosen a mixed bunch of personalities, some timid, others with explosive tempers. Half the battle in the lab was concentrating amidst all the bickering.

Still, I had a couple of days until I had to submit. Surely I could finish a fragrance that would wow them? I had to. We had a perfumery excursion planned the following morning which would snatch a bit of my time. I'd have to hustle as best I could and hope that everything went to plan. The mentoring couldn't come quick enough. Sebastien seemed to understand my need to work in solitude; perhaps we could move to a different studio. But then I'd be alone with him, and that would prove distracting all on its own.

I worked hard for another few hours before exhaustion got the better of me. It was too late to call Jen, and I didn't have the energy, so I sent her a long text and filled her in on everything. Close to midnight I snuck back into my room, with a worried heart and still no closer to perfecting my perfume.

***

Excursion day arrived, and with it our first official visit to *Leclére Parfumerie*. The store was closed, so we had ample time to explore and ask questions and smell everything on offer!

We entered the shop and a hush fell over us. The place was dim, otherworldly, with the thick velvet teal curtains blocking out the light. The beautiful bottles of perfume, art in themselves, stood out, as soft spotlight shone down on them. The space hummed with magic, it radiated from every fibrous pore …

Aurelie called for attention and welcomed us. '*Leclére Parfumerie* first opened its doors forty years ago. Not long compared to some more well-known perfume houses, but long enough to develop a reputation for quality fragrances. Vincent believed that if you loved what you made, from the perfume itself to the handcrafted bottle right down to the parchment label, then so would our customers.' With pride in her voice she smiled fondly at the memory.

I wandered to a shelf that housed their famous *Aurelie* perfume. The thick glass bottle was heavy in my hand and had a purple tint to it and was wrapped in the most delicate gold, latticed-like lacework. It was the type of perfume bottle you'd keep long after you'd used every drop of scent. Handwritten parchment labels were tied on, loping calligraphy detailing the type of perfume and its notes. 'Who writes these labels?' I asked. They didn't look like they'd been printed.

'Our staff,' she said. 'They're trained in calligraphy and every label is handwritten.'

No wonder *Leclére* had made such a name for themselves; every last detail was meticulously thought out.

'What about the perfume itself?' asked Lila. I hadn't managed to ask her if she was the one who wanted to withdraw from the competition yet. 'Surely that's mass produced?'

'We have a lab in the South of France where our perfumes are made. They're made in large quantities, but all by hand, not by production line. Vincent's brother oversees it so our formulas are kept secret.'

I wanted to sniff every bottle and open every jar of dried goods. There was a collection of glass jars full of dried ingredients that you could mix with creams and oils to make your very own moisturizers, exfoliators, face masks. There were scented oils: grapeseed, raspberry, and prickly pear. I'd never seen such a place except in my imagination and I was completely besotted by it.

My dream was to design bespoke perfumes for clients, little bottles of joy made especially for them. Not mass-produced scents, but something personal, that would conjure what they needed most: faith, love, joy ... We relied on our five senses daily, and evocative smells could turn a somber mood into joy quicker than almost anything, that was the magic in perfumery.

Paris had already opened my eyes to new ideas, from bottle design to small touches like packaging that would make my brand stand out. Perhaps a handwritten note would accompany each perfume I made? Instead of a wishing place, like Point Zero, it would be an affirmation, one they could read over and again when they needed it. Almost like a fortune cookie note but for fragrance …

'As you can see,' she said, 'it's not only about the perfume, but the sense of luxury, of a craft learned and perfected over time. We have a product you won't find online, that you won't find in any other store, and that makes it special.'

Tingles raced up my spine. People loved to tell me that designing bespoke perfume would be a mistake. Too limiting. That I'd never make enough money to live, that no one would pay so much for a perfume made by a nobody (let's face it, in the world of perfumery I *was* a nobody) but if Vincent could start from nothing, why couldn't I? He hadn't come from a privileged background, just the same as me. We all had to begin somewhere and build a reputation for exceptional fragrance. If he could do it on passion alone, why couldn't I? Wildcard Perfumery … I grinned at the thought.

I uncapped the bottle of *Aurelie* perfume and was transported to a rose garden. It was exquisite, fresh and lush and sultry, the top note a heavy Turkish red rose, the type of scent that made you reminisce about love …

'Feel free to wander around and I'll be here if you have any questions,' she said.

I raised my hand. 'So what do these sell for?' I asked, noting there were no price tags on any product, and looked up into the baleful eyes of Sebastien himself and my turncoat heart jittered and jived and made talking quite impossible.

He blanched at my question, but took pains to hide it. How stupid of me; the French had this peculiar aversion to discussing money. The American in me just doesn't get that. Leaning close he whispered the amount in my ear. Whoa. Liquid gold, and then some.

He smiled, his features softening. 'You're not going to trip over something, are you?'

My eyes widened. 'I hope not. I don't think I could afford to replace what I break.'

He laughed. 'You're a breath of fresh air, Del.'

I gave a fluttery little laugh, ready to make light of my past clumsiness, because that was what he was implying, right? *Del, the clown jester of the group.* I scuttled away from the intensity of those green eyes of his. But for one lonely second I dreamed he meant it as something more … like I was the cure-all, the tonic to his loneliness.

It was the perfume lingering in the air; those light balsam heart notes could make a girl swoon.

Chapter Thirteen

Deadline day was just around the corner and my nerves were as frayed as the end of an old rope. Each challenge we accrued points, so I wanted to make sure I didn't fall behind, or it would be impossible to catch up, thus losing any hope of winning the competition.

The more I fussed with the scent the more confused I became. It was mediocre at best and I tried to work out how I'd lost my way so spectacularly at such a crucial stage.

I debated whether to scrap it and start over, but there really wasn't time.

With hands on the edge of the bench I stared at the little vial of perfume, hoping an answer would appear. Why wasn't it right? It wouldn't impress the judges, they wouldn't recall it later, and I hadn't taken any risks so it didn't fit the brief we'd been given.

As I'd dallied, the other contestants had slowly flittered away, their perfumes finished and submitted, which had given me the space I needed to work, the air lighter without them, yet here I was. Resident of Struggle Town, population one.

Now there was only me and Lila left in the studio.

Her groans grew louder every hour, and her face got longer and soon I could ignore it no more. Make that Struggle Town, population two.

'Not working?' I asked, as she threw down her notebook.

Scraping back her hair, she said, 'Nope.' Her shoulders slumped south. 'I can't even *think* of why the *Leclére* team chose me! I'll be mortified submitting this.' Lila pointed to a bottle that held a seaweed green liquid, but it hadn't been filtered correctly and was grainy and mottled.

While I debated with how to answer, I wondered if it really was Lila who'd asked to pull out of the competition. It had to be. Somehow I couldn't see it being Clem, Kathryn or Anastacia, and it wasn't me or Lex. So that just left shy Lila. Game playing and sabotage weren't her thing, and it struck me that we were both struggling despite avoiding those tactics.

'Having problems too?' she asked, her brow wrinkled.

'Yep,' I said. 'It's just *meh*.'

'Why?'

'It's a fragrance you'd buy for someone you didn't know very well. A safe blend of … nothingness.' My vial was an innocuous shade of light blue. I'd tried to encapsulate home: Whispering Lakes, earthy rugged mountains, crisp autumnal air and that feeling you get when you're safe, you're comfortable. And that's exactly what I'd managed to do. A comfort zone perfume! Instead of stepping out of my own comfort zone, I stepped *into* it and bottled it. *Gah*.

With no time to start over and a sense of panic arising, I could see the same reflected back in Lila's eyes. Damn it.

'You're too talented to go home,' she said, though she didn't know me or my perfumery really. 'It'll be me who gets eliminated.' She put a hand to her forehead. 'And I gave up so much to be here. My parents, they didn't approve.' Pain tinged her voice grey and it was hard not to offer platitudes to the poor girl. She'd gone against her parents' wishes, so how soul crushing would it be to go home the very first week?

Even I could see her perfume was not up to standard on

aesthetics alone. She was on the verge of giving up but she still had hours left to fix that. I could help her, but in turn would that send me home? I dithered with what to do, until I heard my nan's voice … *I didn't teach you to be selfish, Del, you help that girl now*.

Smiling at the thought of Nan somewhere over my shoulder, I said, 'Lila, you just need to filter it again, use a different technique.' I walked to her bench and opened the stopper, wafting the bottle under my nose. Green tea, orange peel, bergamot, if you overlooked the murkiness it was an evocative perfume. The scent brought to mind early mornings, the first sip of tea, and the beauty of a new dawn, soft sunlight and promise. A couple of the elements needed balancing but it could be fixed in time.

Watching my face closely, tentative hope filled her eyes. 'The green tea is too strong, yeah?'

I nodded, 'Yep, level it out or it takes on seaweed notes. Aside from that the top note is beautiful, and it conjures the quiet joy of a morning perfectly.'

Her face flushed with happiness. 'I'll filter it and try and play about with the combinations. Do you really think I can fix it?'

'Yep,' I said with a smile. The only thing stopping Lila was self-doubt. By second guessing, she'd lost her way. She was mired by the thought of failure because of the pressure, and I knew this because I was facing the same problem.

But I could see that Lila had a real gift, the ability to make a perfume summon a scene, an evocation; it was what the Lecléres were striving for, something *I* was striving for but just couldn't quite grasp.

She'd do very well if she could get the aesthetics under control. 'All you have to do is believe in yourself. Seriously, I'm envious. You'll make your parents proud, Lila. Just you wait and see.' Hope flared, bright like a new dawn.

'Thanks, Del. Imagine that,' she said with a sad smile. 'Them proud of me. They haven't quite wrapped their heads around the fact they paid for my chemistry degree and I chose to make perfume instead of developing a cure for diseases or something noble. But I have to follow my heart, right? And the *last* thing I want is to go home tail between my legs to all those I-told-you-so looks.'

It must've been awful not having their support. It would make the journey incredibly difficult and I really hoped she'd make it to the grand finale to prove to them that perfumery was a viable career. While it might have been all sorts of noble inventing medical breakthroughs, you couldn't be passionate about it if it wasn't your vocation.

Like love, perfumery chose you, and not the other way around. Having the nose for it was a one in a million gift and how could you argue with that? As dippy as my parents were, they always supported whatever whim I had, and I felt sorry that Lila didn't have the same.

Her eyes were glassy with tears and I gave her arm a pat.

'Thanks, Del. Gosh, I didn't expect in a million years that another contestant would ever help me fix it. I really appreciate it.'

I shrugged and gave her a wide smile. 'You would have fixed it, anyway, Lila. You probably just needed to step away from it for a while.'

Lila walked to my bench and uncorked my perfume, piping a few drops onto a scent strip. After a moment, she said, 'I see what you were trying to do,' she said. 'It is comforting, like a homecoming!'

'Not exactly the risk of the century, is it?'

She debated how to answer. 'Well, while it's not mind-blowing, it's still pretty damn good.'

'Not good enough though. It's too sedentary. Like something you'd buy for the old lady down the road who looked after your dog while you were on holiday.'

She laughed, the sound like chimes. 'I wouldn't quite put it that way, but yeah, I see what you mean. Keep going, Del, don't give up now, will you?'

I shook my head. There was no chance of that. 'I'll tinker with it some more and hope I can get some pzazz into it.'

She dropped her gaze and her voice, her shyness reappearing. 'Once this wraps up do you want to grab dinner sometime? I usually eat with the group but it'd be nice to escape that for a while.'

'Dinner sounds great,' I said, feeling a rush of warmth. I too wanted to escape the boisterous group most of the time. I'd managed to avoid dinner by eating cheaply at the little bistros tucked away in the 5th *arrondissement*, or further afield in the 6th, but still caught a handful of them at breakfast when they were usually more subdued. Like Lila, I didn't enjoy confrontation or dominating personalities or being questioned by the management team, who seemed intent on making us sweat by interrogating us for reasons unknown. 'Was it you who asked to leave the competition?' I asked.

A blush crept up her cheeks. 'It was a knee jerk reaction, that's all. I'm glad Aurelie talked me out of it.'

'I'm glad too. You've got such a gift, Lila. Don't let anyone intimidate you. There's some wily contestants here, but you can beat them on talent alone.'

'Thanks, Del. Let's just say I'll never trust Clementine again …'

You and me both.

Chapter Fourteen

Mustering courage, the next day I took my vial of perfume to the *Leclére* office to submit for judging. In the end I'd run out of time and had to submit the comfort zone fragrance and cross my fingers that someone submitted something worse. But not Lila or Lex. I didn't want them to leave, and I had an inkling they'd stay after smelling their perfumes. The other contestants would sell me up the river if it would advance them, but Lex and Lila were of a differently ilk, and already I liked them as people and perfumers.

We wouldn't find the results out until Monday morning, so the next few days would be interminable. *If only, if only, if only …*

Disappointment sat heavily on my shoulders. Still, it would be better to front up with confidence, right? Fake it until you make it and all that.

With a steadying breath I knocked on the door and entered the office to find Sebastien there. '*Bonjour*, Del,' he said, motioning for me to sit opposite him. In the light bright room with only us, I felt exposed and vulnerable as I handed him the bottle. Perfume was so personal; each note symbolizing a hidden depth, a layer of secrets, until it became someone else's and open to their interpretation. 'Can I leave this with you for the judges?'

'*Oui*,' he said. Today his hair was slightly mussed as though he hadn't slept well. But the vivid green of his eyes were bright and focused directly on me, waiting for me to speak. Shoot. I'd never been the tongue-tied sort. It was the long days and lonely nights in foreign locales that had me dreaming in French ... while I was awake.

I dropped into the wingback chair and we gazed at one another for too long to be comfortable, that same rueful smile playing at his lips, as if he could read my mind. It unnerved me that in his presence my traitorous heart fluttered. I reminded myself everyone acted a little foolishly around him. It was the French effect. That reserve of his that we all wanted to chip away at and see what was underneath.

He gave me his full attention like he was reading every nuance of my face, memorizing the curve of my lips, the way my hands quaked a little. Like he'd been waiting for me for the longest time and here I was ...

Lack of sleep was the culprit. He was just a man! Just a gorgeous French man. Even though this was liked being sucked into a bubble where time stopped and all I could feel was the thrumming of my heart.

Sebastien radiated this cool intoxicating kind of charm. I bet he was the type who helped old ladies cross the street and took in stray puppies but he would never say so. He was just a little bit lovely, if you were into the type of man who considered things and held himself in check. I felt there was a deeper level to the guy if you got to know him.

'You were saying?' He wore that same half-smirk he often did around me, like I was amusing to him. Gah.

I set my shoulders and said, 'I hope the judges find my perfume satisfactory.' The phone rang, startling me, but he left it unanswered.

'Please, continue,' he said, in that god damn sultry French accent of his. It should have been illegal to speak in such a tone.

'I was trying to make love ...' I petered off, mortification rushing my cheeks. Holy mother of perfume.

His eyes shone with mirth, and I did my best to recover by speaking really loudly. 'Make a perfume about love.' *Please earth, swallow me whole.* 'Love of homecoming. And, I really have to go now. I've, erm, left ...' *my brain in America!* '... left my electric blanket on and really it's a waste of electricity not to mention a potential fire hazard. And being summer and all ...'

He held up a hand, and I couldn't help but notice it was pretty damn fine as far as hands went, long tapering fingers, a nice olive skin tone, and neat nails. 'Wait, Del.'

I was bent at the waist mid-hover, the desire to escape high; half crouched wasn't my best angle so I sat heavily looking anywhere but him. *I tried to make love?*

'Yes?' He could have asked if I liked rap music and I would have said yes to escape faster.

He cocked his head, sunlight caught the black of his hair and turned it silver. 'You don't have dinner with the group and I wondered why.'

He'd noticed? 'I've been working in the lab late every night. You know, that's my happy place, perfumery, and I've always been that way.' But truthfully I was struggling to make perfume without my nan, and I worried that without her, I couldn't do it. How could I tell him though? I didn't want anyone's pity. Or worse their doubt, that the wildcard was struggling.

'Ah,' he said. 'I understand. As long as you're not having trouble with anyone?'

'No, I'm not.' Besides, I could handle them, even Clementine if I needed to.

'So now you've finished your "making love" perfume ...' He let the words hang in the air between us.

'It's love, just love of home,' I said through gritted teeth. It was one thing to be slightly smitten by a man but quite another to give into it. So my brain might have been on vacation around

101

him at times, that wasn't exactly my fault.

'OK, your love of home perfume is done so you can join us for dinner?' Us? It surprised me he was part of the ensemble at dinner.

'Quite possibly.' *No chance.*

'That's not a yes.'

'I've had a big week, and to be honest I'd rather not spend any more time with some of the contestants. It's nothing personal, just self-preservation.'

'I understand,' he said. 'On Sunday we'll go to *Dans Le Noir*. How does eight o'clock sound?'

'But what if I get sent home Monday?' I saw no point talking shop if I was going home. It would be more devastating to know what I was missing out on.

'What if you don't?'

The phone buzzed again, and this time he picked it up. 'See you Sunday, Del. I'll come up to your apartment to escort you.' He nodded goodbye and then spoke into the phone leaving me no choice but to leave.

As I crept away, his words carried down the hall. '... the management team are ready, and my uncle will take over ...' There was a pause as though someone had interrupted him. '... I'll stay for the duration of the competition because I promised I would but then I'm free and I mean it, I want to be left alone.'

Surprise knocked me sideways. He was leaving *Leclére Parfumerie* for good? Why? What kind of person would desert a thriving business such as theirs? Didn't he want to continue his father's legacy?

The first perfumery masterclass was about to start, so I hurried back the lab, mind spinning. What would happen to *Leclére Parfumerie* without Vincent and his son? Aurelie wasn't a perfumer ... Aside from his uncle no one else in the family was involved. Surely the business would lose its lustre without Sebastien? Part of me wanted to shake the man!

Notepad and pencil whipped from my bag, I raced into the

room, sure my emotions were clearly showing on my face, only to find I was the last to arrive. All eyes landed on me like laser beams. I managed a flustered smile. 'Hey,' I said to no one in particular and then made a show of writing in my book.

He wanted to leave?

Maybe the pressure had got to him, the expectation. Leaving, *abandoning* the perfumery would be a mistake on his part, I was dead certain of it. Grief made people do strange things, and I bet he'd regret this decision later. But what could I do about it? Who was I to him in the scheme of things? No one, that was who. In my heart of hearts, I knew I had to try and help or I'd never forgive myself.

Clementine sidled over. 'Finally found a French lover 'ave we?'

I blanched and said too quickly, 'No!'

'Ooh la la, what a shame. Last night I met a man, but he was, 'ow you say it, a little on the small side.'

My eyebrows shot up. 'Clementine!'

'What? I don't like a man who is skinnier than me.'

'Oh.' I shook my head. 'I thought you meant …'

She nudged me with her hip. 'You 'ave a dirty mind, Del. I knew you weren't as innocent as you seemed.'

I was saved by the master perfumer entering the room. All eyes turned to Jacques Monpellier, French perfumer to the stars, infamous for his love of women and fast cars, but renowned just the same. His perfumes were extravagant and audacious and I was keen to learn from him.

Everyone quietened down; everyone except Clementine.

'I've booked us a table at the Moulin Rouge tonight. You'll come, *oui*?'

'Yes, I'll come if you stop talking so I can listen now.' I held up a hand to stop the inevitable *Pah!* and she closed her mouth. There was no way her invitation was genuine; I knew she wanted information, but I could play the game just as well as she could …

Chapter Fifteen

Shrugging deeper into my coat, I took in the spectacle in front of me – the famous red windmills of the Moulin Rouge. At night the red neon lit up the façade and people streamed past, stopping to take photos. The red-light district was a must-see, Clementine said, and I was happy to escape the apartment and leave the pressure and worry behind. Kathryn joined us and they reminisced about their days as perfumery students.

'We used to get into so much trouble,' Clementine laughed. 'But somehow we always got good marks.'

'You were sleeping with the teacher!' Kathryn admonished. 'That's why you got good marks.'

She laughed. 'So I'm gifted in the boudoir, who are you to judge?'

I wasn't sure if they were serious or not, but sleeping with the teacher seemed highly inappropriate to me. Call me a prude, but I'd want to know I was passing on my own merit, not because I was masterly between the sheets. For some inexplicable reason Sebastien popped into my mind. It would be the same, wouldn't it, if I was interested in him? And not appropriate under the circumstances. As my mentor, surely that was a conflict of interest, not to mention he was the owner of the business now, even if he was trying to leave … What a mess this all was! I hated the thought of him making bad choices because of his grief, but not knowing him well enough to tell him so. It had been years since Nan died and I still suffered the fallout with my own perfumery and I missed her so badly; sometimes a memory took me by surprise and had me bawling into my hands all over again.

'So,' I said, shaking away the cloud in my mind and trying to focus on the moment with the girls. 'What's the show about?'

'It's art,' Clementine said. 'You'll see. You Americans always focus on *les tétons*,' she sighed and cupped her bust. 'But it's not about that at all!'

Les tétons could only mean one thing by Clementine's charade. 'I'm sure it's quite the show.'

'It's about fashion, dance, art and the women are in charge, do you see?'

'OK, you don't have to convince me, Clementine. I'm here aren't I?' I really didn't care one way or the other, I was just glad for a distraction, something that would take my mind away from perfume and all it entailed.

Kathryn sighed and gently bumped me with her hip. 'I'm just here to forget about the competition for a while. It's crazy how exhausting it's been.'

'*Oui*,' Clementine said. 'And *I'm* just here for the men. There's always lots of 'andsome specimens here.' She waggled her brows suggestively. 'And champagne.'

'Champagne! Now you're talking!' I said, and laughed. The two girls could not have been more different, and I was glad Kathryn had come along too. If Clementine took a fancy to someone, at least I wouldn't be sitting alone all night. And Kathryn, while still calculating in the competition, seemed like a nice enough person. She took her perfumery seriously, while there were times I thought Clem relied on other methods to get by and perfumery came second to that.

Inside, music played quietly above. We were directed to a table and a bottle of champagne arrived, as waitresses spoke in rapid-fire French to Clementine. Kathryn and I exchanged a look and left her to it, pouring ourselves a generous serve of bubbles while we waited for the show to start. Eventually the lights dimmed and we settled back to watch. Soon Clementine was nowhere to be found …

Leaving the Moulin Rouge a few hours later, with the bright gaudy lights flashing behind us, we giggled, zigzagging down the streets of Paris, everything more colourful, louder, and brighter than before. The show had definitely been an eye-opener, I'd never seen so many feathers! And sequins! The girls were spectacular dancers and the show was arty, rather than sleazy.

Clementine was right; after the first five minutes *les tétons* and their semi-naked bodies were forgotten and it was more the allure of the dance, the costumes and the performance. Extravagant and burlesque – much like Clementine herself!

As we walked home swaying from a little too much liquid happiness, we chatted aimlessly about this and that.

'Who do you think will win the competition, Del?' Kathryn asked.

'Lex, or Lila.' Champagne should've been called truth serum. It was too late to snatch the words back, and I reminded myself I had to be careful around the two girls when it came to talking about other contestants. I couldn't trust them with any confidences and I worried Clem would home in on Lila if she thought she was a threat. Note to self: don't drink champagne like water, ever again.

'Anyway,' I said brightly. 'I thought we were having a night off from perfumery!'

I caught the pair exchange a glance before they turned to me, big smiles on their faces. 'Yes, yes, you're totally right. So, who wants to have a cocktail at the Ritz?'

'Oh, look at the time,' I said. There's was no chance I was showing my face at the Ritz after the whole running-out-without-paying disaster there. 'It's close to curfew, we have to get back.'

'Oh, look at the little rule follower!' Clementine said sing-songy.

I rolled my eyes. 'I don't want to jeopardize my place.'

I shrugged deeper into my coat, suddenly wanting to escape from the pair. Up ahead, I saw a familiar figure wandering in his particular way, hands in pockets, head down contemplating. Clementine and Kathryn hadn't noticed him, so I begged off, claiming I had calls to make back home. Clementine kept up her volley of teasing but I let the words roll away, and rushed ahead, hoping to catch Sebastien who'd turned up a side avenue.

I hurried to find him, hoping the girls wouldn't notice. The last thing I needed was to arouse suspicion by hanging out with my mentor so close to midnight. But something pulled me toward Sebastien; maybe it was the fact I knew his secret when no one else did.

'Hey,' I said, finding him at another late night bar, phone in hand.

'Del, what are you doing out so late?'

'Sorry, Dad.' The damned curfew!

He smiled, and my heart lifted. 'More rules,' he said laughing. 'Crazy, *non*? What's the difference if you're out during the day or night?'

'I guess they want us level-headed, not seedy after burning the candle at both ends.'

He shrugged.

'What are you doing out so late?' I spun the question back.

'Couldn't sleep. I find it so much harder in Paris to switch off. It's almost like the busier the city, the busier my mind.'

'Is that why you love Provence so much?'

He nodded. 'The fresh air, the lavender fields, olive groves. I could never tire of them.'

'But you have a company to run, right? So I suppose Provence will have to wait?' I held my breath.

'For the next little while.' His features remained closed off, and I knew I wouldn't get the truth from him. Why would he confide in me?

'Why don't you make your own mark on the perfumery? Get rid of the rules and do it your way?'

He was silent for the longest time, and when he finally glanced at me, his eyes were glassy. 'It will never be the same without my papa. The magic is lost …'

And I swear I heard my own heart break for him. His need to flee was so evident in every fibre of him …

***

'No excuses, it'll do you good,' Lex said, pushing me to the foot of a staircase with far too many stairs for this time of the morning. We'd taken to meeting up to tour a different patch of Paris for an hour or two if we had the chance, or a break long enough. But it never involved exercise, nor a staircase winding all the way to heaven, like Lex was presenting me with now.

'But there's a perfectly good funicular we could use!'

'America, what's three hundred steps in the scheme of things?'

'*Three hundred!* Lex, I won't be able to walk for days after this!'

He laughed, and gave me a gentle nudge. 'Tell your story walking, America.'

Lex was more nimble than I thought and bounded up the steps like some kind of athlete. I took a much slower pace knowing it'd hit me hard eventually. Runners jogged by, barely out of breath, and gave me get-out-of-the-way glares.

'Remind me why we're doing this?' I huffed along behind, trying now to stay close to the rail and out of the way of the joggers.

'It's one of the best views of Paris. It truly shows you how huge this bustling city is. And Sacré-Coeur is up there too. The artists' square. The wall of 'I Love You's'. Cobblestones so big they bite into your shoes. It's like its own little world, looking down on the sprawl of Paris.'

'In the funicular I could have seen the view of the city, Lex. Not the view of my own feet.'

'Ach, America, where's the fun in that? This way you know you're alive, your blood is pumping and you worked for the view.'

'Right.' I couldn't speak properly as my breathing grew heavier with each step.

He laughed. 'So tell me, how is it really going?' He paused and gave me time to catch up.

'What?' I puffed.

'The competition. You don't seem to be very friendly with the management team and you're friendly to everyone, even Clementine when she doesn't deserve it.'

When I caught up to him, I leaned back on the bannister, my chest heaving. I waited a minute or two to catch my breath. 'The management team irk me no end,' I laughed, a little shaken I'd made my feelings for them so obvious. 'I just feel that for such a romantic business, one so full of whimsy and charm, that they're so … austere. I mean, I get it's a business, and it can't all be fun and games, but they just seem to be at odds with what Vincent set out to do. And OK, Luc mentioned that I was only in the competition as a wildcard, so I'm still smarting over that little tidbit.'

Lex wrinkled his brow. 'But you're only a wildcard because you haven't had professional perfumery training.'

'Who said my nan wasn't a professional?'

He tutted. 'In their eyes, America, professional perfumery training means at an established university, or school. You know that. You're here because despite that, you're good, damn good, and they don't care about where you were taught, just that you know your stuff regardless.'

I hadn't considered it that way before. 'Maybe.'

'They think you've got the goods and you've been freezing them out.' He cackled high and loud.

'Jeez, Lex, do you think they've all noticed?'

'I wouldn't worry, America. They work for Sebastien at the end of the day … He makes the decisions not them.'

I bit my lip. Not for much longer. As much as I trusted Lex, I couldn't tell him about what I'd overheard. It didn't seem right. Lex turned and ran up the next level of stairs.

I trudged slowly behind. I'd been so damn sensitive about being called the wildcard that I hadn't been able to see past it. Was I making other stupid choices because I lacked confidence in myself? There was Jen, and the issues between us. The more time I spent away from her the less we spoke, but that was life and being busy, right? This whole time I'd been blaming her, but really I had to shoulder half the responsibility too. People change and just because we were twins, it didn't mean she had to put me first. Why should she? But there'd always be that piece of my heart that wondered what could have been if only James hadn't wandered back to Whispering Lakes. And that was OK.

'Lex,' I said between heaves. 'How many more steps?'

'You don't want to know.'

There was something strangely healing about my lungs burning, my muscles aching, that gave me the ability see a little more clearly. Not that I'd be hurrying to race up the steps to Montmartre again, not when there was a perfectly good funicular close by.

'Lex-x-x!' I called just to annoy him.

'America, I've seen Colombian sloths that are faster than you. Get moving!'

I laughed. 'There better be a nice big piece of apple *tarte tatin* waiting at the top for me!' Exercise would do me good before the big date with Sebastien, the big *meeting*, the following night. It might help shift some of that nervous energy I had when I was around him.

Later that day I called Jen. She'd been on my mind since my walk in Montmartre with Lex. No two ways about it, I missed her with all my heart, and wondered if I was on her mind as much as she was on mine.

'Where have you been? I was about to send a search party,' I said, a classic Nan-ism, and one we'd heard time and again growing up.

'Aww, sorry, Del. Things have been super crazy! I got your messages but with the time difference and all it's been hard to catch you. I've been so busy I've lost track of days.'

The love-struck fool couldn't eat, couldn't sleep and I secretly hoped she'd be back to normal soon.

'Why so busy? Extra shifts at Woodfired?' Jennifer worked a few night shifts at the local pizzeria, and did accounts for a local building company during the day. Often the pizzeria would call her last minute to fill shifts and she'd always accepted the work in order to save for NYC … but now I wasn't sure what she was saving for.

'Yeah, work, and life in general. It feels like a lifetime ago you left and there's still so much time to go …'

'If I'm lucky.' I missed my twin so badly but she was distracted, which was becoming our new normal.

'You don't need luck, Del! You've got talent.'

I explained about the trouble I had in the first challenge and how my perfume wasn't as spectacular as I'd hoped, and how competitive some of the contestants were.

'Are you sure it's not spectacular? Or is it the pressure talking? That's the whole point of this adventure, to push you out of your comfort zone, and see where you land. Give yourself more credit, Del.'

'I wished I'd taken a bigger leap out of my comfort zone. It's like I am close to figuring out—'

She cut me off. 'Yeah, I see.' There was a deep voice in the background, she covered the receiver, and there was some gravelly static before she came back. 'What were you saying?'

It was hard to gauge her emotions when she was in a different country. 'You were talking.' I made my voice bright. 'How's Pop?'

Again, there was that voice in the background. Was James, the boyfriend, hovering by her so she was only half-listening to me? 'Pop misses you, we all do, but this is your time to shine,' she said. 'I have to run. Love you lots and keep the faith, yeah?'

'OK, well one other thing …' But she'd gone. What the hell? Out of sight, out of mind! Or was something wrong back home and she didn't want to tell me?

Chapter Sixteen

Sunday night rolled around quickly. Too quickly. Who wouldn't want to go out to a fancy Parisian restaurant with one of the hottest men on the planet? Me! It complicated things and the contestants would be talking out of turn about it in two minutes flat. But maybe it meant I was safe from elimination. Why would he want to get to know me if I was leaving the next day? Or maybe the judges were still ruminating and the decision wasn't made yet, in which case this could be my last night in Paris.

Clock checking, I still had fifty-five minutes to wait.

OK, yes, I'd taken a bit more care with my make-up. And my clothing, choosing a tight ruby-red dress that Lila had insisted I buy from an antique market on the bank of the Seine, and perilously high black heels. My feet would be screaming if we did any real walking but they made me feel like a million bucks. The women here dressed so elegantly, and with Lila's assurances I was on my way to a slightly more stylish version of the elegant French woman. We'd found the heels in a little emporium in the upper Marais, half price and my size, so what was a girl to do?

I'd straightened my wavy hair, then I'd tied it up, then pulled it down, and then gave up. I spent a few minutes pouting in the mirror before catching myself and wiping lipstick off my teeth.

Honestly, what was I doing? The waiting sent me batty.

And then, finally, a knock at the door. I opened it and his fragrance hit me first, a blend of juniper berry, orange and a base note of pepperwood. It conjured quiet nights, a G&T, a cabin in the woods and the type of man who'd stoke the fire, a book of French poetry left open on the armrest. Or so I imagined …

We locked eyes, and for a moment the world stopped turning.

He could be anyone, I hardly knew the guy, so why did my heart beat triple time? It was absurd. And I took pains to hide it, fluttering my hands and fidgeting. You *could* fall in love with someone on scent alone and what that triggered for you! Every perfumer hoped to make a scent like that, but I hadn't expected to fall into an olfactory trap. It was a blend of aromas, that was all! Ooh la la, Paris was making me crazy!

'Hello there!' To recover after the long silence, I greeted him chirpily as if this was any night (*which it was*) and he was an old friend. A *platonic* old friend. Was it being in Paris watching lovers stroll hand-in-hand along the boulevards, or girls on tiptoe by the Eiffel Tower kissing their flush-faced beaus? Couples walked, arms entwined, by the river Seine. Love was everywhere here in the romance capital of the world; perhaps that made even the closed-hearted among us dream.

'*Bonsoir.*'

'Come right in, I'll get my handbag.'

I went to step around him to grab my bag from the hook as he stepped forward to give me the double whammy cheek kiss and we bumped heads with a resounding crack. 'Ow,' I said, grabbing my forehead.

'*Désolé*, Del. Let me see.' He cupped my face, and surveyed the damage. My eyes watered from the pain; would there ever be a fiasco-free moment with the man?

'I'm OK,' I managed, his proximity all I could think of. I made the mistake of gazing into his eyes, the deep oceanic green of them, and stopped. He was so unlike the men of my small town, so wholly different to any guy I'd ever had a flutter for. He enthralled me by scent alone and it painted a picture of what could be. Crazy. A possible concussion speaking. At this rate I'd have to buy a helmet to wear with all the pain I managed to inflict on myself.

As he searched my face for damage he moved closer, his lips barely an inch from mine which had no bearing on anything. They were just close, that's all. Closer than they'd been previously. But if you were into lips, then these would have been right up your alley. They were pretty luscious for a guy, and had that quirk to them, even when he was serious like he was now, that made a person feel like he'd be quick to smile. Quick to laugh. Would the pine-y juniper notes of gin linger on the softness of them? I wondered if I'd be able to taste the botanical liquor on his tongue. A moment later I was horrified to find my index finger suddenly millimetres away from his bottom lip as if I was going to … what? Hook him in for a kiss?

I snatched my hand back, my eyes wide. *He hadn't had a G&T*, that was all a fantasy created by his scent, so I wouldn't be able to taste it anyway. It was his fragrance taking me on an olfactory journey of discovery that was FICTIONAL. I, of all people, should have known how that worked!

He was still staring intently at me, and my legs almost gave way. I wasn't cut out for this level of scrutiny.

'I …'

'Del …' Just then the door burst open and in walked Clementine, babbling away at top volume.

We jumped away from each other like we'd been zapped.

'*Ooh la la* I forgot my—' She stopped and a hand flew to her mouth before she recovered, and smirked. 'So that is 'ow it is.' Crossing her arms, she waited for an explanation, and I grappled with what to say. It was innocent, damn it!

Sebastien put a hand to the small of my back, '*Bonsoir*, Clementine,' he said to her without a hint of embarrassment or the need to further explain. 'We're going to dinner. Enjoy your evening.'

'Dinner, together? *Fantastique.*' Her eyes glittered and the fine hair on my arms stood on end.

'More a mentoring session,' Sebastien said smoothly.

My heart sank. What a fool! My cheeks flamed, it was never a date, it was always about perfumery … but I knew that didn't I?

Chapter Seventeen

Outside, stars sparkled in the inky night as we made our way through the 8th *arrondissement*, and down to the 7th taking in the spectacular sight of the glittering Eiffel Tower, which lit up on the hour.

In his linen blazer, Sebastien looked every inch the urbane Frenchman, and attracted a number of second glances from women walking past. About twenty minutes into our walk I started to hobble in my heels and tried my best to breathe through the pain. Everyone walked in Paris – it was probably why they could all eat the freshly baked baguettes and mountains of profit-eroles and stay slim. While I walked my fair share back home, it was usually around the lake wearing comfortable attire and hiking boots. I didn't know how women coped walking or cycling in heels from one end of the huge city to the other.

Ever observant, Sebastien noticed my wobbly gait and said, 'We should catch a taxi.'

'A taxi would be great.' So much for being French. I couldn't last twenty minutes in heels where Parisian women could prob-ably hitch up their skirts and run a marathon in them.

We were silent in the car. I was unsure what to say, being alone with him; even small talk didn't come easily, so instead I leaned close to the window, taking in the sights of the beautiful city at night-time. His phone rang incessantly, and he cursed under his breath and switched it off.

When we entered the restaurant, I grabbed hold of Sebastien's hand as I was thrust into absolute darkness. 'I can't see!'

'Exactly,' he said, giving my hand a squeeze. 'That's the concept of *Dans Le Noir*. In the pitch black your senses will guide you; instead of sight, you'll have to trust taste and scent. So much like perfumery, *non*?' Perhaps he *was* going to put effort into mentoring me? The situation smacked of a perfumery lesson.

There was a French voice and Sebastien replied, and then with a palm in the small of my back led me to a table. He pulled out a chair and helped me into it. It was all very hands on, and I certainly wasn't going to complain, lest I fall on my face or end up sitting with the wrong man – I wouldn't put it past me.

'The staff are visually impaired,' he said softly. 'It's an insight into their world too.'

Wow. 'They're so sure-footed.' I could hear them walking around, the glug of wine being poured, the clink of plates, their low French voices as they served in total obscurity.

'They're very adept at what they do.'

Without vision the world shrunk, but what was fascinating to me was how my other senses were heightened, especially my sense of smell. The table closest to us were drinking a red wine, the notes of cherry and clove spiced the air between us.

It was strange and liberating all at once. 'How will we know what we're eating?' I asked into the void. Whatever preconceptions I had about food would be turned on their head as I negotiated eating and drinking in the dark.

'It's a surprise,' he laughed.

And with that a waiter approached us – I could tell by his footfalls, and the whoosh of air as he stopped at our table. 'The chef would like to know what you *don't* eat.'

Sebastien touched my hand across the table. 'That's the surprise part,' he said, his voice full of warmth. 'You don't know what you're getting but they won't use ingredients you don't enjoy.'

I was so taken by the concept I was happy to try anything. You wouldn't find a place like this in Whispering Lakes. 'I'll eat whatever the chef recommends,' I said.

'Very good, and the wine?'

'Whatever pairs with the menu,' Sebastien said. The waiter thanked us and left, taking a whoosh of air with him.

I kept blinking as if I'd suddenly see again, until I caught myself. It was so strange to be in the space, knowing you were surrounded by people but not able to see them.

'So, Del, how do you see your future in perfumery?'

The question was delivered lightly, almost innocently, but I felt it held more weight than he let on.

'Didn't you watch my audition video?' We'd all sent videos about our lives and where we saw ourselves slotting into the world of perfumery. It had been the most excruciating ten minutes of my life getting Jen to shoot me blathering on, trying to sound impressive, knowledgeable and inspired. Like I was coping just fine without Nan. It had been Jen's idea originally for me to submit a video and see if I made it in.

I sensed Sebastien was smiling, but I couldn't be sure. '*Oui*, of course, your video was one of my favourites. *Parfumerie* is such a solitary job, it was quite magical to see your workspace, the perfume organ, and hear about your nan and the way you formulate fragrances. Everyone's journey is so different.'

He removed his hand with a quick apology as if he'd forgotten he'd put it there. My skin cooled without his touch.

As I grappled with something to fill the awkward silence he spoke up. 'You haven't answered my question?'

Was he trying to break the bad news gently to me? Why was he so interested in my future once I *left* here? My heart thudded at the thought I might be going home tomorrow.

'My plans are still dreams, Sebastien, but they're within

grabbing distance.'

'Why so shy suddenly?'

How to say that, without the prize money, I'd struggle making my dreams come true? That the grand plan I had with my sister had gone up in smoke? The money I'd saved for years was only half of what I needed; without Jen's contribution I couldn't afford it. And mostly that deep down I lacked the confidence to go it alone.

'I'm not being shy. Just cautious. Why? Should I start packing my bags?' The darkness made me bold, I could easily have gotten used to it.

'*Non, non*, I don't know to be honest. And of course I couldn't tell you anyway. I have yet to see the judges' scores. I won't know until tomorrow morning, just before *Maman* makes the announcement.'

'I can imagine how hard it will be to send someone home; the thought of leaving so soon makes my chest tight, like I can't breathe. I can't go home – there's nothing there for me.'

'It's funny you say that – I loved the footage you shared of your home town. All that pristine water, not a soul in sight.'

'That's the problem, there's nothing there. It's so quiet.'

'Peaceful.'

'Boring.' I shook my head. We were so different. That kind of peace was the reason I wanted out. You couldn't sell perfume to wildlife. I needed people, a busy thriving metropolis.

'Why did you decide to hold the competition? I know you promised your father, but why now?'

Another weighty silence fell, and then finally he spoke. 'Part of the plea bargain was to hold it within the year. If I held the competition as per my papa's wishes, then I could leave. The management team would take over running *Leclére*, and I was free to go, signing away all my rights.'

I hadn't expected he'd confide in me. I had to remember I supposedly didn't know and this was a shock. 'But *why* …? I know how hard it is to keep going when you're grieving, but perfume can save you, you know. Isn't it the place you go to get lost, to put all thought except formulas from your mind? Why would you throw it all away?'

'It goes deeper than that, Del. And I can't stand to be here and face the memories every day. What's the point? Without Papa there is no *Leclére Parfumerie*, there's only what once was.'

Part of me was sad I'd never get to meet the enigma Vincent himself, by all accounts an unconventional man who had been trying to create not just a scent, but to conjure the feeling that went with it. Like capturing a visit to beach: sandcastles, laughter, brilliant sunshine, and the salty fresh smell of rolling waves, but most of all, the euphoria that overcame you when you were sunning yourself and watching life drift by from the comfort of a sandy perch.

How could you recreate laughter by smell? Or the intoxicating sense of first love? Was it possible?

Vincent had reportedly said that when he worked, the world around him faded to black, and he relied only on his nose; his olfactory sense: the concoction, an aromatic journey limited only by imagination. And I recognized the same trait in myself. I lost days making perfume, and only came up for air when hunger pains got the better of me. It was about more than the fragrance, it was about where that scent took you. How it changed you. Sebastien could surely continue his research, and maybe make something nobody had ever imagined was possible.

'How can you be sure that you won't love it again? Doesn't it inspire you, all these perfumers with new concepts and techniques?' I so wanted to say something that would make him change his mind, but he was so closed off, so sure he wasn't suited to this life.

'It *is* intriguing watching everyone work,' he said. 'And I'm impressed by you all, but once it's over then I am free and I'll sign my rights away. And as selfish as that sounds, that's all I can think of.'

I couldn't wrap my head around it. I understood he was being pulled in a million directions, but surely he could get help in and create perfume locked away alone, if that's what he wanted? He could even do it from his little village in Provence! So why sign all his rights away? It just didn't make sense.

'What would your father say, knowing you were throwing away his life's work?' Perhaps I'd put it too bluntly, but the man was walking away from a lucrative business where he could do anything he chose fit. Being in the depths of despair so long after Nan died, I understood his need to flee, but I *knew* he'd regret it later.

The waiter returned, and poured our wine, and I tried to decipher it. Gooseberries, grassy and herbaceous. 'He'd be heartbroken,' Sebastien said, his voice firm. 'And he wouldn't understand.'

'Why? What was he like?' Had he been similar to Sebastien? Resolute when he wanted to be? With that need for privacy?

'My papa was ridiculed as a young perfumer, told he'd never make it, that he had no talent because he didn't follow the "rules of perfumery". But he had this grim determination about him and never gave up.'

I smiled, thinking of *le savant fou* and all those who tried to stop the incredible man from sharing his gift.

'And yet, he became one of the most famous perfumers in the world,' I said, wistfully. In a way it was nice to know things hadn't come easy for Vincent, but they'd still eventuated. He proved you could make it in this business if you worked hard enough.

'Perseverance,' Sebastien said, 'and passion. He had those qualities, and the more people turned him away, the more he persisted. It came at a cost though. His marriage broke down because he was so intent on perfume. Witnessing *Maman*'s heartbreak made me realize just how fragile love is. We perfumers get lost in the world of perfumery, but he went so far that he never really came back. It taught me what *not* to do.'

Sebastien's *eu de parfum* undulated in the air between us, the peppery, orange zest and dark balsam notes, while I contemplated. Was he not as close to his father as I presumed? 'It's so easy to fall down that rabbit hole when you make fragrance; you can lose days, weeks …' I said lightly, unsure of what else to say.

'*Years*,' he said, a touch of bitterness creeping into his voice.

The picture I had of Vincent was not the one Sebastien painted. 'But wasn't he a dreamer, a gentle soul?' The man I'd imagined had white wispy hair, magic in his eyes, the kind of secretive smile when you know you've made a perfume so great people revered it for decades …

'*Oui*,' he said. 'If you could steal a moment of his time, you felt as though you were the stars to his orbit. But his door was always locked.' Loneliness leached from each syllable.

By the sounds of it, Vincent had indelibly bruised his son's heart. Changed the course of his life by being absent. It occurred to me we both had some broken pieces of our pasts rattling inside our hearts.

'So that's why you want to leave …' *Leclére* was a prestigious, famous perfumery for some, but the holder of bad memories for Sebastien.

'What people don't know is, when I'm in Paris working all I see is that locked door, and the little boy standing on the other side, wondering why he can't go in. Please don't think my papa was a cruel man, he wasn't. He was just so distracted, so invested in his work that all else paled.'

The image of a young Sebastien standing by the thin strip of light by his father's door, waiting for attention, was almost too sad to contemplate. Was the old man really that busy he couldn't make time for his son? Did he know the only legacy he left behind was one of loneliness? It was devastating that Sebastien wanted to flee instead of continuing his father's work, but it made more sense to me now.

'But when you got older you worked together?' I hoped for a

happy ending, a change in circumstances …

'No, not really. I worked in my own studio and he in his. Mine is in Provence. And I only came to Paris when I was needed.' Why was communicating so hard for these people? Why couldn't he have bashed on the door as an adult and asked for attention? But I knew it wasn't as simple as that. By then walls were up, pride had to be protected.

I shivered in the cool room. 'What happened with your parents?' I knew that they'd divorced a long time ago and Aurelie had only returned to Paris after Vincent's death.

'She fell in love with another man,' he said, his voice level. 'Papa was devastated, but in his usual quiet way, he let her go without a fight. I've always wondered if she wanted him to fight for her, to really *see* her. Maybe her plan to get his attention backfired.'

'Surely not, surely she would have told him?' Perhaps all families had their skeletons and it wasn't just my parents who'd acted irrationally, it was just that my parents did everything in full view of the world, totally transparent.

'My *maman* had her pride. She still does, and refuses to talk about what was said at the time. I think she grew tired of coming second to *parfumerie* and remarried and moved away. Papa loved her though, right to the very end. His last words to me were, "*Tell your* maman *even if she loved me for only a minute, it was worth it.*"'

'That's heartbreaking.' How could he have let her go? Why didn't she tell him to fight for her? Why let real love slip through your fingers? It was a tragedy.

'He had so much regret. And the saddest part of all is that *I* regret not telling him how I felt, and now it's too late. Maybe he just didn't know how deeply his absence affected us all. We needed him, yet he couldn't be that person. Anyway …' he let out an embarrassed laugh, 'I don't know why I'm confiding in you like this. It must be the dark that makes a person share their secrets … Forgive me.'

'Don't apologize.'

We lapsed into silence. I considered my parents, and the regret I felt almost every day. Regret that they weren't responsible, that they didn't conform to what being a parent meant. But they were still around, when they weren't adventuring, and in their own way they showed us they cared. And they'd never pretended to be anything other than who they were, and I loved them despite their follies, though it was easier to think that way here, while I was out of the fishbowl that was Whispering Lakes.

'So, I'd better get down to business,' he said. 'You have a wonderful gift; your perfumery is exceptional. Yet, you hold back. Why?'

I stifled a groan. He was my mentor and this is why we were here, he'd obviously tested the perfume I submitted. Embarrassment flared and again I was glad for the darkness. 'I played it safe, and when I realized my mistake it was too late to change it. Since I lost Nan, I've lost some of the magic and I can't seem to find it no matter what I try.'

'I'm so sorry, Del. And your nan taught you well, so why don't you take those lessons and make them your own. Take a few risks. Experiment. Like in this restaurant, you have to trust your instincts. You can't see the food you're eating, but your senses will guide you, just like perfumery.'

I sent up a silent prayer to the perfume gods to give me one more chance at the competition. I'd take risks and be better organized. I'd get my mojo back. I'd beg for it if I had to.

'I will, I'll take risks, and I'll think outside the box. I hope I don't go home – I'm just getting started.'

'I know. I don't want you to leave,' he said, as our entrees arrived. It was an incredible experience determining what it was from the taste and textures. Scallops with salty sea foam, and fresh herbs, or so I guessed. What an intense way to eat food! I took it slow, each mouthful another foray into an abyss.

Our main meal arrived; a rich cassoulet of confit duck. It melted in my mouth and it was all I could do not to sigh with happiness. I tasted the silkiness of white beans, saltiness of pancetta, crispy duck and a thick and rich sauce.

'Open your mouth,' Sebastien said. I did as bid in the pitch black. A hand cupped my chin and he slowly, delicately, fed me a forkful of his meal, which was different to mine. I tried to guess what it was but I was distracted by the sensuality of the moment. I hadn't tasted anything so intense before. The evening had been a revelation on so many levels and I was bewitched with it all. Maybe this was just another French foible, though. Maybe they all shared forkfuls of food and there was nothing untoward in the gesture.

'What do you think?' he asked.

'It's slow-cooked beef, ah, with caramelized onions, herbs ...' Was this some kind of mentoring test?

'*Oui*,' he said and I heard the smile in his voice. 'A classic French dish, beef *pot-au-feu*.'

The taste lingered on my tongue, as the slow-cooked dish offered up levels of flavor, and he fed me another mouthful which I took my time discerning. This time I could taste the base of the broth, an almost umami taste of the bone marrow used, and the body the gelatinous cut of meat gave the dish. It was bursting with flavor, and I thought I'd never taste anything so delicious ever again.

'Exceptional,' I said, warmed by the comfort of the food and sharing the experience with Sebastien. He'd sure managed to surprise me, and I felt like a different person in his company. As though I was slowly unfurling from small town girl to worldly traveler.

Chapter Eighteen

After dinner we strolled along the boulevards in the 7th *arrondissement* down to the banks of the Seine. I paused and wrenched my heels off, not giving a damn about French etiquette. Sebastien gave me a side look, and tried to hide a grin but I caught it anyway. Hell, there was no point being anyone other than me.

Paris had its own blend of scent – earthy, damp, elemental – and it was stronger at night-time with less people hurrying this way and that.

We made our way through cobbled streets and came to a patch of gravel rocks where some roadworks were set to take place but had halted for the evening. Just as I debated how to walk around it with bare feet, Sebastien lifted me with surprising ease, making me gasp.

'Sorry to startle you,' he said. 'I didn't want you to hurt yourself on those little stones.'

I blushed to the roots of my hair, his lips were mere inches from mine, and up close he was even lovelier. How could that be so? I quashed the urge to rest my head on his shoulder and gaze up at him. Gaze up at him? It was the wine talking.

'Thanks, I should be OK now.' In his arms I was suffering the strangest malady; shaky, hot and tingly. If I didn't know better

I'd have suggested I was in the first stages of love, but I knew that was impossible, he was my mentor for god's sake. And that was that. When he gently stood me back on earth, it shook just a little, spun on its axis for the briefest moment of time. What was in the wine I'd drunk? *Get a grip of yourself, Del!*

I wandered just ahead staring at dark shopfronts, their shutters like eyes closed against sleep. Oceane from the bookshop was right, Paris had an ability to burrow under your skin and make you fall slowly, inexplicably in love with it. It wasn't all pale pink blooms, and silky sunlight, there were scars on the city like any bustling place – overflowing rubbish bins, and the stench of waste in parks and gardens – but somehow it made it more real, finding the beauty in the urbane, against the backdrop of night sky.

'It's almost midnight,' Sebastien said, glancing up from his watch.

My curfew! 'It's not!' The evening had raced away after our first bout of awkwardness; we'd chatted nonstop and I felt as though I'd really got to know him as a person, not just as the competition organizer and son and heir of the family empire.

'Will you turn into a pumpkin?'

I laughed. 'Maybe!' Part of me wanted to walk with him into the dawn, but the practical, sensible side of me prevailed. 'I'd better head back. If I don't get eliminated tomorrow, I know from experience I'll need my wits about me for the coming week.'

'You're due for the rest of your facial, *non*?' His eyes twinkled with mirth. Damn it! She *had* mentioned me to Sebastien!

'It was sabotage!'

He pursed his lip in jest. 'Sabotage?'

Shoot! I didn't want to mention the lengths some contestants were stooping to in case it turned back on me. It didn't seem right to tattle so I changed tact. 'A case of mistaken identity and I had some trouble extricating myself from the situation. I really don't think I should have been billed for such a service and I intend to tell them that.' I folded my arms and stuck out my chin.

He laughed. 'I haven't met anyone like you before, Del. I hope you stay. Laughter hasn't come easily lately and then you turn up.'

My chest seized. What was he saying?

'It wouldn't be the same without you and your disasters.'

Oh god. Disaster girl, that was me.

'I aim to please.'

'You think I'm joking,' he said, with a rueful shake of his head.

We headed back to the apartment, chatting about Paris and perfume and everything in between. Our pace was slow, despite my bare feet, my heels swinging by my side and I vowed never to wear them again, even if that meant not quite keeping up with the French women, and their effortless style.

At the foyer, we turned to face one another.

'Thank you for dinner. It was quite the experience.'

'My pleasure,' he said, giving me that same intense stare that I found so compelling.

'OK,' I said, rooted to the spot.

After sharing confidences, I felt closer to him. Enjoying dinner in total darkness had bonded us somehow. I knew it was all a mentoring session, albeit framed not to look quite so sedate, but still, it had been better than I expected.

'Until tomorrow,' he said.

'Yes, tomorrow.' *Please perfume gods do not send me home!*

'Sleep well.'

'You too.'

He moved to peck my cheek but I turned my face and caught his lips. For a few seconds we pressed into each other, his warmth, the softness of his mouth against mine, his proximity sending tingles of desire up and down my body. I hadn't meant to do it, and we both registered shock on our faces.

'Sorry!' I said.

'*Pardon!*'

'That was my fault, sorry, I only meant to …' Was I supposed to kiss to the left or the right!

'Don't apologize,' he said. Did he think I meant to kiss him? It was a simple mistake, those double-barreled French kisses always muddled me up …

Upstairs, Clementine snapped on the light, starting me.

'Ten past twelve …' she tutted and flicked off the light once more.

The last thing I needed was a lecture from her. I washed up quickly and jumped into bed, mind spinning at the events of the evening.

After tossing and turning for hours on end, I gave up, dressed and wandered around Paris in the hazy light of pre-dawn. It was achingly beautiful, all shuttered up and quiet, streets bereft of cars, pavements shy of pedestrians.

The city was a music box whose song had come to an end, waiting patiently for someone to wind it up again.

I walked aimlessly, lost in thought as the minutes slipped away. Soon it was nearly time to have breakfast and face the possibility of elimination. Quick as I could, I did an arc around my favourite places, returning home via the Champ de Mars to the Eiffel Tower, across the Pont d'Iéna to the Trocadero gardens saying a private goodbye to Paris as I went, just in case.

It was just after eight when I got back to breakfast, surprised to find almost everyone in the dining room – even the night owls had woken with the birds. The atmosphere was tense; Kathryn had a wooden smile, Lila was jittery and fidgeting, and Clem was quiet for a change. Nerves had got the better of everyone.

I found Lex in the group, and made my way over to him.

'America,' he said, with a slow smile. 'You been pounding the pavement?'

'Couldn't sleep,' I said, returning his smile. 'What about you? This is a first, having breakfast with us mere mortals.'

'Right?' He gave me his trademark grin. 'I thought this old dog was past all that senseless worrying that laypeople feel. Couldn't sleep either – guess this means more to me than I thought.'

I gave his arm a reassuring pat. 'Guess it does,' I said.

'Battling the demons about it all though, like why bother at my age? What do I want out of this? But being able to mix potions like an old wizard again makes me remember why I love it so much.'

I felt a deep sense of paternal warmth for Lex. I felt like I could trust him, that if I did right by him he'd reciprocate, and it would be as simple as that. And I still wondered what had set him on his nomadic path all those years ago. While it sounded fun, traveling the globe, being a world citizen, I was sure there'd be fallbacks too. Loneliness and never putting roots down.

Before I could ask him, Aurelie appeared and told us to assemble in the salon for the results.

'Good luck, America,' he said, giving my hand a squeeze.

'Thanks, you too.'

Clementine caught my eye and gave me a wink. In the blink of an eye she was back to her incorrigible self, you could sense her devious side just from the sparkle in her bright blue eyes. Pushing her way over to me, she linked her arm through mine and managed to whisper loud enough to draw the attention of everyone.

'Let's hope Anastacia is sent home, *non*?' She glared at her and then snapped, 'I'm 'aving a private conversation 'ere, or can't you tell?'

Anastacia rolled her eyes and volleyed back, 'Then why don't you keep it down to a half-bellow, Clementine? Pretty sure everyone up at Sacré-Coeur can hear you.'

Clementine scoffed. 'As I was saying.' She turned back to me. 'I 'ope it's Anastacia, three ingredients do not make a proper perfume where I come from. The birth place of *parfum*, *non*?'

I grabbed Clem's arm tighter and motioned for her to zip her lips, but she took no heed.

'And imagine setting you up in the Ritz like that, Del! We should 'ave told Sebastien a long time ago about how she tried to sabotage you.'

Anastacia leaned over and stuck a finger in Clem's face. 'Keep out of it. Or I'll mention how Lila was given directions from the Parisian herself, and managed to get all the way to Versailles. *That* is cheating if you ask me.'

They bickered heatedly and I did my best to stay out of it despite Clementine pointing and gesticulating at me. Really, they'd both been underhanded, and worse they seemed to enjoy it.

Sebastien entered the room and a hush soon followed. My heart thudded so hard I was sure everyone could hear it. He was soon followed by Aurelie.

Panic skidded in my chest. Suddenly I was sure I'd be sent packing and I rued the fact I'd played it safe. Leaving would be heartbreaking, and how could I ever go home after this?

'Welcome,' Sebastien said, gazing at us all in turn, skipping over me far quicker than the rest. Did he regret confiding in me?

Aurelie spoke next: 'It's come time to say *au revoir* to one of our perfumers, regretfully, as we must. Please know it hasn't been an easy decision. The votes were close. You should be very proud of yourselves, no matter what happens.'

While outwardly Sebastien radiated calm, his eyes were clouded with worry, as if he too was nervous about delivering the results. But if he lost his protégée, me, then he'd be free, wouldn't he?

I threw Lex a pained look, and he shook his head, as if to imply it wasn't going to be me this time.

Aurelie laced his fingers and said, 'Without further ado, I will read the scores from highest to lowest.'

There were murmurs and the air grew thick with apprehension.

'The perfume that we found most incredible belonged to Lex. A scent that managed to take us to an exotic place, tropical and lush, full of hope.' I risked a glance at Clem whose mouth was an 'O' of surprise. 'Second was Lila; we loved the celebration of a new day, a breathtaking fragrance. In third we have Anastacia with a striking fragrance that captured the brilliance of stars themselves. A truly atmospheric perfume.' To which Clem let out a guffaw. 'In fourth place we have Clementine who concocted our only masculine scent, spicy and herbaceous, almost primal – the judges loved it.'

I couldn't look at Lex or Lila but I felt my friends' worried eyes on me. There were only two places left, it was either me or Kathryn.

Aurelie paused and glanced up from his sheet of paper, sorrow etched on her face. 'The next two contestants were *very* close, almost too close to call. The judges weren't in agreement which made the decision a little more difficult. After much deliberation we believe we've made the right choice.' Her gaze fell back to the sheet. 'In fifth place is Del, so I'm sorry to say, Kathryn, your time here is over, and we wish you all the best for the future …'

I risked a glance at Kathryn, whose mouth hung open.

Golly, that was close … I closed my eyes as relief rushed me. But I knew my perfume hadn't hit the brief, and disappointment sat heavy on my shoulders.

Hanging back, I waited to hug Kathryn and say goodbye. Her pale face was whiter still. My heart broke a little for her.

Kathryn's mouth was a tight line as she fought tears, and everyone murmured farewells and promised to keep in contact. Her devastation was obvious; the space around her pulsed with it.

I gave Kathryn a hug, 'I'm so sorry,' I said, guilt nudging me, knowing how close it had been.

'It's OK, Del.'

Kathryn left with a backwards wave, and the room fell silent.

I desperately wanted to call Jen but I wouldn't get a chance until much later this evening as our next challenge was imminent. But I felt like if I didn't step up, I'd be the one going home next. Could I leave so soon? I had so much more to learn.

Chapter Nineteen

Once Kathryn had left, Aurelie clapped her hands together to get our attention.

'Challenge two is here. This week you'll work with your mentor creating a perfume together. There's no gallivanting around Paris for this one.' To that the room let out a sigh of relief. While it had been great to see the sights, we'd run some miles, and my legs had been heavy as stone for days after. 'Instead, you'll be driven to different destinations around France. Vincent believed that quality perfume started at the source.'

I'd read about Vincent and his beliefs about sourcing products for his perfumery. Elements like lavender were from chemical-free fields in Provence, and rose petals from organic farms in Normandy – in that instance a rose was *not* just a rose. *Leclére* had strict quality control processes and it reflected in their fragrances. Some larger perfumeries used hothouse roses to save money, but this was against every principle Vincent held dear.

He had searched regions of France himself, taking time to find the right lavender fields, the best flower farms for resins, balsams, spices, grasses and fruits to name but a few. After harvesting, then came the extraction process, then the blending where we perfumers came into it, and then the ageing process. All of this depended on the high-quality producers.

'So,' Aurelie continued, speaking over excited whispers. 'The locations are as follows: Grasse, for Lila, that's where you'll find our factory, and Sebastien's uncle who runs things there. You'll be given instructions once you arrive. Provence for Del, Nice for Anastacia and Bordeaux for Lex and Clementine.'

'Why are we both going?' Clementine asked pouting.

'Why not?' Aurelie threw back, giving Clementine a long stare to which I hid a smile. Clementine would have her hands full trying to sabotage Lex. He might have come across as laid-back but he was no one's fool. Perhaps the management team knew exactly what Clementine was up to, and were putting Lex in her way. Besides, their mentors would be there alongside them – but could they survive a week with Clementine? I shook my head just thinking about her and her ploys to get ahead. Nothing was sacred.

'You have an hour to pack, your drivers are outside waiting. You'll head back Friday for a class with another esteemed perfumer.'

I tried to catch Sebastien's attention but he was conferring with a *Leclére* employee. I didn't want our visit to Provence to be awkward after our near-miss kiss. But this morning it was almost as if he was purposely ignoring me. Well two could play at that game! I didn't have time for these ridiculous feelings, these clumsy altercations. But with him being my mentor it made things difficult.

As we left the room, I hung back to congratulate Lex. 'Hey, well done, Mister. I'm so proud of you.'

He grinned. 'Ah, luck of the draw and that's all it was.'

'It was amazing perfumery skills, so don't downplay it. You deserved to win. What was your perfume called?'

'Hope.'

'And what does hope smell like to you, Lex?'

'It's the cool of the shade under a palm frond, the juice from a fresh mango, sand and salt and light and shade, but most of all it's the waft of hope itself on the breeze, and the girl of your dreams a few steps away.'

I smiled. 'So there *is* hope?' I said. 'With the girl?' I sensed Lex had unfinished business somewhere. Just occasionally I caught him downcast, as if he was reminiscing about someone. The woman on the beach perhaps?

'Nah, just an old man living in the past.'

'You're not that old, Lex!'

'Compared to you young cats, I am.'

Obviously he wasn't ready to share his woes. 'So how do you bottle hope, and have it interpreted as such?' This whole bottling a feeling idea still bamboozled me. I understood the value of it, but how did you know it would translate for someone else? Like Nan had wanted to bottle love ... How? What if love smelled different to everyone? Sure, what we made was inspired by the notion of it, but it wasn't tangibly *it*.

'That's the thing, Del. It's everything and nothing. You just have to be bold and hope they understand what you're trying to do. It was just damn luck on my part, but I *hoped* ...' he smiled at the word '... that they'd understand.'

I shook my head, knowing I had to solve this damn riddle myself. But that was the thing about perfume – sometimes it was unsolvable like the most complex mathematical equation. And it was all subjective too.

'Enjoy Bordeaux.'

'I'm gonna dash out now and buy some earplugs, all the burgundy in France can't dull that voice of Clementine's.'

I laughed, imaging the fireworks.

'Off you go, America. Kick ass, yeah?'

I gave him a quick hug. 'See you at the end of the week.'

Packed and ready, I headed to the car to find Sebastien standing stiff as a toy solider, his hands in pockets as he surveyed the avenue.

'Del,' he said. 'There you are.' Four simple words that had my heart hammering. Damn it.

'Here I am.'

'Safe, for another week.'

'I'm so relieved.'

'It was very close.'

'Yes. Too close. I promise the judges made the right choice and I'll prove it to them this week.'

'I know you will, Del. You have a gift, there's no question about that.' He gazed so deeply into my eyes, all thought of perfumery leapt from my mind. He stared at me like I was the only person on the planet. There was such an intensity about him and I had to remind myself to speak, and not just stare back like some dumbstruck fool.

My distractions had got the better of me so far, and I was determined not to break my focus again. But damn the man, he made my heart rhumba of its own accord, and what the heck was I supposed to do about that? I went to touch my lips, remembering the accidental kiss, before I thought better of it. I blamed it on his perfume, that's all it was. He smelt so dang good and it was lulling me into a false sense of …

'So, Provence,' I said. I mentally added great conversationalist to my repertoire.

'You'll enjoy it, Del. At least I hope you do. About last night—'

Oh god, the about-last-night talk. I held up a hand to stop him. I didn't want to hear him tell me it shouldn't have happened because I *knew* that. And I was mortified by it. I'd asked Clementine what the kissing etiquette was so I'd never mess up again. Kiss left cheek first, and then right. Whose left though, yours or theirs? And in some parts of France it was a three-barreled kiss but not for Parisians. Confusing or what?

'I wanted to apologize for that. I didn't realize there's a certain side to kiss, well not kiss, *peck*, and I got muddled. I am a walking disaster, you said it yourself. Let's just be glad I didn't kiss, I mean, *peck* your ear or something.'

His eyes reflected the confusion I felt. '*Oui*, a mistake. I'd hate

137

for people to accuse me of anything untoward. It would not be appropriate as your mentor and head of *Leclére*.'

'Of course.' I wanted to cover my face and run. 'This competition means everything to me and I won't jeopardize it, nor your reputation.'

With an apologetic smile. 'It's … it's for the best.'

Trust me to feel a sizzle for a man I couldn't have. But it was so clearly one-sided with him letting me down gently, just like I'd seen him do with Clementine and anyone else in his orbit.

Before I started bemoaning my fate, I said, 'Definitely.' And hoped he'd let it drop so my mortification wasn't obvious.

I jumped in the car, greeting the elderly driver with a '*bonjour*'. In order to appear unflustered, I texted my sister, suddenly missing her. I wished I had the privacy to call and pour my heart out, but Sebastien soon joined me so that was that.

Chapter Twenty

Jen, I'm safe for another week, but only just. It was so close even the judges deliberated over it until finally sending Kathryn home. I'm thankful, but I feel like I have to work a lot harder than I have been. I have to think differently and push myself to try alternative techniques. It's like I've got this block and I just can't seem to work out how to go around it. Guess that's all part of this adventure! I'm off to Provence for the next challenge – can you believe that? Lavender fields, sunshine and fresh air … Will call as soon as I can. Del xxx

I hit send and settled back into the seat. Before long, my phone pinged with a message.

What aren't you telling me? I'm reading between the lines there's something else … What is it? Why can't you talk now? Jen xxx

Pesky twin intuition. My twin sister often had the unique ability to guess how I was feeling.

I'm in the car with Sebastien … Not sure what the challenge entails, so it might not be today. I'm fine, really, just sometimes it's all a bit lonely without you. And it was a pressure cooker of a week.

P.S I kissed Sebastien, accidentally. More of a peck than a kiss. A light brush of lips. Very minor. And then he gave me the face-to-face Dear John talk ... I could die from embarrassment, and guess what, he's my mentor so I have a week alone with him. Kill me!

Love you xxx

We left the bustling streets of Paris and were soon speeding down a motorway. Soft sunlight shot filmy spirals through the tinted windows.

My phone beeped, like I knew it would.

Oh, Del, I hardly think anyone would give you the Dear John talk! Are you sure you're reading the situation right?

I'd expected some kind of jokey reply. Some over-the-top missive about the city of love, best man speeches, and pregnancy cankles; not that, what *was* that?

I'm sure. And the elimination was so close, I really have to knuckle down. Feel like crying and laughing all at once. Whew, what an experience.

My desire to get ahead, my ambition – all of it stemmed from fear; fear that I'd turn into my mother and dance through my days in some kind of daze. Let responsibility slip through my fingers and bray to the moon, just like she did living in an alternate universe. I didn't want that for myself. Like Sebastien wanted out of the world of perfumery, I wanted in. But we were the same in that we wanted to step out from the shadows of our parents, and live life on our own terms. If I let my guard down I'd be eliminated, I knew that for sure. So there was no question it was time to switch on and put anything else out of my mind.

Follow your heart. Call me when you can. xxx

I am following my heart – and it's going to lead me all the way to 5th Avenue. I'll call you later. xxx

The driver made eye contact in the rear-view mirror. 'We have a long drive ahead, so please let me know if you need anything. You'll find some champagne in the ice box. We'll stop halfway for lunch.'

Champagne in the ice box! The French, they celebrated everything, even long drives.

An hour later and our silence sat heavily in the air. Sebastien fielded phone calls, and spoke in rapid French. They were all business related from the words I'd picked up. How one little store was so busy amazed me, but their clients paid top dollar for their lotions, potions and perfumes and couldn't seem to get enough of them.

I opened the window and settled back to read a guidebook about Provence on my Kindle app, figuring a little research into the area couldn't hurt, and the more I read, the more excited I was to arrive. One of the books described the abundant lavender fields, colloquially known as 'blue gold' because of the amount of uses lavender had, and what it meant for the economy.

It was used in perfumes and bathing products and strangely enough even in bistros dotted around the countryside who used the fragrant flower in *crème brûlée* and ice cream.

And as for *vin*, rosé was the wine of choice in Provence, and the region was famous for it. Wine was huge in France, taken with most meals with much less pomp and ceremony than back home.

When it came to cuisine, the *Provençal Bouillabaisse*, a rich fish stew, was lauded as a must-try. There were also the UNESCO heritage listed Pont Du Gard aqueducts that crossed the Gordon River. Amphitheaters, arches, and ruins were thick and wide across the region, and while we wouldn't have time to see them (they spanned a huge section of the area), it was still nice to know I'd be in the vicinity of such historical importance.

Much later we arrived in Provence. The driver negotiated some hairy turns until we came to a villa surrounded by olive trees and fields of lavender. I jumped out of the car, glad to be free of the confined space. Zapped from the long drive, I yawned and stretched. I took in my surroundings; the light was different here, filmy and luminescent. All at once I understood why Sebastien loved it here. It was worlds away from the chaos of Paris, and if you were a solitude seeker, it would be perfect.

The driver shook our hands and said, 'I'll be in the cabin out back if you need me. Enjoy.'

'*Merci*,' Sebastien said. In the fading Provençal sunlight Sebastien's face was paler than usual, as if the long drive had sapped him. He'd had barely a moment away from his phone, and when he wasn't speaking he was checking emails and replying. Was it a ploy to avoid talking to me? Any conversation was stilted, awkward.

It occurred to me we'd be alone inside the villa for an entire week. If it was going to be this awkward I didn't know how I'd stand it. Why, oh, why had I kissed him like that? Truthfully, it meant more to me than a simple swipe of the lips, accidental or not. 'Is everything OK?' I asked. His harried expression said otherwise.

'Yes, just work issues. Come inside, Del.'

He ushered me inside the stone villa, which was more like a cozy little cabin, less grand than the Parisian apartment. While the place was spotless, it also had a lived-in, homely feel, from the weathered and crazed leather sofa, to the scarred wooden bookshelves, filled with haphazardly stacked novels. It was the kind of space you could relax in, be yourself.

'Make yourself comfortable and I'll get us some coffee.'

While he did that I wandered around the room, stopping at the mantle. There was a grainy black and white picture of Sebastien with his father Vincent, their heads bowed close as if they were discussing the secrets of the universe. Was it taken here?

'That's one of the only photos I have with him,' Sebastien said softly, handing me a mug of steaming hot coffee.

'It's lovely. Looks like you're plotting something magical.'

He gave me a half-smile. 'He'd asked me to make a perfume about love, but I failed miserably.'

'Why?' It was eerily similar to what Nan had asked of me. Maybe it was a perfumery test we all took.

With a shrug he said, 'According to Papa all he could smell was cynicism.'

Before I could ask more his phone rang again. 'Sorry,' he said, sighing. I waved him away, and sipped my coffee, itching to find out what was going on.

'What is it?' I asked when he ended the call.

'One of our formulas has been copied, and sold in a well-established perfume house. We're trying to get them to pull it from their shelves.'

'Does this happen often?'

As much as you could guard your formulas, in this day and age it was easy to break down the ingredients in a perfume and copy it.

'Every now and then,' he said, a touch of anger in his tone. 'But for a respected perfumery, it's unforgivable.'

'In Paris?'

'*Oui.*'

My eyes went wide wondering who they were. 'And will they pull it from their shelves now that you know?'

'I think so, but then we have all the legal ramifications to deal with. Why can't they just design their own? It's embarrassing for them. They're trying to save face by saying it's "inspired by".' He made air quotes with his fingers. 'But, of course, it's a replica of the real thing.'

'They don't deserve to be in business!'

'No, and the headache it creates …'

'I can imagine. So do you need to head back?'

'No, but let's get to work, if you're up for it after the drive?'

'Of course.'

Sebastien carried those business burdens so heavily on his shoulders. He stood, his green eyes dark with worry. I felt like I was another distraction for him, another concern. It became clear, the difference between being a perfumer and running a company, just how committed you'd have to be. Naively, I hadn't banked on that for my perfumery boutique. I'd only imagined the fun part – blending perfumes for happy people. Not the messy side of things, when problems cropped up. That was to be Jen's domain; without her, could I cope alone in my own dream business?

Sebastien sat opposite me and spoke almost robotically as if he just wanted to get it over and done with. 'Challenge two is all about region. About raw materials used in perfumery, and where they're sourced. Provence is famous for the abundance of lavender fields. Your challenge is to make the humble purple flower shine.'

If anyone could make lavender shine it was me!

According to the guidebook I'd read on the way down, we were at the beginning of the lavender season, and I noted from the drive there were beautiful purple fields as far as the eye could see. I imagined walking through paths of lavender, arms outstretched, fingertips fanning the heavily scented flowers as I passed.

Lavender perfume, though. It was such a strong, distinctive scent. The memories came thick and fast, Nan placing silky sacks of dried lavender in her lingerie drawers. Lavender misting spray she used on her pillow to help her sleep. I had to take it further than its humble origins. I had to reinvent it.

But how … I took a notepad from my bag and grabbed a pen. Once again, I was grateful for my stay of execution and fired up with this challenge.

'Tomorrow we'll take a walk around town so you can get a feel of the place and see if you can't think of a concept around Provence,' he said.

His phone trilled again, and he sighed. 'Sorry, I have to get that.'

'Go for it.'

Darkness had fallen while we'd been here but I desperately wanted to see what was outside the villa. In the utility room I found a torch and headed outside, amazed at the hush and the span of night sky. Perhaps Paris had become part of me now; I was used to that noise, the lack of space and could now enjoy this solitude for what it was. In the distance there was a field of lavender, the scent shimmied on the wind. An olive grove stood somberly nearby, tree trunks grey-white under the moonlight.

Gravel crunched underfoot as I made my way around the property until I came to a little log cabin. A perfume studio? Fragrance leached from every fibrous pore of wood. I tried the door, which I found unlocked. Inside, I groped the wall until I found a switch and flicked it on. In pride of place sat a perfume organ, similar to my nan's but slightly bigger. They were hard to come by these days, antiques that they were, and it was a beauty all right.

If I closed my eyes, I could picture Sebastien and his father as they were in the picture I'd seen inside. What magic had they made side by side, heads bent conspiratorially? What an honor it would be to sit and work where they had. This was Sebastien's quiet place, his refuge when Paris wore him down.

I sat at the perfume organ, each shelf with every kind of essence you could imagine, French handwriting scrawled on each label. Edging closer, I attempted to translate the words, running a finger along the bottles. *Lavande* was lavender, *lis* was lily …

Feeling altogether silly, I sent a silent prayer up to Vincent and asked him to help me. Help me learn to work without my nan. Help me grow and be brave with my perfumery. Keep me safe in the competition for as long as possible. Help his son find his passion once more …

The studio had a fireplace set with wood, ready to be lit. In front of it were a couple of wingback leather chairs wrinkled with age, the slight impressions of someone's shape. It was a comforting little spot so markedly different from the sterile lab in Paris and it felt more like me, more like home.

Chapter Twenty-One

We were up early, and had breakfasted on fresh baguettes with salty butter and steaming hot black coffee. Light spilled across the sky and the day felt heated from the ground up. Did Vincent spend much time here? For some reason I could picture *le savant fou* waking with the sunrise, muttering to birds as they stole olives from the trees.

'Did you spend summers here with your family?'

Sebastien nursed a cup of black coffee.

'Occasionally,' he said. 'Papa would join us for a day or two. They were some of my best memories, working in the studio here with him.'

I smiled, remembering the sense of calm I'd felt in the studio the night before, almost the like old man was there.

As if reading my mind, Sebastien said, 'When I work here, I get this strange feeling like he's standing to the left of me, whispering in my ear. Crazy, *non*?'

I reached across the table and found his hand, giving it a supportive pat. Whatever stress he felt yesterday was slowly dissipating in the Provencal light. 'Not at all. I feel that too with my nan. For me Nan was always there, just off in the distance.'

'What does she say?' he asked.

'Usually she starts with, *I didn't teach you to* … insert diatribe from *be selfish*, or *be a quitter*, to *hide away like this*. I spent all my time with her growing up and into adulthood; she was more than just my nan, she was also like a best friend, and it was hard to lose both. It's easier to pretend she's near me, dispensing advice, showing me the way.'

'That makes me feel less crazy,' he laughed. 'On bad days when I feel the break in my heart, I pretend Papa is in his studio, just a few steps away from our apartment, lost in his perfumery and tinkering about. It does help, at least for a little while.'

The break in my heart. I just loved the way he described it and his honesty. 'You're not crazy, you're just muddling through grief the best way you can. We're lucky though, at least we have their perfumes, and they'll always live on through those.'

He nodded. 'I have a collection of my papa's last formulas – perfumes that haven't been made public and I often wonder what to do with them. Keep them for myself, or make the range, knowing they'll become bestsellers but then they won't be only mine?'

'I can tell by your voice what you want to do.'

'And?'

'Keep them for yourself. Keep that one thing; after all, *you* can always design a new range and keep your famous clients happy.'

'Maybe.' He let the comment slide. 'What about your parents, what do they think of your perfumery ambitions?'

Where to start? 'To be honest, Sebastien, they wouldn't really have a clue. Of course they know I love it, but they don't know much else. They weren't around much for me and Jen, and Nan and Pop were more like parents.'

'Why, what were they doing?'

'Healing the world one tarot card at a time. They only came home when they ran out of money. It was tough, living in a small town when they blew back in, older but not wiser.'

'Is that what gives you that drive, why you're so determined?'

I nodded. 'I guess so. I just always wished they were more normal, just your average suburban parents. But I guess we don't get to choose and they're sweet in their own way; they just live life on their own terms. But I want more. And I don't have anyone to fall back on if it doesn't work out.'

The driver knocked at the door and offered to take us into town, but Sebastien took the keys and told him to take the day off. We wandered the Provençal streets of Saint-Rémy, the bright sunlight warming my face as I turned it toward the sun.

Already Sebastien had lost that tension in his face; he was quick to smile, and enjoyed sharing the history of the town. 'Nostradamus was born here. And Vincent Van Gogh was treated in an asylum at the monastery Saint-Paul Mausole asylum in 1889 for two years. He painted a collection of works while he was in Saint-Rémy; one of the most well-known is *The Irises*. You may know it?'

'Yes!' I said, amazement coloring my voice. We were walking in *his* footsteps, the legend that was Van Gogh, another Vincent ahead of his time. I knew the painting he spoke of; it was iconic – a patch of purple irises in a field with daubs of yellow and green.

He continued, '*The Irises* is truly remarkable in that Van Gogh thought that it was saving him from insanity. He started it a week after being admitted to the asylum, and he fought valiantly to pull himself out of ill health. It's nothing like his other paintings, it doesn't have the same intensity, and I love it all the more for that.'

What had happened to the almost broody Sebastien? He was chatty, and animated. Could a change of place really have that much effect on a person?

'What happened after he was discharged from the asylum?' I asked.

Sebastien dipped his head. 'He died a few months later.'

I'd always been fascinated by Van Gogh, and the loyal and inspiring relationship he had with his younger brother Theo who supported him through so many hard times. And I found it tragic that his extraordinary artwork was never appreciated while he was alive and he struggled financially until his death. If only he could have seen what a legacy he'd left behind. I couldn't recall much about his passing though, and found it inordinately sad it had happened so soon after he left the asylum, supposedly cured.

'How did he die?'

'Gunshot wound,' Sebastien said. He was as morose as if he knew Vincent personally, and I warmed toward him because of it.

'Suicide?'

He gave a small shrug. 'It's believed to be that way, but there's always those conspiracy theories that he was shot by an enemy of some sort.'

'People believe what they want to believe. I remember reading that his brother died not long after.'

Sebastien nodded. 'They say he had a disease of the brain but it was not so. He died of a broken heart at only thirty-three years of age.'

Goosebumps raced the length of me. Those poor brothers, both so young.

After a couple of hours walking around the beautiful town, we got back in the car and went to visit our first lavender field. Sebastien was testing me. Out of the five fields we were to visit, he wanted me to tell him which one *Leclére Parfumerie* used for their lavender. Just how the heck I'd know was beyond me, but I was up for the challenge, and secretly relishing spending time with him when he was this carefree, this happy.

'So,' I said. 'This first field, how long has it been operational?'

He gave me a quick *as if* glance.

'Too obvious?'

'*Oui.*'

We exchanged grins. 'I wonder if I'll get a sense, you know, or if after a while all I'll see is a purple-blue blur.'

'I think you'll surprise yourself.'

'Shucks, what faith you have in me.' We shared a meaningful

look, and I quickly turned way. Focus. I told myself not to read into a feeling that wasn't there.

We turned down a pebbled drive, with sprawling fields of lavender as far as the eye could see. As we got close you could make out the blue sprigs dancing on the wind, a burlesque just for us. 'Gosh, it's absolutely breathtaking.' Lavender was distinctive and with such abundant fields of it, I wondered if I'd be able to really mark those few variations in scent.

Sebastien parked the car in front of a stone villa and a couple came out to greet us.

'Welcome,' the man said. 'We're the Miliots. Let us show you around.'

We did a tour of the property, and they showed us how they harvested the crops, and some of the products made from the oils extracted from lavender.

I picked a bud, sniffing it, then broke it to release the oils. I wasn't sure this was the right place; it didn't ring true for some inexplicable reason. We thanked the couple and moved on, and I crossed that farm off the list.

When we reached the fifth field, home of the Lillettes, I'd made up my mind. This was the place. The mistral, when it came, would blow hard from the north, but the fields were protected by a mountain range nearby. The flowers wouldn't suffer the wooly weather as much as they would in the other fields; here they'd keep their spikes and buds intact.

This farm gave off a certain vibe, almost cocooning the blue dream.

Another couple came to greet us, rugged types dressed in old jeans and tees, and plastic boots, their smiles as certain as I was.

Still, I questioned them about their processes and did a tour out of genuine interest.

After effusive thanks we left them and headed back to the villa.

We sat across from each other at the kitchen table. 'It was the last farm.'

'How can you be so sure?'

I explained about the mistral winds and the damage they could wreak, and how the mountain range protected the lavender.

With his poker face, it was impossible to tell, but I pressed my lips together and waited. Which lasted exactly half a second before I burst out with, 'You're enjoying this, aren't you?'

He bit down on a smile. 'Far too much to be healthy. And you're correct, we chose that place because of the protection the mountains offer. The mistral is fierce and can damage the buds or ruin crops completely.' His eyes shone with a sort of pride. 'It's organically farmed and the property has been in the Lillette family for three generations.'

'Yay! Who knew I'd have farmer material written all over me!'

He raised a brow.

'OK, maybe farmer is a stretch.'

We laughed. 'I can see why you love it here.'

'It's not just the quiet,' he said. 'It's a sense of belonging,'

'Lavender fields, olive groves, sunshine and friendly locals. I can see the appeal.'

He uncorked a bottle of wine and poured us two glasses of rosé. 'But you only have eyes for the bright lights of the city?'

In the fading light of Provence I felt relaxed, dozy as a cat in sunshine. Time moved slower here; there was no rush, people meandered, unlike Paris where everything was a desperate rush. Don't even get me started on catching the Metro at peak hour. That was a mistake I would never make again. You could really think in a place like this. 'I *thought* I knew what I wanted, that my plan was foolproof, but doesn't life just surprise you when you least expect it?'

We locked eyes and the air grew heavy. 'It certainly does.'

Chapter Twenty-Two

In the little Provençal perfumery studio I was doing as promised, taking risks, blending notes I usually wouldn't pair up, experimenting, and thinking outside the box. As a mentor Sebastien had given me something money couldn't buy – confidence! He made me think about perfumery in a completely new light. Every stage was crucial from the farms themselves, to the extraction techniques, and even the mood of the perfumer. Suddenly the block that had been holding me back lifted, and I felt like I had half a chance of staying in the competition, if only I could hit the brief.

'You must be happy in the moment of mixing, and shut off any outside worries. If you're angry, sad, frustrated, it will show in the perfume. It's all about temperament.'

'What?' I cried. It was such a whimsical thing for him to say. 'What do you mean, temperament?'

Sunlight shone in the window behind him. 'If the perfumer isn't happy, it reflects in their product.'

I cocked my head, and held a laugh in check. Nan and I had a few fragrance quirks between us but I didn't expect Mr Serious to believe in something so frivolous. Secretly I felt the same, but I couldn't help tease this whimsical side of him out more. 'And how can that possibly be?'

'Well,' he said, his cheeks pinking. 'It's like cooking with love, that's a common saying isn't it? If the cook is rushed, or harried, the food tastes bitter. The same with fragrance. If the perfumer isn't happy, then their sense of smell is off, and they can't blend perfection. It will always be tinged with that unhappiness.'

Somehow I managed to keep a straight face but my heart just about exploded. *That!* That was passion! That didn't sound like the words of a man who wanted no part in perfumery … My nan would have jumped up and cuddled the guy. The idea crossed my mind too.

'I agree,' I said.

Goosebumps prickled my skin, and I had the most curious sense someone was standing just off in the distance … It dawned on me that Vincent knew all along what his son needed.

While Vincent might not have been as available as he should have, he still knew his son's heart. Aurelie too had had a hand in it. I had to resist the urge to clap a hand over my mouth as all the puzzle pieces fit into place. The competition was *never* about finding an unknown perfumer, even though it would open doors and be a great benefit to us, it was about helping their son rekindle his love for perfumery, without his father.

The man who broke his heart was attempting to put it back together – from the afterlife.

That's why they suddenly opened up their long-closed doors to us. For their son – the boy who'd stood at that doorway lost and alone. Vincent knew he'd made a mistake in not spending time with Sebastien and he was trying to fix it the best way he knew how …

Instead of feeling duped, I felt this great sense of complicity. I could be a cog in the machine that helped Sebastien let go of his past and live for his future. The love he had for his craft shone in his eyes, and I knew he just had to open his heart to it once again.

The Lecléres had sacrificed the one thing they cherished – their anonymity – by offering the winner a chance to design a perfume range for the house. It seemed a fitting compromise, and I loved them all the more for their foresight.

So now, under the guise of mentoring me, I had to lead him back to the world in which he claimed he wanted no part of.

'So shall I leave you? To experiment some more?'

'*Oui*,' I said, watching him walk away, a smile on my face. I needed time to think! How would I go about helping him rediscover his love for fragrance? Perhaps I could make a restorative for him to wear that would help things along … An oil blend of black spruce, coconut, vanilla, and juniper would invigorate his senses, give him clarity once more. I set to work, shelving my own perfume for later, and made it with all the love I had in my heart.

When it was done, I sat back, smiling. I had the feeling things were on the up for Sebastien, but he just didn't know it yet.

My phone beeped with a message. Jen!

Hey Del,

I'm just falling into bed after a long shift but all is well here in sleepy-ville. Grandpop says hi. Mom and Dad are on some road trip to visit some of their tree-hugging hippy friends for a full moon party … James and I are going well, too well, and sometimes I wonder if I'm dreaming it all up. How can a man make you feel just so? Anyway, I know we're both busy, but let's talk as soon as possible? Miss you like crazy.

Jen xxx

I replied: *Miss you too. Give Pop a hug from me and tell him to keep an eye on the snail mail. And about James … you deserve a guy who sweeps you off your feet and makes your heart sing. May it long last.*

Urgh, may it long last, sounded like a line from *The Hunger Games*. Suddenly I understood her a little better though. As if this time apart had given me room to grow without her.

I spent the next few hours with my lavender perfume, happily lost inside my mind, concocting this and that, hoping to find a balance between risk and reward. As it often did with perfumery, time slipped from my grasp.

When I finally came up for air, he was there, a silhouette in the doorway, Sebastien patiently waiting for me.

'Would you like to take a walk, Del?'

'Sure. It's just what I need,' I said, tidying my things away. 'I made you this.' I handed him the little bottle. 'It's just an experiment, nothing to do with the competition ...'

His lips curved into a deep smile. '*Merci.*' He removed the stopper and dabbed the oil on his pulse points. 'A perfect blend ...'

'I hope you'll wear it and it makes you smile.'

He thanked me again and I beamed, hoping the blend would do its trick and awaken the dormant perfumer in him.

We wandered through rows of olive trees, their trunks reflecting a diaphanous orange of a setting sun. Down to the lavender fields, the flowers waving in the wind like they were saying hello. Something had changed, and I couldn't decide if it was me, or my perfumery, or Sebastien and his journey. But I felt lighter, like I was letting go of the reins, and that was OK. Or maybe it was trusting in the process more and enjoying the ups and the downs.

The sun sank behind the mountain range, orange glowing above it like the tips of a jeweled crown.

He turned and looked so intensely at me, a flush crept up my cheeks. He was so close, a half-step away. I knew right then, I needed to express these feelings, one way or another. The sun had set and the blue of sky deepened to lilac. I wanted to feel his lips against mine. Just this once, just to feel the emotion in my heart, my soul.

'Del ...' he said my name like an invitation.

Before he could say anymore I stood on tiptoe and pressed my mouth against his. I could taste the sun and the sea, the earth and the sky on his breath. His fragrance was musky with desire. I kissed him as long as I could, melting against him.

I broke away, breathless, but he caught me again, and kissed me back softly this time. My legs, already jelly-like, threatened to bow under me, so I held him tight, and all the while wished the moment would never end. But of course it did. Abruptly.

'Del, we shouldn't. It'll ruin everything.'

I blinked back surprise. What had I expected? He'd already told me in so many words! The unfairness of it all made my chest tighten. Why now, why him, and why could it not be reciprocal? Mortification colored me scarlet.

Seriously what had I been thinking? 'Sorry,' I said. 'You're right. It would complicate things.'

'It's not that I don't feel ...'

I pressed a fingertip to his lips. 'I know.'

That wasn't in the five-year plan, was it? Silence fell and I reminded myself of it, to get it through my thick knucklehead once more.

Step one: win the competition. Step two: find a job as a perfumer. Step three: build own perfume empire. Step four: be fabulous. Step five: I'd forgotten step five. But regardless, there was no love on that list. And no time for it.

And yet ...

The next day I waited for Sebastien in the perfume studio, but he didn't appear until mid-morning, once again with his cell phone pressed to his ear. He wore a besieged expression as if Paris was pulling him back.

With a sigh he hung up the phone, pocketed it, and opened the studio door.

'Del,' he said apologetically and I knew what was coming.

'Good morning,' I said, having noted he was wearing the oil

blend I'd made for him the day before. 'Why the long face?'

'I have to head back to Paris, the situation with the copied formula has become more complex, and the management team have asked me to return to talk to our lawyers. I'm so sorry about this. I'm not being much of a mentor to you.'

My heart dropped at the thought of him leaving, but I understood. 'It's fine,' I said, waving him away. 'We had a great session yesterday, and I think I'm on track anyway.'

'Would you like to continue working on your perfume here, or in Paris?'

'I'll stay,' I said, staring past him, through the window, to where lavender shimmied and swayed in the breeze like a hula dance. 'This perfume is all about Provence, and I'm inspired here.' As much as I'd miss him as a mentor, a friend, and whatever else I couldn't quite name, I wanted to soak up the atmosphere, and pour that feeling into my work. The quiet sort of crept up on you here and seeped into your bones, making you relaxed and sort of starry-eyed with it all.

'You'll be happier, Del.' He had a sparkle in his eye I hadn't picked up on before. Was he relieved I was staying and he was going? That we wouldn't have to sidestep around each other? And then we'd avoid talking about a kiss that shouldn't have happened? 'Jean Marc will return for you.'

I turned away. 'Safe travels.' With a lump in my throat I went back to work, only stopping for a moment when I heard the crunch of tires on the gravel as he left.

Stop kissing him then, Del!

I returned to my perfumery, but had to stop and let that lonely feeling pass, lest I taint my perfume with it. While I contemplated it came to me – what I should have known all along. Lots of people dealt with heartbreak, loneliness, fear, and grief, and I'd been trying to make a blend to help them heal – making tonics, tinctures, aromatherapy oils. But surely they needed a perfume that bolstered them, boosted their mood and made them remember the good times, the fact that love was always worth it no matter what it cost you?

Invigorated, I set to work, recalling the mentoring session from the day before and everything Sebastien had taught me …

Chapter Twenty-Three

Back in Paris, Provence was just a lavender-scented memory. The quiet had done me the world of good; I felt recharged and relaxed and ready to tackle the competition in earnest. I'd had an Oprah light bulb moment, and I felt I could achieve anything just as long as I remained focused.

My lavender perfume had hit the brief, and I felt a surge of confidence. It was such a change from my previous submission that I felt like I should celebrate the moment. Maybe I was becoming a little French, enjoying the good of every day.

Out front of the *Leclére* apartment I waited for the other contestants to join me for our group excursion to the Musée du Parfum. Aurelie was to be our guide, and I was relieved I wouldn't have to face Sebastien today. Time apart had made me realize I was muddying my perfumery dreams with my involvement with him, and it wasn't appropriate.

What had happened to the clear-headed ambitious girl? She'd had a wobble, the first flush of what love could be, and been so easily distracted, but that was over now.

I shot off a text to Jen to pass the time.

Hey sleepyhead, while you're catching Zs, I'm waiting for the group. We're off on an excursion which are always fun. The week went well, and I'm looking forward to the judging this time around.

Why haven't you called or texted? I miss hearing your voice, and listening to your terrible jokes. Is it James? He's stolen you away from me, hasn't he? Next I'll get a call saying it's time to knit baby booties, and can I be home to help you rush down the aisle. Imagine that! It's hideous, isn't it? Anyway, call me when you can. Love you xxx

Clementine was first to arrive, and wore a thunderous expression. 'Del,' she said, sashaying over in a satin teal dress, and white faux-fur coat, quite the ensemble for a summer's morning. She air kissed my cheeks.

'It wasn't so bad,' I said. 'How'd you do?'

She rolled her eyes, taking a deep breath, chest heaving. It was monologue time, and I couldn't help grinning as I waited for a dramatic retelling of her week with Lex. 'That man, that … *old* man, well he tried to tell me what to do, 'ow to think all the time, like I don't 'ave a brain in my own head.' She pointed to her temple. 'Does it look like I don't 'ave a brain?' she demanded. 'Because that's 'ow he was treating me! *Brainless!*'

It was hard not to laugh, but I kept my mouth clamped closed and gave her a nod to continue.

'And 'e talks and talks at me. Says we have to think on our feet, and then I get this picture of 'e's feet and I'm disgusted and I lose track. And in the end I just give in, *not* because 'e knows what 'e's talking about, just for my own wellbeing.'

'So, it was a tough week but you made a perfume and you're happy with it?' I asked, trying to untangle the accented words.

'*Oui.*'

'So …?'

'So, I'm just telling you 'ow it is, Del! Do you 'ave a brain in *your* head?'

I laughed and gave her a hug. 'I've missed you,' I said and was surprised to find I meant it. It was hard not to love Clementine, drama, backstabbing and all.

'I missed you too, *ma cherie*. And there might 'ave been one boy, but better that stays in Bordeaux, *oui*? It was only an 'oliday fling!'

I shook my head – she was a man-eater, all right! It was a wonder she'd got any work done, and I bet she had Lex to thank for keeping her on track. He didn't have to help her but by the sounds of it he did.

Eventually Lila, Lex and Anastacia joined us and we were driven to Musée du Parfum.

When we arrived at the museum we were ushered inside by our own private tour guide. We had special access and, excitingly, we'd get to see many relics from another era up close, not from behind a chain link like everyone else. Sebastien must've pulled some strings to make it so.

Our tour guide led us through and explained perfumery through the ages, and the different methods used hundreds of years ago to make the elixirs.

The museum was ripe with perfumery antiques that still held the merest whisper of scent, from a kohl perfume vase, believed to be circa 3000 BC in the Mesopotamia early dynastic period, to a seventeenth-century Louis XIV perfume burner in gilded bronze and ebony. They hummed with memories of the past.

It astounded me that these special relics from all over the world had survived. Fabergé bottles, sixteenth-century pomanders worn on belts like a pendant or boxes held in the hand that were used to ward of epidemics, tiny ring flasks from the Czech Republic that held precious perfume, and couture bottles that were so elegant and well-crafted they made me catch my breath at their delicate beauty. There were perfumery workshops for tourists who were busily blending their own fragrances to take home.

On the way back to the lab we were buzzing with all we'd seen.

'I want that ring flask,' Clementine said. 'I've never seen anything so beautiful.'

These excursions were shaping us as perfumers, opening our

eyes to the world of perfumery in a way we'd never imagined. Scent was about so much more than oil collected from rose petals, or seeds gathered from a vanilla bean pod. It was about the history, the memory and what it evoked, and finding one that conjured a feeling unique to you. A spritz swept you up, made you believe and those around you translated it.

After the excursion I ran into Sebastien in the lab; he was chatting to Lex about Bordeaux. He was spending more time with the contestants ... Were we inspiring him? By the way he focused on Lex you could see he was truly interested; such a difference from those first weeks where he answered questions curtly and was gone in five minutes.

Aurelie wandered in and called Lex over, leaving me with Sebastien. Instead of dithering, or acting the fool, I steeled myself and smiled.

'Did you sort everything out?'

'*Oui*,' he said, scrubbing his face at the memory. 'And let's just say our lawyers will probably be vacationing for years with the money we've invested.'

I shook my head, imagining the amount of money they'd lose, and all because another company took what wasn't theirs. 'It seems so unfair.'

'It really does,' he said. 'But I suppose it gets our name back in the papers; it's good for business in that sense.'

The papers? Wasn't that the last thing he wanted? 'But you hate that don't you? The limelight?'

'I thought I did,' he said with a rueful grin. 'But I'm beginning to understand my papa better.' He dropped his voice to a whisper. 'We shunned the press for years, because they wanted stories about us, fabricated or not, and why would we go along with that when it should've been about our perfumes ...'

'Yeah, so what's changed?' I'd have bet the press would've still done anything to get inside information about Sebastien, the intensely private, broody hot French guy – I'd buy that!

He sat at the bench opposite me. 'All this time, I thought my papa was on the other side of that door, lost in the magic of making perfumes, when really he was crunching numbers, doing the neverending paperwork, stopping his collections from being copied, keeping *Leclére* afloat ...'

'And he did it all behind closed doors so he was the only one who shouldered the worry?'

Sebastien double-blinked, a sign he was moved by something deep. I gave him a minute to compose himself. '*Oui*, he did it for me and not once did I have any idea what running *Leclére* entailed. He did it so I could design perfume without hindrance, without any stress or pressure. I had no idea, none at all, what sacrifices he made so I could concentrate on what *he* loved, perfumery.'

My skin prickled again, like the old man was leaning over my shoulder. 'And now you know, it wasn't that he *didn't* love you, it was because he loved you so *much*.'

Sebastien's eyes grew glassy. 'I had it all wrong. He gave me the space he thought I needed, but I only needed him. What an intricate web we humans weave when we don't speak our truth.'

Our truth? But it wasn't always so easy to speak the truth ...

'Sounds to me like someone has found a scrap of passion amid the paperwork?' I said, waggling my brows, trying to lighten the mood.

'*Oui*.' He gave me a wide smile. 'It was because of you, Del.'

'Why me?'

'I wasn't going to go through with the competition. That's why I wasn't there for the welcoming party. I was all set to leave, I'd decided I wanted no part of it. That it had been a terrible idea, and I shouldn't have promised. But then I kept running into you, literally,' he laughed. 'And you gave me pause. Not just because you are disaster girl but because you were so obviously out of your comfort zone, so alone and yet you were here, and I felt I owed it to you – to this girl who wore her heart on her sleeve and had come all this way, and truthfully made me laugh, really laugh for the first time in forever.'

He had planned on abandoning the competition? But fate, or ghosts, or whatever you want to call it had stepped in by throwing me quite literally in his path. *Three times*. I slapped my forehead at the memories of that day. If I didn't know better I'd have guessed we had a couple of people pulling strings from above …

'Well,' I said, 'Disaster Girl at your service.' I saluted, and grinned at the man before me with dazzling eyes and a smile that lit up his face.

He'd come such a long way in the time I'd known him, and I felt so attuned to him. Grief and its myriad layers had the ability to knock a person's world on its axis in such a way it wasn't evident to them, they just felt unbalanced all the time, and now here he was righting himself once more.

'It's not only that, Del,' he said, spots of pink appearing on his cheeks. 'It's the way you believe perfume can fix everything, like it truly is medicinal. I knew what you were trying to do when you handed me the oil in Provence. I've never met anyone that believes so wholly in scent, except for my papa. You think you're ambitious, you have this drive to succeed, but I think you underestimate how you succeed every single day just by being you. By sharing your gift when you diagnose what a person needs.'

My mouth opened and closed and I grappled with what to say.

'I'm sorry, I've dropped all this on you,' he said, but soon the smile fell away and was replaced with something deeper, more real.

Standing there, staring into his eyes, had a hypnotic effect on me and I wanted to reach out and touch him, to feel his arms around me, to feel his lips pressed against mine and I knew then that I was lost to it. Lost to the intensity of want. Why him, it was hard to know, but when I was near him there was a charge in the air, a force that compelled me to throw caution to the wind and admit that I couldn't function for thinking of him. Surely when there was an ocean or two between us I wouldn't feel the same. He'd made it clear he didn't feel the same way, and he was ready to leave and I'd just arrived …

When he spoke, his voice was husky. 'I'd very much—'

Anastacia chose that moment to wander over and I stiffened. Sebastien took my lavender perfume from me, as if we'd been discussing that and removed the stopper. The scent drifted between us, lavender and orange, a hint of smokiness. Together, we'd made lavender shine but we'd also brought it kicking and screaming smack bang into the twenty-first century. Instead of focusing on theme, or on bottling a feeling, or conjuring a mental picture, we'd concentrated on blending the right accents to modernize lavender, make it contemporary. At least that was the goal, until he'd left, and I hoped I'd managed to succeed. I knew it was good; I felt it in my bones as the scent eddied unseen in the air.

Swirling the vial, he waved it under his nose, but his expression didn't waver, he didn't give anything away.

'So, if you're happy then I'll submit it for judging?'

'I'm happy,' I said, giving Anastacia the side eyes as if she was interrupting an important mentoring session.

'Enjoy the rest of the afternoon, Del, and tomorrow you have a class with perfumer Louisa Elliot.'

'Thanks,' I said, rearranging my face to appear casually indifferent while Anastacia stood so close.

'Louisa Elliot!' she cried out, her features radiating joy. It was the first time I'd seen Anastacia crack a smile. Louisa was an American perfumer who'd made a name for herself making perfumes for Dior before leaving and setting up her own business. She was well-known for fits of temper, but it was her passion spilling out, her need for perfectionism.

'Yes, it was quite a coup having her agree to visit,' Sebastien said.

'I better go study up on her.' Anastacia dashed off, her hair blowing backwards in her haste.

'Wonders never cease,' I said, shaking my head at the sudden change in her.

'I'm going to my papa's studio,' he said. 'If you need me, that is.'

Need him for perfumery or need him in my life? But I realized he was fired up again, inspired and ready to work, to get back to his real passion: perfumery. I couldn't tangle that with my needs or wants, could I?

'Enjoy,' I said, giving him a quick hug and feeling a zap in my heart.

Chapter Twenty-Four

'You must think of perfumery like a dance, like you're making love!' Louisa Elliot said in a saucy voice and cackled high and loud. She was quite the comedienne and had us all falling about laughing most of the morning. It was nice to have a relaxed session, one where our shoulders weren't bunched up around our necks in fear we'd make a mistake in front of one of the masters. While Louisa was indeed fiery and passionate, she was helpful and articulate and had shown us a great deal already that morning.

She talked about everything from how to choose the right bottle to get our message across, to designing marketing campaigns and finally how to design a perfumery collection that marries together well.

'Now your task is to blend me a dream … How you interpret that is up to you.' She fluffed the back of her short curls. 'I'll give you an hour to mix and then we'll see what you've managed to do in that time.'

An hour! This was my downfall, struggling to capture a *feeling* rather than aromas I knew worked well together. I'd expected perfumery at this level to be more about balancing than evocation but I was being proved wrong time and again.

Thirty minutes into it I was struggling. Dreams were hard

to nail down and different for everyone. Plus my head was wooly with them, if I was thinking of my own goals. New York, perfumery, love ... Since coming to Paris, I dreamt about romance a lot. I'd tossed and turned in slumber, lost in a realm where love was simple and you followed your heart, but when I awoke it was never that simple. Real life came crashing back and the knowledge I couldn't act on the impulses that crowded my mind. So if I closed my eyes what did I dream of ...

Louisa came to my bench. 'Why the glum face?'

With a sigh I said, 'I struggle when it comes to this kind of thing. I can fix a malady, but when it comes to bottling a feeling itself, doubt creeps in.'

With her heavily kohled eyes, and shiny red lips Louisa looked every inch the sophisticated Manhattanite that she'd once been, though she now was based in France. 'OK, so tell me what you're trying to do here.'

'Well, when I think of dreams, I think of my own ... Love, ambition, a place to call home.' I hastily tucked a tendril of escaped hair back. Nan's advice flashed in my mind. Until I'd said the words I love you in three different languages, or figured out exactly what the language of love was, maybe I'd never get it. How could you bottle a feeling, an emotion?

Louisa crossed her arms, and surveyed me. 'So why the troubled expression? It sounds like you know exactly what you're doing and what you mean to express in fragrance, you just need to toy with it, right? What does a dream mean to you? Do you dream of light, of love?'

'Well,' I laughed nervously. Do I dream of love? Is love a dream or a state of being? 'That's just it, when I come to bottle *that* tenuous type of idea I lose my way, and it never quite translates. That *wow* gets lost somehow.' It was easier to just pick essences and blend them rather than tie them down to an evocation. 'If we were talking about love for instance ... Love might be roses, but what else? A dash of this, a splash of that, but it's not really love is it? It's roses, vanilla bean, you know? I find it hard to pretend it's something that it's not.'

Taking a moment to smell my blend she jotted some notes, and then clicked her fingers. 'I see,' she said. 'You have to separate what you *think* from what you *feel*? Does that make sense to you?'

It did, but it was easier said than done. She must have seen the reluctance on my face and spoke again. 'You're blending elements that you *think* work together, that you *think* will balance but what you need to do is mix a perfume that makes you *feel* an emotion. Don't use your head, use your heart, see?'

As I pondered, the answers came thick and fast. Perfumery should be about more than the sum of its parts.

I was thinking too literally.

Too linearly.

Had my nan been right all along?

Was I doing my perfumery a disservice by *hiding* behind my true feelings? By not laying myself bare?

I had to be brave.

Be bold.

So many questions buzzed around my mind but I felt I was whisper close to solving the riddle that had puzzled me for so long. The only way to know for sure was to try to bottle another emotion, one I'd felt before and see if I could make that work, then I'd have my answer. If I could capture another feeling then I knew it wasn't that I was clueless, it was that I just couldn't capture something adequately because I hadn't truly lived it yet.

'Thanks, Louisa! I understand! I think …' It would just be a matter of believing it, believing it was possible. But I wouldn't bottle love, I'd bottle a dream, my dream. Living in a new city, discovering the world around you and delighting in it. Taking a chance on yourself!

She gave me a tiny nod. 'I knew you would. And my advice for the future is, risk it all, you have to, to be a great perfumer. You must find that passion, extract it from every nuance of life, live with great gusto, and never, ever look back …'

I smiled a great big corker of a grin. Never ever look back seemed like great advice to me, and something my nan would have agreed with. I set to work, this time concentrating on capturing a different emotion, the *joie de vivre* of a new life, a new challenge. Living in the moment, grabbing joy with both hands and holding it tight to me. It was the scent of freshly cut grass. Sunshine after rain. Coffee beans. Sugar and spice. The expectation tomorrow would be even better. The sweet smell of success!

New York …

My hands flew across the bench, my heart racing because I was close; I was close to achieving my own dreams, knuckling down that theme which had alluded me for so long and that to me was the biggest win so far.

Thirty minutes later I brandished my little vial of perfume for Louisa. She wafted it under her nose, her scarlet lips breaking into a grin. 'Ladies and gentleman, we have a winner!' she said. 'Del has managed to conjure big city living, the elegance of Paris! Long lazy days, wandering the boulevards, stopping for *café au lait* … This,' she said solemnly, 'is the start of great things for you.'

Wait, what? Paris!

'Ah, Louisa, I was actually …' My words petered off as I grappled inside my mind. I'd meant to bottle a perfume that represented my dream, my NYC dream, but somehow it had morphed into a Parisian perfume.

Had my dreams changed and I hadn't realized until now?

Louisa stared at me, head cocked, so I hastily responded. 'Thank you, Louisa …' Capturing love would have to wait, it was still too hazy a notion for me, and now I had to work out why my subconscious had changed course so dramatically. I trusted in perfumery, in the magic behind it, so I just had to figure out what this all meant.

What my subconscious was telling me.

At the end of the afternoon we sat together and chatted about everyone's hopes and dreams. Louisa must have sprinkled some kind of comradery dust over the group. We discussed what had worked and what had failed and I was beyond happy that mine had been chosen as perfume of the day. Louisa hugged me tight and told me to follow my instincts. It gave me hope for the future.

By winning, I was given use of Vincent's studio for an entire week. I didn't waste any time, and snatched the key and headed there and caught the sillage of Sebastien's perfume, as if he'd just stepped out and I sort of fell in love with the damn guy on scent alone.

It was like a dream come true, being able to walk among his papa's things, sit where he once did. Sebastien had left his papa's notebooks out, with a handwritten message giving me permission to read them. It was an honor reserved for the winner, so I couldn't help but feel special, as though he trusted me implicitly. I used Google translate to help me decipher the words, and was soon cast under his spell, reading the old man's musings.

As I read through his words, one sentence jumped out at me, and I wrote it in my own notebook so I could reread it later and recite it like a mantra. '*Compose the perfect perfume and it will live on like a song, forever.*' The old man was poetic in his scribbles; he wore his heart on his sleeve and was open and honest, almost like it was more a memoir than just perfumery notes.

In the little studio, on a floor above *Leclére Parfumerie*, I thought of Vincent and everything he achieved in his life. A man who was shunned by the greats at the time, told he'd never make it. And yet he'd proved them all wrong, he'd succeeded and still kept that same humble eccentricity that made people take him into their hearts. It was a lesson in perseverance and I vowed to remember it always. But also to stop and take time to enjoy the people in my life, not just perfumery.

I took a break from reading and went and stood by the window and pictured Vincent doing the same.

In his mind he'd still be blending; a dash of this, and splash of that. The fine hairs on my arms stood up; perhaps the old man was still hovering in the place he loved best. Here in his studio just off the Champs-Élysées where the hustle and bustle of city life was only footsteps away, gastronomic scents wafting upwards as if tempting the residents. Could I stay in this city, the city of love …?

Chapter Twenty-Five

'You didn't!' Jen screeched down the phone. 'That must've been totally amazing!'

I'd finally caught her and told her all about the previous week – being able to spend time in Vincent's studio and read his notebooks, tinker at his perfume organ and soak up his greatness. With hand to chest at the memory I said, 'I did! And it was. A real highlight. I can't explain how connected to him I felt in there.'

'Del, it all sounds so incredible. You must never want to come home.' She was right; part of me wanted to stay on this magic carpet ride forever. I knew I'd learn every day, and keep growing as a perfumer.

'Aw, I don't know,' I said. 'It's one of those things, like an enchanted interlude in real life and soon enough it will be over and then the real work starts. Being here has opened my eyes, made me realize that home isn't so bad. It'll always be the place I go to when I need comfort, but to follow my dreams I'm going to have to be brave and believe in myself.'

'You can do anything you set your mind to, Del. You think you're like Mom and Dad because you're a dreamer, a creative, but you're not. You've got huge ambition and with your work ethic, whatever you want will be yours. It might not happen overnight, but you will get there in the end. I just know it.'

'I do wonder …' My voice petered off. 'You'll stay on in Whispering Lakes?' Part of me secretly hoped that first flush of love might've waned and she'd join me. It was a selfish thought, but I still missed her so.

She didn't respond and my heart banged against my ribs. It dawned on me, blindingly, like I was staring at the sun. It had *never* been her dream. She had only humored me because she loved me and wanted me to succeed. I held my breath and waited for her to confirm it.

'Del, I love you and would do anything for you, you know that right?'

I closed my eyes bracing for it. 'Yes.'

'I was happy, more than happy to go along with you and help build that great big empire you always envisioned. Maybe because I just wanted to be where you are, maybe because I love you more than I love myself. But then things changed, and I suddenly realized I couldn't tag along and pretend it's what I wanted too.'

'But I thought …'

'It's not because of James, if that's what you're thinking. Well, it is and it isn't. Being with James opened my eyes the fact that I was only ever going because of my love for you, not my love for perfumery. I can't even smell the damn fragrances!' She let out a hollow laugh, and a stray tear rolled down my cheek. How could I have been so blind to my sister's own wants and needs?

'James has proposed.' Her voice was brisk. 'And I accepted. I wasn't going to tell you until after, I didn't want to distract you while you were competing.'

I gasped. 'You're engaged?' So much for knowing each other inside out. Her whole life had shifted and I'd been none the wiser. Didn't we share everything? Every secret, every promise? Every joy, every sorrow?

'Yes.' This time her voice was colored with joy. 'He popped the question not long after you got to Paris. And I gave it a lot of thought. Made him wait a week for an answer, poor boy! But I was worried about letting you down, and if I'd made the right choice. After much soul searching, it was suddenly crystal clear to me that I was planning for the life *you* want, not the one I want. I hope you understand.'

It was hard to catch my breath. I was winded by her confession and felt guilty I hadn't seen that I was manipulating her life even if I wasn't doing so with any malicious intent. Flashing through my mind were all our conversations about men, boyfriends and relationships. I kept landing on the messages she always sent, jokes about marriage and babies, and I realized they weren't jokes as such but maybe something she genuinely yearned for, but I had been too stuck on my own direction to notice. It made me feel a bit of a farce as a twin sister to only see that now.

'Are you OK?' she said softly.

Choked up, I nodded, even though she couldn't see me. I wanted to reassure her, but I was still hurting, still processing it. This completely shattering news. 'It's just a huge surprise, Jen. The engagement, everything.'

'I know, that's why I've held off telling you. The timing isn't great, and I'm sorry for that. But I sort of figured we had to grow on our own, you know? We can't be joined at the hip forever, as much as we want to. Without Nan you struggled to make perfume, and yet, by leaping into the unknown, taking the risk and leaving me and heading all the way to Paris, you fixed that broken part, Del. Don't you see? We both needed this.'

Gosh, she was right. And I hadn't seen it at all. 'Yes,' I said, as tears stung my eyes. 'I guess I hadn't thought of it like that. As scary as it was to leave you, we had to do it, for our own sake.'

I loved her and I wanted her to have the life she deserved, the life of *her* choosing.

'You can still go to New York, I'll still support you from afar. I can do your accounts and help out online as much as possible.'

I appreciated the offer, but she had to do what made her heart sing, not mine. 'Don't worry about NYC,' I said. 'And anyway, we've got a wedding to plan!' Marriage seemed so adult, so grown up, when I was still finding my way in the world. As twins we'd hit every milestone together, and this just felt so foreign, so strange, but also like maybe things were panning out for us in this new, indistinct way.

'We do! And who knows, maybe you'll fall in love and we can have a double wedding?' The jokes were back. My Jen lived in a parallel universe. One where we all fell in love as quickly as the click of fingers, got married and had adorable well-behaved babies, and set up perfume empires practically while we slept.

An hour later we rang off, after much talk about bridesmaids' dresses, flowers, wedding vows and everything in between. It was almost a relief to finally hear her say it. I could move on and know she was following her heart and I was following mine. God, I missed her. But she'd seen what I needed all along, and pushed me to do it for my sake as well as hers. The true love of a twin sister.

***

It was elimination time, but I was still dazed from speaking to Jen. I walked to the *Leclére* apartment and took my place in the sitting room.

Lex must've noticed my expression because he frowned and came straight over to me. 'America, what is it? Are you worried you're going home?'

'No, it's not that,' I said. 'It's my sister, she's engaged.'

'And that's a bad thing?'

I gave him a wobbly smile. 'No, not at all! It's just I feel so guilty about things. I was always pushing her to follow my dreams and it hadn't really occurred to me that they weren't hers ... I guess it's just a shock. She's getting married!'

'Ah, the twin thing,' he said. 'I bet she'll visit you in NYC every chance she gets.'

I was embarrassingly close to tears, happy tears, as well as a few bittersweet ones for good measure, but I was grateful to have Lex to talk to. He always made things that much clearer, wise man that he was.

'But without her NYC won't be the same. What I think is, I painted myself this future, based on bloody *Sex and the City* or something and I was Carrie and she was Charlotte, or maybe I was Charlotte and she was Carrie, but the point is, we'd have this great modern fabulous life brimming with possibility and cocktails. I'd be able to saunter in heels not shuffle and it'd be a roaring success, and my perfumery would start small and grow into this empire, and I'd move from a grimy bedsit to a loft in Tribeca, and those songs, those songs you hear about New York, would be about us, and we'd have made it. Against all odds, the girls from Whispering Lakes would have made it big … But that was just fantasy, right?'

Lex took me in his arms as I sobbed for what would now never be. I felt ridiculous, as though I'd envisioned a life based on a TV sitcom. How silly could I be? I wasn't ready to open up a perfumery boutique. I wasn't even ready for New York! I could barely find my way up and down the Champs-Élysées without getting lost. So much for my five-year plan.

'You know it's OK to alter course. You set your sails but the sometimes the wind changes.'

I sniffed and tried to compose myself, aware the room was filling with others who would think my crying was about the competition. I kept my face buried in the fleece of Lex's sweater, not wanting to face them with a tearstained face but knew I'd have to eventually. I was an ugly crier from way back. It took about three seconds for my eyes to puff up and turn an unflattering shade of bloodshot.

Pulling myself upright again, I threw Lex a grateful look while surreptitiously patting my face dry. 'Thanks, Lex. I just can't help but feel a little sad things aren't the way I imagined, but I am happy, I do feel like this is all part of the journey I'm supposed to take.'

'Don't be so hard on yourself, Del. Life is all about swings and roundabouts, and sometimes you just gotta go where the momentum takes you.'

'Yeah, that's it. Time to make a new plan. And I need to grow up a bit. Stand on my own two feet.'

He rubbed the tops of my cable knit covered arms. 'Don't go growing up too much. That leads to madness.'

I laughed, wishing I had a tissue. 'True. All the best people are a little zany, right?'

'Right.'

Sebastien entered the room with Aurelie.

Taking a few steadying breaths, I sent up a prayer that I wasn't eliminated. I needed to stay even more now.

'Welcome.'

We quietened down and all eyes were on Sebastien. He flicked his gaze around the room before settling on me, a frown marring his features. I shook my head, almost imperceptibly as something passed between us. His concern was evident, and it made me feel a little lighter. I tried to convey by look alone that I was OK without making it obvious for the likes of Clementine.

Aurelie spoke in her cool clear voice. 'We hope that you enjoyed your foray into other parts of France. We chose locations that were special to *Leclére* for various reasons and gave you challenges to suit. Once again, we were impressed with the high quality, the risks taken to produce such astonishing, evocative perfumes. It's not easy to do so under so much pressure and in a new environment, so we want to acknowledge that.'

Anxiety filled the air as the contestants' worry got the better of them, including me.

'I'll get right to it. This week Lex took first place with a sultry Bordeaux-inspired perfume, rich and bold and very special indeed.'

Clementine whooped and clapped, throwing herself on Lex who let out a grunt.

'Next we have Del.' Thank you perfume gods! 'Her lavender perfume took the humble purple flower to new heights. It was bold and contemporary and one of their favorites this week.'

'So, that leaves us with Clem, Lila and Anastacia. Again it was a close decision. All perfumes were pleasing and fit the brief, but of these three, the one that really wowed us was Lila's ode to the French Riviera, a complex aquatic perfume that perfectly conjured a South of France lifestyle. Clementine, you just managed to hang on, so I'm sorry to say that means it's time to go, Anastacia ...'

The room sat in shocked silence.

'*Au revoir!*' Clem crowed.

'Clem ...' I said in a warning tone. There was no point in rubbing it in. Why gloat?

'What?' she asked faux innocently. 'Isn't it true she tried to sabotage you, Del?'

That was many moons ago in the scheme of things and what was the point of bringing it up now?

'Leave it be, Clem.'

'What? I'm just saying we shouldn't shed a tear for someone who would break the rules to get ahead ... That kind of behavior is crazy, *non*?' She leaned close and whispered in my ear, 'And you, Del, you've broken the rules too, *oui*?'

Sebastien noted the tension in the room and clapped his hands for attention. 'Please say your goodbyes, and take the rest of the day for yourselves.'

All I wanted to do was get the heck out of that room and away from Clementine who was really showing her true colors and they were black and angry with bitterness. She wasn't the person I thought she was at all ...

Chapter Twenty-Six

There was no sign of Sebastien the next day, only Aurelie standing gracefully awaiting us. 'Dear friends,' she ushered us in. 'This week we ask you to create a scent that transcends time. How? That is up to you. Define it however you wish. Of course, it's called a challenge for a reason, so it won't be quite as easy as it sounds. You only have one hour to make it. How fitting it seems to be limited in the very thing you're trying to interpret. I guess what Sebastien and his papa set out to do, when they dreamed this little scenario up, was to test the limit of your creativity and see if you could still produce quality in a short space of time. I know you can, so let's get to it. The lab is unlocked and you have until ten o'clock this morning to hand in your bottle.'

An hour! An hour was OK to toy with a perfume like I'd done with Louisa, but not long enough to make a proper perfume, and not when I was being judged on it. I ran just behind the others, my mind going a million miles an hour trying to figure out what I'd do, and funnily enough the only thing I could think of was the lack of time, and how it would hinder me. That's when I had a brainwave.

My heart hammered as I set my bench up, half from running to get there, half from adrenaline. Could I make this work?

Time.

I managed to block out Clementine's voice as she bickered with Lex who was having no part of her teasing. 'Clem, enough!' I said exasperated. She just wouldn't quit. Why couldn't she focus on her perfumery? It was almost as though she riled people up to put them off.

Right, focus, Del. Time to me was having one more day with someone you loved. When that someone had gone, never to return, it proved how time was finite, and that we had to enjoy the now, this moment right here. It was fresh like the smell after rain, it was the hush before night fell. It was the twinkle of the first star in the inky sky. It was one more hour when there was none left.

Stolen time.

I blended like a woman possessed, feeling a buzz in my fingertips that I was on the verge of something incredible. A breakthrough. Or maybe just a way to be closer to those who I'd lost.

Time, as it was wont to do, was up before we knew it. Aurelie was back and took our vials of perfume with a gracious smile. We were free to leave. I tidied my station and grabbed my handbag.

'A success then?' Clementine asked. I couldn't wipe the wide grin off my face no matter how hard I tried, but her whispered threat remained unspoken between us.

'I hope so.'

Clem's eyes were clouded with abject misery so I reined in my feelings. 'What happened?'

She let out a long, loud sigh. 'I ran out of bloody time, didn't I? I've made a whole cheese about it!'

'You made what?'

'I fussed too much!'

I'd never understand her little idioms. 'But you did manage to submit something?'

'Barely. I really don't think it's enough. Del, I'll be furious if

I'm sent 'ome before 'er.' She jerked a thumb to poor Lila who avoided Clem like she was contagious.

'Don't waste your time with that sort of talk, Clementine. If you hadn't spent the better part of the hour mocking Lex, you would have got it done.'

She gave me a shove with her hip. 'It wasn't that,' she said. 'I don't like being rushed, that's all.'

'None of us do, Clem, but if you actually focused on the task at hand …'

'Pah! Not all of us have a Leclére to help, *non*? We can't all break curfew, can we?'

'Clem,' I said warningly, returning her challenging stare. 'I'm fairly certain you've broken curfew too,' I bluffed and walked away, my heart pumping. She could make things difficult if she wanted. It wouldn't take much for her to convince the others that I had an advantage. And I had broken curfew, but it had seemed like such a pointless rule. I never missed a session, I consistently turned up early.

'I'll drink my own blues away then, you traitor!' she called after me, and I shivered. I'd avoid her as best I could for the next little while, but I felt certain I was next in line for her bullying.

With the afternoon stretching blissfully in front of me, I walked into the bright Parisian day. I was almost back to the apartment when I ran into Sebastien.

'*Bonjour*, Del. I'm so sorry I missed the challenge today. How did you go?'

I gave him a broad smile.

'That good?' he laughed.

'Yes,' I said. 'I felt like it came naturally, I didn't have to force it, it was instinctive. And I can breathe again! Where are you going?' I asked.

'To a friend's shop, will you join me?'

'Sure.' Gone was the plan of changing into a summery dress, and flip-flops. I didn't want anyone to see him waiting for me.

Better if we hightailed it from there fast. I'd have to make do with my jeans, and sneakers – not very glamourous, but more comfortable for walking.

'What kind of shop is it?'

'It's a little antique shop under the shadow of the Eiffel Tower. Anouk, the owner, thinks she's found one of the very first perfumes my papa ever made when he worked for Coco Chanel. Of course, everything he made stayed in the lab, he was just an underling then, but apparently this has his initials on it. We will see.'

'Wow, that's exciting. Do you think you'd recognize his style, even if it was from back then?'

'*Oui*. I will know.'

Sebastien strode purposefully, turning down a small avenue, and leading me along cobblestoned laneways, the Eiffel Tower visible above the rooftops.

'Maybe I can find my sister a gift. I haven't had a chance to buy anything for her yet.'

'I'll have to get permission for you, but it should be OK.'

Confused, I asked, 'Permission for what?'

'For you to shop there.'

A gentle Parisian breeze blew, bringing with it the scent of the Seine as we got closer to the centre of Paris. 'Why do I need permission to shop there?'

He laughed, his sea-green eyes brightening. 'It'll sound crazy, but you see, Anouk is traditional and very particular about her clientele. She cherishes her antiques and will only sell to certain people if she feels she can trust them. She also prefers them to stay on French soil if possible, so there's always this sort of distrust with strangers, especially foreigners. She's quite formidable but her heart's in the right place, I guess.'

Another French foible? 'Trust them with what?'

'Trust them with the antique, knowing they'll treasure it and protect its heritage.'

Laughter burbled out of me. Was he spinning me a story? What kind of businesswoman only allowed certain shoppers? 'I don't believe you.'

He raised a brow but his lips twitched as though he found it an amusing anecdote. 'She's quite famous for it these days. Her shop is in all the travel guides, people are drawn there because of Anouk's beliefs. All joking aside though, she does procure a number of antiques that would otherwise be lost and with it their history. She doesn't like the spotlight, but people are fascinated by her.'

I had never heard of such a thing. Surely a shop sold its wares and that was all there was to it? How did she make a living if she turned people away?

'Will she let me in?'

'Ah.' He held up a finger. 'You need an introduction from a loyal and trusted customer … and then she'll scrutinize you. You might get inside but you probably won't be able to buy anything.'

The idea fascinated me, and I suddenly wanted to be given the right to shop there and I hadn't stepped foot in the store yet. What if she deemed me not worthy? I wanted to prove myself but I hadn't the faintest idea what that might entail.

We came to a pastel pink shop, the door firmly closed and a sign announced it was only open by appointment. I turned to Sebastien. 'Looks like we're out of luck.'

He shook his head. '*Non*, it's just a deterrent.' He pushed open the door, and said quietly, 'Just be yourself.'

Well who else would I be? Was my hesitation obvious?

A beautiful blonde woman with curled hair and bright pink lipstick came to the counter, her gaze piercing as she gave me the once over. My toes curled, but I was distracted by all the wares on sale. Gilded ornate mirrors leaned against walls, reflecting my surprised expression. A couple of antique world globes spun softly in the breeze we carried in, and I watched transfixed as they both halted on the outline of Australia. A gramophone sat patiently in the corner, its brass bell polished to a shine. What music would it make?

The shop had a peculiar smell; it was dust of the ages, the lemony tang of polish, brightened with the perfume of fresh roses in bloom. My gaze fell on a table of knick-knacks; gold letter openers, jewellery boxes in burnished silver, and the most exquisite antique perfume atomizer, with a beaded silver pump and ruby red tassel. The bottle itself was adorned with clusters of diamantés which blinked under the dimmed lighting. I had to have it. I had never wanted anything more in my life.

'And who have we here, Sebastien?' Anouk came around the counter and gave Sebastien the three kisses, left cheek, right then left again. I noted ruefully she knew exactly which way to turn her head. But weren't three kisses for other parts of France, not for Paris? I would never understand!

'*Bonjour*, Anouk. This is Del, a very good friend of mine. A gifted perfumer.'

'*Bonjour*,' I said, unsure of the protocol; did I kiss her, did she kiss me, or should I hold out a hand to shake? Instead of doing anything sensible, I clutched onto my handbag like a safety blanket and tried not to impersonate a deer caught in headlights. The woman intimidated me, there was no two ways about it. It was the stare me down tactic she used. She was good – I was absolutely terrified she'd send me back in to the square out front.

Anouk continued to survey me like she could see into my soul, and I found it all a trifle amusing and worried for a second that I might burst out laughing. The French and their foibles never failed to delight me.

'Bonjour,' she said, her expression haughty. 'You like the atomizer?'

'Erm, *oui*,' I said. I'd only looked at it for a split second, but I guess a perfumer and a perfume bottle were an easy match to make.

'It's not for sale.'

'Oh.' What the heck?

'It might be later, I don't know.'

'Of course. I understand,' I lied.

I'd been dropped into a parallel universe; nothing quite made sense. I tried not to fidget and watched as Anouk picked up the atomizer and lovingly untangled the tassels. 'This piece came from a woman in Montmartre,' she said. 'She cleared out a storage room in her art gallery and found a trove of wonders from the previous owner. Being an artist herself she recognized the craftsmanship of the items and knew they were valuable, maybe not in a monetary sense but valuable in a sentimental way, and she wanted to protect these trinkets.'

The atomizer was empty of perfume but its faded oriental notes were still discernible.

'It's beautiful,' I said. 'And good of her to bring it to you.'

She smiled and her face softened. 'The previous owner of the gallery was around Paris in the Twenties. And so this is part of her story, this is a layer of her life we can hold on to, and remember her by.'

I was touched that Anouk thought so deeply about her antiques and their owners. What did any of us really leave, if not memories – and what if no one was there to protect them? I suddenly understood with a bright clarity how important Anouk's eccentricities were, and why she was careful about her antiques. They were more than just things, they were a bridge to another life. A link to the past.

'I find out the history of every piece I own,' she said, her voice wistful. 'Otherwise how can I find the right buyer for the next stage of the heirloom's life?'

Wondrously, I gazed around the shop, knowing that each piece here had its own unique story, that people long since gone from this world once cherished these things so completely. The lives they lived weren't forgotten, at least not by Anouk, who was biding time until the right person came along and a new life started afresh in a different house, with another owner who knew the history and respected it.

'How do you know if they're the right buyer?'

'I can sense it, I can see it in their eyes, the way they move their hands, the way their gaze darts back to a piece. And then I have to decide if they're trustworthy, if they want something for its history, or for its monetary value. I can usually tell. I've been wrong before of course, but most often a feeling washes over me, almost like a daydream and I know why they're looking for something. It's usually more about what they lack, a hole they need to fill, than materialism. Or on selling for a hefty profit.'

'And with me, can you tell what I'm lacking?' The words escaped before I could snatch them back.

She cocked her head and measured me for the longest time that I hardly dared to breathe.

'You feel like the atomizer will bind you to someone so when you touch it, you're almost touching them. And you want it very much.'

My nan. My breath left my body with a whoosh, and a fine trail of goosebumps broke out on my skin. How did she know that?

She placed a hand on my arm. 'It's not so hard to see if you take the time to really look at a person.'

'I understand.' I smiled. 'I have a similar theory when it comes to scent. It can be a tonic, a cure all, if you understand the person well enough.'

The Frenchwoman leaned her elbows on the counter. 'Interesting. And what do you feel with me?'

I studied her for a beat. Her cheeks bloomed as though she was in love, her eyes sparkled with a vitality that suggested good health and wellbeing, but there was something bubbling just below the surface, something she yearned for … But what was it? My gaze dropped to the drumming of her bare fingers on the counter top. Ah! 'You're wondering if he's The One?'

'Perhaps.'

'You want to propose?'

She stood and folded her arms across her chest. 'It might have crossed my mind. Why can't women be in control of their love life? Why should we wait for a man to ask? But what if I'm wrong about him? I've been wrong before …' While Anouk tried hard to mask her vulnerability by clipping her words, you could see she was at a crossroads.

'What's the worst that can happen?'

'So many things! What if he changes, or isn't who he seems?'

'What if I told you I could make you a special perfume that would give you clarity? Would you wear it?'

She scrunched her eyes as if she was suspicious, but even I could tell she'd give it a shot. 'I would give it a try … perhaps.'

I smiled. 'Perfume has a miraculous way of awakening the mind and body and with the right blend, it can also erase doubt. What you need, Anouk, is a fragrance that will clear your confusion; a blend of clove, orange blossom, green tea, sweet musk, and melon will do the trick.' I gave her a little eyebrow waggle for good measure. I sensed Anouk was a whimsical soul just like me, and we were merely playing our parts by not admitting we were similar in that regard.

'It sounds like a charming fragrance, I would like to try something like that …' Anouk smiled and this time there was real warmth in her eyes, like I'd passed some test I didn't know I'd been taking. 'And, Del, you may come back again soon. Perhaps I'll put the atomizer to one side just in case.'

I nodded my thanks, understanding that I hadn't quite proven myself to Anouk, or perhaps she couldn't give in straight away to save face, and loving the subterfuge of it all the more.

'I'll come back soon,' I said. '*Merci.*'

After we left we walked along the river Seine. Sebastien had the bottle of perfume that had indeed belonged to his father. Something so special Anouk simply gifted it to him and refused to take any money for it. She claimed he was the rightful owner and it had been restored to the person who always should have had it. There'd been a real happiness in Sebastien's eyes. It linked him to his father once more, so brilliantly, that it took my breath away.

Sebastien's mood changed and rippled in the wind, while the delicate cherry blossom note of flowers along the Seine mingled with his *eau de parfum*. He radiated the love of a son for his father, and even if I hadn't been able to sense it by smell, I'd have been able to see it in his eyes.

This precious relic from the past was helping him close another door on his grief. Almost like a gift from his papa, a message to say *continue on, I am always with you*. At least that is what I took from emotions dancing about.

With the unshakeable knowing, I slung a friendly arm around his waist to comfort him, and tell him without speaking that I cared. That I understood. The scent of butterscotch permeated the air and with it came his bittersweet smile. Sebastien wandered down the long road of acceptance and had just come out of the darkest tunnel to the light brightness of the other side. He had a way to go but he would get there.

***

There was a knock on our door. Clementine buried herself deeper under the blankets, but I'd been up for ages, the curse of a morning person. I opened the door to find Aurelie standing there, her eyes twinkling.

'Surprise challenge,' she said.

'What?'

She raised a brow. 'You and Clementine are to head to *Leclére Parfumerie* and spend an hour there. Who knows what's in store for you?' Her voice had a mischievous trill to it.

'OK, so should we …?'

With a shake of her head she pressed a finger to her lips. 'I won't say another word about it. Go there now and see.' With that she turned on her heel and sauntered away.

'Clem!' I said, wrenching the covers from her. 'We have to go! Did you hear Aurelie?'

She groaned, the warmth of sleep evaporating. '*Oui*, I'd better hurry. Why could they not give us more notice?' She grumbled but even in her half-dozy state she smiled at the mystery.

'Quick,' I said. 'We'll go together.' I still hoped there was a good side to Clem, and I was determined to keep things friendly.

Clementine got ready at Olympic speed (praise merciful gods) and soon we were at *Leclére Parfumerie*.

The shop assistants whispered behind their hands before strutting to us, their lips twisted into smirks. Oh lord, what did they have planned?

A girl with soulful brown eyes, and glossy hair said, 'So, we are to let you take control of *Leclére* for the next little while. What the customer wants, the customer gets, so do your best to fulfill any need they have. *Oui*?'

'OK,' I said, glancing around the store trying to familiarize myself with the perfumes, and where everything was situated. If I had to work the cash register, which was all computerized, how would I manage the French? I didn't know if Clem and I were supposed to work as a team or against each other, but I could guess she'd look out for herself before me. 'What about …?'

'We will be back soon,' the assistant said, grabbing her handbag from behind the counter. 'Do not upset our clientele now, will you?'

'Of course not!' I said, but then remembering I was in fact lumped with Clementine, and anything could happen with the likes of her. She'd been short with me lately, impatient, but I'd let her moods roll right off me.

Clementine yawned prettily and then set about spraying herself liberally with perfume.

'What do you think this about?' I asked. 'Surely, it's not

simply serving customers? None of our challenges have ever been straightforward or easy …'

She shrugged. 'What this entails, I do not know.'

I walked around the store, delighting in having the time to cradle each bottle and read the story behind the fragrance. In the dim light of the store it was easy to be transported by smell alone; a summer fragrance, salty and sandy, took me straight to the beach. And then a grassy, herbaceous thyme scent and I was wandering in the wild of northern France. My favorite was a bright, punchy citrus scent that conjured fresh fruit so ripe you could almost taste it.

There was no time to test them all as a group of customers entered the store. Before long I was chatting away to a variety of people from all over the world about perfume and the various lotions and potions on offer at *Leclére*.

They exclaimed when I showed them a picture of the perfume wheel, everyday people who had no idea that each fragrance had certain elements that grouped together as part of scent family.

There was a tap on my shoulder and I turned to a woman with a grave expression, and anxious eyes.

'Can I help you?' I asked politely.

'I need a perfume,' she said, in a thick French accent.

'Well, you've come to the right place.'

'*Non.*' She shook her head. 'I need you to make it for me now. I want something that no one else has.'

I frowned. Were there even ingredients here? *Leclére* didn't make bespoke perfumes, did they? But I did, and I knew suddenly this was the test. Could I think on my feet, keep the customer satisfied, and have her leave with a high-quality fragrance that might just fix her problems?

'Of course,' I said, and motioned for her to follow me to a small chamber behind the front counter. On the desk sat a box I hadn't noticed before and I picked it up. Sure enough, it was filled with everything I'd need to make a perfume oil on the spot.

I glanced over my shoulder, Clementine was chatting to customers who milled by the door. She shot me a questioning look but I let it pass. I had to concentrate.

'Tell me what you'd like,' I said.

'You tell me.'

I hid a smile and surveyed the customer. The woman's stony face gave nothing away on first glance, but if you looked closer the clues were obvious. Anxiety, eyes that darted here and there, the inability to sit still, a busy life with the thought there was always something to catch up on, more work to do. Fatigue.

'You need a buoyant perfume, perky, energizing. A sunrise. A burst of orange for energy. Ginger for clarity, jasmine for steadiness. Cucumber and grapefruit for awakening. What do you think?'

Her face dissolved into a smile, and it lit up her features, making her appear much younger and handsome in that elegant French way. '*Merci*,' she said. 'That is exactly what I need.'

With a nod I set about producing a perfume oil that would invigorate the woman, so even if she had to stay on that never-ending mouse wheel of life, she'd have a perfume that would transport her elsewhere and give her enough stamina to get through. That's what I loved about perfumery, its ability to free a person just on scent alone, transport you elsewhere while you got on with the business of living.

An hour later, I was done and Aurelie appeared, taking the perfume from me. As ever her presence stopped me in my tracks and I only hoped I'd read the woman correctly and made the right choices. She took the woman off to the side and they spoke in hushed whispers.

Clementine sidled over, a perplexed look on her face. 'We are to make a perfume here? But 'ow?'

'There's a box behind the counter for you.'

She folded her arms, a customer standing awkwardly behind her. '*Oui*, but 'ow am I supposed to do that in 'ere? It's ridiculous!

This isn't a place to make perfume!'

I grabbed her by the arm and pulled her close. 'Clementine, don't leave your customer standing there like a fool. Use your charm and find out what she wants. Do your job, in other words.'

She grunted. 'Follow me,' she said to the woman, who by the frown marring her features wasn't too impressed by Clem's customer service.

What could I do? It wasn't my job to save her. I knew she wouldn't do it for anyone else.

Sebastien arrived, and had a quick exchange of words with his *maman* before coming to me. The customer vanished outside after waving her thanks. 'Do you see what this means for you, Del?' He spoke just above a whisper.

'What?'

He stood staring at me for an age, long enough that my chest constricted with his proximity.

'You don't need anyone, Del.'

'Well, thanks but …'

He saved me from making a gaffe by saying, 'On your perfumery journey. You've grown in such a short amount of time. Some perfumers work best by themselves, and it seems you are one of them. The incredible, complex perfume oil you made for Mme Loire proves it. The judges will decide of course, but I would start thinking about what winning this competition means to you …'

My heart hammered at the realization. If I won, I'd stay in Paris for a few months more to design an exclusive range for *Leclére* … That, coupled with the prize money, would make moving to NYC a breeze. But suddenly I was torn. Had I fallen in love with a different city, or was it just the excitement of the competition and learning to think about perfumery in a new way making me second guess everything?

All I wanted to do was blend perfumes for strangers, conjuring a perfume that fixed them, replaced something that was missing in their lives. Made them smile, reminisce, and invigorate their days …

'You underestimate yourself, Sebastien. Without you, I wouldn't be here today.' He'd helped me find my way without Nan, and what greater gift could you give a person than that?

'I think you're exactly where you need to be.'

There was magic in the air at the little perfume shop off the Champs-Élysées.

Chapter Twenty-Seven

Judgement day arrived for the 'time' perfumes from the week before, so like always I went for a long walk to clear my head and quash any stray nerves.

Paris gave a person the ability to blend in, to be one of many going about their day, so different from back home. I still hadn't quite gotten used it. It made it so much easier to gather my thoughts which far too often drifted to Sebastien. Each day I found it harder to lie to myself. I was falling for the guy, an impossible situation. But he gave me no clue that the feeling was reciprocated so I focused on the task at hand, and tried to ignore the erratic beating of my heart.

This morning, I felt a lightness descend. Perhaps because I was truly confident the 'time' perfume I'd submitted was exquisite. Meaningful. Even if I didn't win, I felt I'd taken a great leap forward and I was proud of myself.

At the apartment I made my way inside and took a seat as the others wandered in. Lex found me first and saluted. 'America, the gleam in your eye suggests you're pretty happy today.'

I smiled at such a Lex-ism. 'Paris makes me happy,' I said. 'It's a bit like living in a dream. What about you, Lex? Are you confident about your perfume?'

Tiny spots of pink colored his cheeks. Lex wasn't big on bragging and hated admitting he was happy when he was pitted against us. 'I like what I made. An hour to mix sure was a test, but I think I got there. I hope so.' That same weariness sat heavy on him today, like whatever was bothering him had kept him from sleeping and turned him to the bottle to cope. One day he could run steps at Montmartre like a teenager, the next he looked like he'd spent the night tossing and turning. From my bag I took a small lavender vial and only hoped it would work. A sleep blend to wash the worry away, a little more naturally, so he'd fall into a deep slumber and rest properly.

'I made you this,' I said, and handed it to him.

'A perfume, and to what do I owe the honor?'

'Let's just call it medicinal. It's your new go-to when you're wide awake at midnight.'

He raised a brow and took the stopper off, swishing the vial under his nose. 'Makes me think of the minute just before you fall asleep, when your worries float away and you become part of the mattress.'

I gave him a wide smile. He was so prescient, so sensitive.

I still wasn't sure about Lex's past, but I sensed he was tough on himself over it, hence the drinking when all else failed. 'Will you wear it?'

He grinned. 'With pride.'

'Report back, OK? Let me know if it helps.'

'Sure, and thanks again.'

Sebastien and Aurelie wandered in, followed by Lila and lastly a flustered Clem who must've slept in. She tried to catch my eye but I ignored her, pretending to study my nails. We all grew quiet.

'Last week you were asked to make a perfume about Time. And given its significance and the fact that it was a challenge, we decided to make it a little harder by taking the one thing away that you most needed. Time itself. An hour to make a perfume is a hard task so we knew it would show us how well you worked under pressure, and what gifts you have instinctually when that pressure is turned up,' Aurelie said.

I lost a moment staring intently at Sebastien, soaking up every nuance of him, every smile line, the exotic color of his deep green eyes, the perfect symmetry of his face, the curve of his kissable lips, before he caught me and I turned away, heat rushing my cheeks. Whoops. *Focus, Del!*

'The judges were amazed by what some of you did in those sixty short minutes, and more so by what Time evoked for you,' she said.

There were a few murmurs amongst us before she continued: 'Our winner this week is Del, with her fragrance Stolen Time. The hope for an interlude, for one more day, one last embrace.' Aurelie's voice cracked and she stopped and took a moment to gather herself. 'It's one more moment to declare your love, and give thanks. A truly extraordinary perfume that manages to stop time. Congratulations, Del.'

My eyes went wide as everyone turned to face me. I'd managed to bottle a feeling, a real emotion and it had translated so much so that Aurelie had teared up at the memories the perfume conjured for her. Lex gave me a pat on the back and Clementine gave me the thinnest of smiles. Lila leaned over and said, 'Well done, Del.'

I nodded my thanks, suddenly too shy to speak. Like a whisper on the wind, I felt Nan's presence, as if she was right beside me. I bathed in the warmth of her love and pride for one lonely second. Maybe she could reach through time? Maybe I'd summoned her? The thought made me smile.

'In second place we have Lex, with his perfume Future Time. An almost apocalyptic fragrance, the likes of which I've never experienced. It was explosive, fiery, smoky, thunderous. The type of scent you'd wear going into battle, metaphorically or not.'

I returned the pat on the back, and couldn't contain the grin that split my face no matter how much I tried. If I was sent home next week, then I'd always have this moment. And sharing it with

Lex was a cherry on top.

While I wanted to win the competition I also wanted Lex to succeed. I felt he needed the win, needed to know he was gifted in a way others could only dream of. Nomadic Lex was running away from something, I could sense it as easily as I could coming rain. But what exactly was it, and why did he not pursue his passion for perfumery until now when he was so talented?

My ruminating was cut short by the next announcement. 'Lila was third with Once Upon a Time, a fragrance for booklovers.' Ah, she'd visited the lovely little bookshop on the Seine and had the same idea I'd had briefly when I'd stood in that dim room, wanting to pull up a chair and pull down a book.

'That leaves us with Clementine with her perfume Time Off, about enjoying the break in your day ...'

My stomach flipped. That meant she'd come in last?

'I'm sorry to say it, but your time in the competition is over, Clementine.'

'What!' She was up on her feet, hands on hips, shooting Sebastien a glare so frosty I expected he'd freeze on the spot. 'Are you mad? Honestly, who would choose Del over me?'

My mouth dropped open.

'Del has broken her curfew a number of times, and that is cheating if you ask me! Isn't it in the rules? We all have to be home before midnight, and I have a log of each time she came home late, waking me up and distracting me!'

Aurelie frowned. 'Is this true, Del?'

Shoot. My high plummeted to a low. 'Well, I might have missed curfew by a few minutes, but I didn't wake Clementine, or distract her at all ...'

Clem cut me off. 'Oh, *non*? Then how do I know?'

I narrowed my eyes, as anger bubbled up, but Sebastien cleared his throat and spoke. 'I'm sorry, I should have mentioned it earlier, but with my schedule at *Leclére*, we've been forced to have our mentoring sessions whenever I can fit them, and sadly sometimes that means late at night. Del has been at a disadvantage having me as a mentor, as I've been called away so many times, including while we were in Provence. Missing curfew by a few minutes is nothing compared to being left without a mentor for most of the week …'

Aurelie smiled. '*Oui*, of course. I'd forgotten about that.'

Clementine glowered at me. 'So because she has a Leclére on her side, the rules are different?'

Sebastien stared her down. '*Oui*.'

She flounced out and I hoped we'd seen the end of Clementine.

***

The next day Lex found me in the shared kitchen. 'Hey, America. It's so god damn quiet around here.'

I gave him a sad smile. 'I know, I kind of miss her in this weird way, despite her nasty side.'

Lex grunted. 'You know, I don't think it was ever about the perfume for her.'

'Hmm,' I said, considering it. 'Maybe you're right. She was far too invested in making waves. Still, she'll pop up somewhere again.' The world of perfumery was small, hadn't he told me so the first day we met?

With a grin he said, 'Yeah, in my nightmares. Speaking of which I had the best sleep I've had in years.'

'The lavender worked?'

'Like a charm.'

'I'm glad to hear it!' But there was more, something I couldn't pinpoint. Another problem.

'Did she break your heart?' I remembered. The girl under the palm tree! Lex had come here for escape, and surprised himself by reigniting his love for perfumery, but he still had to reconcile his past.

He raised a brow. 'Don't hold back now, America, will you?'

I laughed. 'Just tell me. Did she? Who was she?'

He rolled his eyes. 'Fine. Her name was Arunya. I left Thailand to escape but not because I wanted to be here.'

'What happened?'

He shook his head at the memory. 'She had this little fruit stall by the beach, she sold mangoes, bananas, rambutans. I'd never met a woman as lovely, with her long black hair blowing in the breeze, the way she laughed always covering her mouth and hunching her shoulders. She was weathered though too. Sort of ravaged by the hard grind of life, you know, a bit like me, and I wanted to protect her, to save her. But she was happy as she was. Earning a meager income, sitting under the shade of a palm tree for hours on end every day. She didn't want or *need* rescuing.'

I could picture Lex at the beach; the smell of tropical fruit wafting on the wind, the salty ocean spray.

'I'd made a classic Westerner mistake. Walking on in like I had all the answers, like I was her savior. I hate that kind of person, I should have known better. But with Arunya, I had blinkers on, tunnel vision. I know it came from a primal place, I only wanted to shield her from hurt and pain and instead I caused it, by implying her life needed fixing when it didn't. She'd been at that fruit stall for decades; who was I to come waltzing in saying it wasn't good enough?'

'So you made a mistake, but you made it with good intentions. Can she give you another chance to redeem yourself?'

'Nope, it's over. Well and truly kaput. She gave me this look like I was a disappointment, like she'd made a mistake trusting me and that put paid to us. She never spoke to me again, took her little shanty stall of thirty years further down the beach away from my homestay. I tell you, my heart broke for this woman, for the love I imagined we'd share.'

'Did you try and sort it out, Lex, after that? It's not like you did anything horrible, your heart was in the right place.'

'I tried, again and again. She told me we were a mistake.

After that I backed off. Maybe it wasn't love for her, so I had to respect that. Then I heard about the competition through an old friend and I got out of there quick smart – it felt like the perfect opportunity to be elsewhere and lick my wounds for a while. I never expected I'd enjoy myself, that it would spark my passion for perfumery again. Now I've got to forget her and forget I made such a mess of it. Read it all so wrong.'

'Oh, Lex. You're being awfully hard on yourself.' Lex didn't read people wrong, he was too sensitive, too attuned for that. But maybe with love hearts for eyes, he'd misread the woman. Lex was one of the kindest men I'd ever met and I knew he would never intentionally upset anyone.

'I deserve it.'

'No, you don't. Maybe she wasn't the right woman for you, but that doesn't mean you should give up on love altogether.'

He shrugged like he had the weight of the world on his shoulders. 'I'm too old for love, anyway, America.'

'Pah,' I said, and we laughed the mood lightening.

***

I called Jen, and she answered chirpily. I spent the better part of half an hour catching her up on all that had happened. She didn't say a word, just gasped or sighed or laughed depending on which part of the story I was up to. When I came to a close she said, 'Oh, Del, what an exciting time it's been for you. What will happen with Sebastien do you think?'

Again I checked myself, expecting jokes about marriage and babies, but now she was secure with her love and her marriage plans, she didn't goad me like normal. 'Nothing,' I said. 'The guy is still grieving, he's so lost, you know, like we were after Nan with all this pressure and regret on top. It's just not the right time.'

'You can choose love over perfume, you know.'

It was my turn to gasp. 'Jen, it's not love …'

She let out a sigh, long and lengthy, to let me know she didn't believe me. 'But you admitted it to me, you've kissed him a couple of times.'

'After that kiss he couldn't race back to Paris quick enough.'

'Del, honestly. This thing you do, it has to stop. Why can't you just admit you really, really like the guy?'

'Because I don't, Jen. There's definitely a spark between us, an attraction, but what would be the point of pursuing it? I've got this one chance here and I can't mess it up. After the death of his father, and all he's had to deal with, I might just be the tonic, but it wouldn't last, would it? He needs to sort himself out first. And so do I. I need to make a new plan armed with what I've learned here.'

She clucked her tongue in a motherly way – not our mother, mind you. 'Why not stay in Paris? Why not drop the plan and see what happens? I promise you won't wake up in the morning and have turned into Mom. I *promise*.'

I scoffed. *Have no plan!* 'Just no.'

She huffed and puffed. 'You've loved every single second there, even when you've struggled, so why would you leave when you've got connections in Paris, you've got opportunities and friends!'

'I'm not changing my plans on a whim.' No way was I going to be that girl. Once I let go of the big things, then next thing it would be the little things and my life would just be a series of events out of my control. I didn't want to end up like my mom, flitting through life as if she were in a maypole dance. I had to have goals, and I had to chase them, otherwise I'd be stuck in Whispering Lakes forever, and as pretty as it was, I wanted more.

Chapter Twenty-Eight

I poured another coffee, contemplating what we'd be in for this week, and hoped I'd survive.

'Imagine winning,' I said, shaking my head. Reading through Vincent Leclére's precious notebooks properly, making perfume for a month side by side with Sebastien. The prize money, enough to set me up. Everything I wanted and more.

'Don't get your hopes up,' Lila said, waggling her eyebrows. 'I plan on taking the prize.'

We laughed. I'd got my wish of forging a true friendship with Lila, and knew no matter where we ended up we'd continue to support each other.

And then there was Lex. Leaving him would be like leaving a favorite uncle. We'd keep in touch, but I'd miss his quiet contemplation, and compassionate nature. The last few days he'd been happier, smiling more, gazing off into the distance like he was remembering something beautiful. Maybe it was the sleep blend, but I didn't think so. Whatever it was had given him reason to be happy again, that weight he carried had lifted.

It took me a few moments to realize, I hadn't smelt alcohol on his breath for a while now. He wasn't as rumpled as he'd been. His clothes were pressed, his once ruddy skin clear. Had he quit the booze!? How could I have missed that?

'We have to get through the semifinal first. I don't want any of us three to go,' Lila said, her gaze downcast.

Lex arrived, his hair combed back, eyes bright. 'Let's go do this, hey? May the best perfumer win. And truly, I hope it's one of you,' he said kindly. And I knew he meant it.

'From your mouth to God's ears.'

'Let's go, America,' he said, proffering his arm. We wandered down the stairs, that same delicious aroma wafting through walls as it had on the first day, and headed outside to our meeting point.

We took our places in front of Sebastien and his mom, Aurelie.

Sebastien wore the smile of a man who was inspired. 'Welcome to our final challenge before the grand finale next week.'

We whooped and cheered.

'You will need to show the judges just how much you want it.'

Nerves flared.

'Today you will have to make one final perfume. You'll have the week to complete it. There are no rules, no restrictions, no themes. Just make a perfume that will live through the ages, appeal to the masses. What that means to you, well, only time will tell.'

Appeal to the masses. What would appeal to the majority of the world …?

'That's it,' he said, cutting his usual talk short. 'Head to the lab when you're ready!'

We raced away, knowing we'd need every single second to outdo each other. As I ran, and then slowed to a jog, and then a brisk walk, and then more of a hobble, I debated various themes. Outdoors: sun, sand, sky. Nope, been done a million times. What did everyone yearn for? Want? Need? Crave?

Aha! Love! But I stopped short. I'd tried to bottle love, hadn't I? And it scared me that I'd waste the week, and get stuck still missing that crucial element. What if I did that again and then had nothing to submit? I couldn't fail this time. There could be no room for error. Did I trust in my ability and all I had learned here to make it work?

There was no question that love would appeal to the masses. But bottling love? That was another thing. Still, I had to try.

I heard Nan over my shoulder … *love is the answer!*

Well, OK then! I began to interpret my own feelings of love, and poured them out of my soul, feeling bold and brave, ready to lay my heart out for all to see.

***

A few days later, I was at breaking point. It hadn't worked! I'd painted myself into a corner and for the life of me I couldn't see where I'd gone wrong. Just when I'd been doing so well! I'd managed to make a bottle of puppy love. The type of perfume you'd buy for the twelve-year-old girl next door.

Next to me Lila put down her own work and edged over. 'What is it, Del?'

'It's not working! I really thought I'd managed to bottle a feeling, evoke emotion, but it hasn't translated. Not in the way I wanted. I've managed to bottle puppy love!' It was hard to keep the angst from my voice. I only had two days to fix it or start over and from the contented sighs and sporadic happy dances going on around me things were going well for Lex and Lila up to this point.

She took my perfume and sniffed it and then went to speak but hesitated.

'You can say it,' I said. 'I won't be offended.'

'When I think about falling in love, especially the first time, it's explosive, like fireworks. It's passionate, and romantic, but thorny too. You're missing the intensity, that overwhelming feeling you have at the beginning, those emotions that are so strong you think you're the only person on the planet to have ever felt such a way.'

My nan had been right, how could I make a fragrance about all consuming love without having experienced it myself? But I had felt it, unrequited or not, hadn't I?

'Explosive … yes. I'm missing the *wow*.' She was spot on. I'd played it safe and made a bottle of puppy love, the first flush you have when you're a teenager, when what I really needed was something more adult.

'I don't have time to start over,' I said, my shoulders slumping at my mistake.

'You have this,' she said, holding my puppy love perfume. 'If all else fails.'

I considered it. 'OK, so fireworks, thorny red roses …'

And then it hit me.

'Thank you, Lila!'

'I owed you,' she said, and smiled.

Just because I hadn't admitted my love to the man, that didn't mean I hadn't felt it. Or dreamed of it too many times to count. I took a pen and notebook and scrawled my ideas down. Love was …

Moonlight, the sweet release of sleep after rapture. Heartbeats. Breath.

What else did love consist of? Not just the elements but the mood – the feeling …

We all wanted to love and *be* loved, but you couldn't just snap your fingers and choose. You couldn't order up a Mr Right. Until then you needed faith. The almost ineffable *knowing* that true love would find you, and until then you just had to believe. And what was true love? For some it was love of a person, for others a place, or a spiritual quest. Love was more than words, it was waking up in the moonlight. The desire to have just one more day with someone. French kissing and breakfast at dinner time. But how to bottle that? Could it be done? The language of love wasn't a specific language, it was a feeling! And it buzzed in my fingertips as I worked.

***

We handed in our perfumes, emotions getting the better of us, knowing our time in Paris was coming to an end. Sebastien didn't make eye contact with me when I handed mine in so I left feeling heavy with regret. What had I expected anyway? For him to throw his arms around me?

Lila noted my long face. 'Want to go to eat your body weight in chocolate?'

'I have never wanted anything more,' I said.

Outside we wandered slowly along the Champs-Élysées, past the Place de la Concorde until we got to *Les Chocolates Yves Thuriés* on Rue Tronchet. The heavenly scent of rich dark chocolate wafted from the small shop and my mouth watered accordingly. Surely there was no problem too great that couldn't be solved with *grand couverture* chocolate. Well, no problem of mine, at any rate.

'Shall we pretend we're going to skip dinner?' I asked Lila.

'Of course,' she said. 'And we can pretend we're going to walk it off too.'

'Great,' I said and turned to the man behind the counter. '*Bonjour*! I'll have the …' I tried to read the French names. '*Bouchons Pralines noir.*' Dark chocolate pralines, get in my belly! 'And a box of *truffelines.*' He nodded and got my order together. 'And one tub of *fondue au chocolate.*' I wasn't sure what that was but it looked like a tub of chocolate mousse or ganache. Either way, I intended on spooning out every delicious morsel. 'And …' Lila shot me a sideways glance. 'That should be enough for now. I can always come back,' I said hesitantly.

Lila laughed at my suddenly desperate expression. 'We can come back every day until we go home,' she promised.

'And you?' the man said to her.

'I'll have the same.'

We took our goodies and wandered to the Tuileries and found a spot on the grass. People were reading, chasing small children, eating ice creams, or resting their weary legs a while.

'So,' Lila said, choosing a truffle from the box. 'How did it go in the end with your perfume?'

I took a truffle dusted in cocoa. 'Good, really good, thanks to you. If you hadn't stepped in, Lila, I'd be gone, I know I would.'

'I'm only here because you stepped in for me with the whole filtering debacle I had back in the first week.'

I smiled and bit down on the truffle. 'Can we take a moment to appreciate this man is probably married to some lucky lady who gets to eat chocolate like this every day?'

Lila laughed. 'She probably hates chocolate. Too much of a good thing can do that.'

I sighed. 'I don't think that applies to chocolate somehow. It would be cruel.'

'Yeah, maybe. It's not like we ever tire of perfume or wearing it, is it?'

'No.'

We ate until we could stomach no more. 'I think I over-ordered.'

'You definitely did.'

I laughed.

She laid back on the grass shading her face. 'It's been a helluva ride, huh?'

'I wish we could stay.'

'Paris has got to you,' she said.

I laid down beside her and closed my eyes against the sunshine. 'I don't know if it's Paris or the perfumery, but I never expected to feel so alive, so independent. Sad, right? I'm almost thirty and this is the first time I've been away from my home town. But somehow I feel like I finally belong. But why? I don't have anything here.'

'You can fall in love with a place, you know. So what happens next for you, once this is all over?'

'I was all set to move to New York,' I said but the words didn't ring true even to me. 'But now I'm not so sure. What about you?'

'Slovakia. Back to parents who want to control my life.'

While my parents were the epitome of unreliability at least

they encouraged me in anything I chose to do. I felt for Lila, following her passions without any support. It wasn't like she was wasting her life away, she was striving for a future in perfumery, a lucrative career if you made it.

'Why don't you say no to them, Lila?'

'They're strict, controlling. I find it hard to speak up around them.'

I turned to face her. 'Do you have to go home? Why don't you stay here?'

'Ah,' she said rolling on her side. 'In a perfect world, I'd never leave. I'd stay in Paris and open up my own perfumery and eat chocolate for breakfast and adopt a rescue dog and walk when I'm anxious and sit on the grass at the Champ de Mars with a bottle of wine and some cheeses from the market and wait for my friends, the ones I haven't made yet, to join me.'

I grinned. 'That sounds like a damn good life to me, Lila. So what's stopping you?'

'Money, what else?'

For the first time ever, I realized I wasn't the only one whose perfumery dreams hinged on the prize money. In a way I wanted Lila to win it so she could do everything she wanted to do. Live a life of *her* choosing. But her winning would put paid to my dreams.

'If you won the prize money would you stay here?'

A tear rolled slowly down her face, and the scent of hope, bright and breezy filled the air. 'Yes. Please god, yes.'

What could I say? It meant freedom for her.

That evening I found Sebastien alone in the *Leclére* dining room. He was staring into the distance with a lost look on his face. I debated about whether to retreat but he heard me and turned around.

'Del,' he said. 'Come and join me.'

'Where is everyone?'

'Enjoying Paris, I suspect. Everyone is on edge about the

semifinal results on Monday.'

'Yes, it's daunting.'

'And then we'll have only one week left.'

'It feels like I've been here for years, I can't imagine leaving. I bet you'll be happy to have your quiet life back. You can leave and never look back.'

He gave me a sad smile. 'I'm not so sure, anymore. Maybe Paris isn't as bad as I thought.'

'Maybe you can have the best of both worlds.'

'*Oui*.'

'Who would your papa have liked? Not just for their perfumery, but for their personality.' I wasn't fishing, I genuinely wanted to know more about Vincent and the type of people he had been drawn to.

'Ah, that's a good question. Truthfully, I think he'd like Lila, her reserve, the way she can focus and make a perfume spring to life. But you, he would have loved you, Del. He'd have squirreled you away and questioned you, eking every last piece of information from you. And Lex. In a way, Lex reminds me of him at times. That need to distance themselves. Their ability to let love go, even when they shouldn't.'

'You know about Lex?'

'*Oui*, it's not hard to see. My papa wore that same look for decades.'

'Today, it was gone though. I bumped into him this afternoon and he was almost a different person.'

'And why do you think that is?' Sebastien grinned and it lit up his face, his eyes sparkled with a secret.

My breath caught. 'Oh!' I remembered the day the last challenge was announced, and the way his expression changed, but I couldn't pinpoint what it was. A waft of rose, but more, of faith, and hope, and ... love! 'Your *maman*!' I cried out. It changed when Lex caught sight of Aurelie. 'Does she know?'

Sebastien shook his head. 'I don't think so.'

It all made sense. He'd given up the booze, which he'd prob-ably only started as a way to alleviate the pain of a broken heart. 'That scent, it's the one I bottled with Nan all that time ago!' Instinctively I'd captured that nebulous essence. It didn't have a description, it was a tangible mood, a feeling; if I had to name the ingredients, I could. Bergamot, pink peppercorn, rose, musk and more, but it wasn't about that, it was more tangible than that. It was creating something when you understood it, when you felt it in your very bones, when you radiated it and that shone out of you and straight into your work. Oh, god help me. I was in love too and I only recognized the bouquet of love now.

I was woozy, giddy, and dizzy all at once. Sebastian's scent morphed as he moved closer to me. And I recognized it at once. Love was in the air. Literally.

My nan had been right all along. Hadn't she said I wouldn't know until I'd said I love you …

'*Je t'aime, ti amo, te amo*.'

'Did you just say "I love you" in three different languages?'

I whipped my head around, sure it was my nan who'd just spoken and blushing to the roots of my hair to find it had come from my own mouth.

'Umm.' I couldn't think straight. His proximity had that effect on me, it turned my brain to mush, my mouth to speak of its own accord. But how to get out of this?

Just as I was about to speak he pressed his lips against mine and I was lost to him. At that moment all I could do was respond, my heart thumping against my ribs, and kiss him back with all the love I had in my heart.

When we parted we stared at one another, and I realized I'd been searching for Sebastien my whole life. I just hadn't known it. The big question though, was he searching for me?

The spell was broken when Lila walked in, headphones in, staring at her phone. We pulled away from each other, and I blushed and fumbled with my earrings, while Sebastien busied himself at the table.

'Oh, hi,' she said, taking her ear buds out. 'So we can have dinner after all?' Even after all that chocolate!

'Yes,' I said, giving her a toothy smile that felt wooden. 'I guess so!'

The real world came crashing back. What the hell had I been thinking? I kissed him again! And love, what did I know of love? How ridiculous. So it might have been the first flutterings of romance, but that was all. And yet, surreptitiously I touched my bottom lip; that was one hell of a feeling, and I yearned for more.

Would I be the girl who risked her future on a whim? I didn't think so.

Chapter Twenty-Nine

Nerves were frayed as we sat in the salon and awaited our fate. One of us would be eliminated ahead of the grand finale.

Lex grinned like a lovesick puppy and I had to hide my smile. He wasn't aware that I knew he had his sights on the glamorous Aurelie. Once this was over I hoped he would give love another chance – if anyone deserved it, it was Lex. Would she be interested in him, was the big question, and I hoped in time I'd find out. Lila sat biting her poor nails to the quick.

'Welcome,' Aurelie said, her usual greeting. 'A sad day for us at *Leclére*, saying goodbye to a contestant ahead of the grand finale next week. I know you're nervous so I'll get straight into it.'

'The winner this week is Del with her perfume called *Love Potion*, a transcendent fragrance, and one we won't forget.' I bit my lip as my emotions threatened to overcome me. It wouldn't do to jump for joy when one of my friends was being sent home. But I'd finally solved the riddle that had stumped me and Nan all those years ago and I felt her there, cheering me on for finally believing and taking those risks she'd urged me to do for so long.

'Next was Lila, with *Sweet*, an inspired gourmand perfume.'

I took Lex's hand in mine, giving it a supportive squeeze. Tears stung my eyes and Lila let out a sob of anguish. Lex was out of the competition.

'Girls.' He took us in his arms. 'It was never about winning for me. It was about finding my way. To come this far has been the greatest joy. And now I get to watch one of you win.'

'I know you're on the up and up, Lex.' I rallied a little, knowing he had found what he needed here in Paris.

'We're in the final!' Lila cried out.

'It's crazy,' I said. It proved all that scheming, all that sabotage hadn't helped the others in the end.

'What will the final entail, do you think?' I asked. Would it be a week-long extravaganza or something deceptively simple?

'Who knows?' she gulped.

Sebastien spoke up. 'The grand finale begins and ends tomorrow. You are required to meet in the lab at nine a.m. sharp. By the end of the business day, we will crown our winner.'

The end of the day! I'd banked on another week in Paris at least. It was too soon. As with the other contestants, as soon as they were eliminated they were helped to pack their rooms, and driven straight to the airport and placed on the next flight. Despair sat heavy in my belly. What was the rush?

'Whoa,' Lex said. 'You're not mucking around, are you?'

Sebastien gave him the ghost of a smile. 'We don't want to delay.'

Was he ready to do that and pack up and leave after? Head for the lavender scented hills of Provence?

Lex coughed and dropped his gaze, 'Well, I'll be moving out of the apartment, but I intend on staying in Paris …'

I feigned innocence. 'You're staying in Paris, Lex? Any reason?' I widened my eyes, and stared at him, hoping he'd admit it.

'Nope, just haven't seen enough of Paris yet.'

'Really?' I narrowed my eyes. 'I think there's more to it.'

He pulled a face. 'All right, America, leave me be. You … you perfume whisperer.'

'I like that,' I said, grinning. 'Del Jameson, *Perfume Whisperer.*'

Sebastien smiled and said, 'Don't do too much today, save your

214

energy for tomorrow, won't you?'

Save our energy! Would we be running all over Paris again? My feet hadn't quite got over that first day of punishment.

We broke away, and I promised to catch up with Lex and Lila later. But first we had to pack up our rooms and make sure we were ready to leave the next day. Whoever won the competition would move into a suite of rooms on the top floor in the *Leclére* apartment and stay on to design a perfume collection for them.

After I packed and tidied the room, I sat at the end of the bed and blew out a breath. Emotions hit me hard and fast. Loneliness, reluctance, worry, excitement. I thought about the other contestants and their stories, how far we'd all come. Lila desperately needed the prize money to stay in Paris, or she'd go back to a life dominated by her family. Lex would probably make a name for himself in perfumery at fifty-five years of age, finally following his passion, and hopefully he'd find a little romance along the way.

But where did I stand now? The more time I spent in Paris the hazier my New York dream became. Could I survive without a plan? Probably not. I wasn't the airy fairy type unless I was making perfume. I needed to know where I'd be in five years, otherwise how would I know I was on the right path?

I called Jen and hoped she'd answer despite the ungodly hour it would be over there for her. With a yawn she answered, 'Hello?'

'Sorry to wake you.'

'You OK?' she asked.

'Sort of.'

'Sort of means no. What is it?'

'I got to the grand finale …'

'WHAT!' she shrieked. 'Oh my god, Del! You made it to the grand finale! I knew you would, I knew you had it in you!'

'Yeah, I know, it's totally amazing, but I'm having trouble envisaging my future now. What do I want? Things have changed and I have changed …'

'Aw, Del, you make things so tough for yourself. Can't you just wait and see? Spend the rest of the summer in Paris, whether you win or lose?'

I exhaled the worry. 'I guess, but what would be the point?'

'To test yourself. Remember you were supposed to jump out of that comfort zone, and as far as I can see, you've jumped right back into it. New York was a great ambition but like you said things have changed, so maybe it's not the right time. Maybe in five years when your name is synonymous with perfume, maybe that will be the time to head to New York and open up a boutique on Fifth Avenue itself, not down some dark little alleyway that you would struggle to afford now.'

'Hmm, yes, yes, I see your point, but I'll feel anchorless, won't I, without a plan? What if I suddenly spend all day sleeping in and I only eat chocolate, and watch movies with subtitles and become lazy ...'

'Then I'd say you're having the time of your life. One summer isn't going to rule your future. Promise me you'll stay there and let a new plan come to you organically.'

'Yeah, maybe.' Maybe not.

'And Seb, what's happening with him?'

'Zero.'

'And you're happy with that?'

'Well, not exactly.' I didn't want to worry about him, not now, especially with the grand finale looming. 'Forget about that for a minute, what about the competition? If I win, then Lila won't get the money and won't get to live her dreams.'

'Oh, Del, I should've known this would happen. It's a competition! You deserve to win just as much as she does! What about *your* dreams?'

I sighed. 'I guess ...'

She made her voice soft. 'Del, just win the competition, OK? Win it for Nan, win it for your future, win it because you love perfume and you deserve it.'

I took a deep breath and did what sisters do best, I changed the subject. 'So, how's James? The wedding plans?'

'Urgh,' she said. 'I think we might have to elope. Mom is talking about some kind of river goddess wedding, whatever the hell that means, and Dad wants to officiate …' And on she went about our cuckoo family.

After our saying goodbyes I stared at Clementine's side of the room for a while. It was so peaceful without her but sort of lonely too.

I changed for lunch and a last long linger around Paris with Lex and Lila.

Chapter Thirty

I was ready, and had accepted my fate. The grand finale was imminent and we waited impatiently for Aurelie and Sebastien to appear in the lab and give us instructions. Lila was busy sending up prayers and Lex was here for support and sat in the window box, knees folded, reflecting silently as he stared out of the window. I jiggled my knees up and down, and toyed with my bracelets, the ones Clementine found so infuriatingly loud, which was ironic coming from her.

When they finally appeared, we froze.

'And then there were two,' Sebastien said, dazzling us with his shiny white teeth. We assembled in front of him, hands behind backs, ready to begin. 'As perfumers you rely on your olfactory sense, so what better way to test you than on your "nose", your gift, and the reason you're here.'

That didn't sound too bad? There must be a catch.

'Soon our staff will bring in a variety of ingredients used in perfumery, from the exotic to the ordinary. It's up to you which you choose. Whoever names the ingredient wrong first, is eliminated. Sounds easy, *non*?'

Yes, way too easy! We'd know on sight what most of them were. I held my tongue.

'To make it a little harder, each ingredient will be hidden under a cloche and you'll be blindfolded.'

'Ahh,' I said. We'd have to rely on smell alone. 'So, can I clarify, whoever gets the guess wrong is out? Just like that?' We had no time, nothing to fall back on.

'Correct. And in keeping things fair, to see who goes first you'll draw straws. Whoever has the shortest straw will pick the first cloche, and so on.'

Lila and I exchanged so-be-it glances.

'Ready?' Sebastien said.

'Yes,' we murmured back. My pulse raced, and my palms grew sweaty. It could all be over in minutes!

Aurelie helped us draw straws and I chose the shortest, so I was up first. Risky.

Sebastien blindfolded me and I might have had one teeny tiny moment of pure fantasy about that but it was soon replaced by cold, hard fear.

He led me to the bench. 'Which number would you like, Del?'

'Cloche ten,' I said.

He lifted the cloche and I knew at once what it was. Still, I groped for the ingredient, and picked it up, smelling it, feeling it to make certain. 'Tiger Lily.'

'*Oui*, very good.'

Next was Lila. 'Lavender.'

'*Oui*.'

My turn again. I chose a number and Sebastien lifted the cloche. Easy. 'Orange.'

'*Oui*,' said Sebastien. 'Lila's guess again.'

Lila mumbled to herself nervously as she approached the bench. 'Oh, my gosh,' she said. 'That is horrible. And it's dimethyl sulfide.'

Dimethyl sulfide was a chemical used in some perfumes, it smelled of sulfur and onions and was noxious in its natural form, not blended.

My turn again, and I knew it at once. 'Phenols,' I said. It was overpowering like cleaning liquid.

'*Oui.*'

Lila's turn again. I held my breath, worried for her. It was pot luck what was under the cloches. She took an age to answer, but then said triumphantly, 'Is it gunpowder?'

Sebastien laughed. 'It is, and it has been used by big name perfumers before.'

The mind boggled. If consumers knew half the ingredients that went into perfumes their heads would explode. These days most of the ingredients were replicated synthetically, but not so long ago lots of seemingly disgusting ingredients were used to build and balance perfume. Once the perfume was blended those strong substances weren't detectable any longer, in their odiferous form. The bad balanced the good and made the perfect blend.

It was my turn and I sensed that it was going to get more difficult from here on out.

Sebastien led me to the bench for the last time and lifted the cloche. I paused for a few seconds knowing this would alter the course of my life. It was agarwood.

'Guaiacwood,' I said, and waited, hoping to god I'd done the right thing. I had followed my heart and not my head.

The room was silent bar the faint pounding of my heart. Could they hear it?

'I'm sorry, Del,' Sebastien said. 'It's agarwood.' His voice was thick with disappointment.

I made a show of being shocked.

'We have our winner, Lila.'

Lila shrieked and bawled at the same time and Lex grabbed her in a big bear hug and swung her around. When he finally deposited her on the ground I rushed in to give her a squeeze.

'Congratulations, Lila! You clever girl!'

'I can't believe it, Del! This will change my life, the *entire* course of my life! But I am so sorry!'

'Don't be sorry, Lila! You won fair and square.' I hid a grin, and knew I'd made the right choice.

***

Our bags were assembled in a tiny line of two. Lex was moving into an apartment in the upper Marais, and I was waiting for Jean Marc to drive me to Charles De Gaulle airport. There'd been much celebrating with Lila, Lex and the Lecléres and it was all I could do to keep the tears at bay.

I'd been part of something so extraordinary, so special, that I'd never forget it. A foray into the private world of the reclusive Lecléres and a magical perfumery journey that would see me in good stead going forward.

What it meant for my own perfumery was endless. What I'd experienced in Paris couldn't be replicated, it would stay with me forever. But there was one last thing I needed to do.

'Aurelie,' I said, finding her in the office. 'Will you call me if Jean Marc arrives? I have to …'

She smiled, the smile of a woman who wanted to love again, and I wondered if Lex had said anything to her yet. If the candy floss *joie de vivre* I suddenly sensed had anything to do with it, then I'd say he had, and they'd both only held back for the sake of the competition.

'Of course,' she said, in her charming French way. 'Take your time.'

I nodded and went on foot to the place it began.

Point Zero.

The wishing place. I stared down at the innocuous little plaque in the ground and had a quick look around me before I stepped in the center of it. Feeling crazy, but owning it for once, I lifted one foot, laughed and with closed eyes spun around three times, wishing for true love to find me.

Please if it's real, give me a sign, I offered up silently to the wishing gods.

I opened my eyes, and found only the curious stares of onlookers. Well, really what had I expected? A homing pigeon to fly in with a message? I turned on my heel, ready to escape the gathering crowd and ran, smack bang into a broad chest. 'Sorry, I'm a little …'

'What did you wish for?' he said huskily.

'You.' Heat rushed to my cheeks. 'I mean …'

'Here I am,' he said, and dropped his lips on mine. I looped my arms around his neck and pulled him closer to me, only mildly aware that the crowd had begun to clap.

'I didn't think it would work quite so fast,' I said breathlessly as I stared into his luminous green eyes.

'Your wish is my command.' He grinned and took my hand. People jostled nearby, lining up to stand on Point Zero, astounded that it truly had seemed like a miracle at work. Who was I to ruin their fun?

We laughed and moved away, giving them room.

'I know you forfeited the competition on purpose,' he said.

'You knew?' Hadn't I been convincing with my downcast face, and glassy-eyed stare?

'*Oui.* Why did you do it?'

'It felt like the right thing to do.'

'Stay, Del. Stay in Paris.'

'Why?'

'Because I want you to.'

I'd told the guy I loved him in three different languages, hadn't I? Did it mean I was giving up my dreams, or making new ones?

'I made you this.' I took a small bottle of perfume from my bag.

He laughed. 'And I made you this,' and took a small pink vial from his pocket.

We uncapped our bottles and wafted them under our noses. The perfume he'd created for me was explosive like fireworks, and French kisses, love under the moonlight. The sweet rapture of release. It was his promise that he was ready to step from the shadows of grief and to love.

Sebastien spoke first. 'It's a bundle of love letters, a rose before it blooms, still warm linen, the sun as it crests the earth, and an invitation to your heart?'

We were so in tune, it couldn't be wrong.

And for once in my life I was going to follow my heart, just like Lila desperately needed to do, and now she'd have the money to do so.

'Will you stay?' he asked once more.

'Well, Paris is the perfume capital of the world.'

'I have something of yours.' From his pocket he took my scarf, that errant scarf from the very first day, but now it smelled like hopes and dreams.

'You kept it?'

'I fell in love with you at that very moment …'

It was always meant to be. It was written in the stars, in the sky, in the shape of a perfume bottle. In the scent I held in my hand.

We fell into each other's arms and I wished for time to stop so I could stay there forever. True love always finds a way …

Acknowledgements

We lost our best friend right around the time I got *Little Perfume* back for the final read. It struck me how relevant the words I'd written were to how I was suddenly feeling. Grief plays a big part of this story, and I hope I managed to convey the sentiment that while those we love might not be here in body, they're always around. They are there as the sun sinks, burnishing the sky amber. They're the smell of ozone after rain. They're in our dreams and there when we first wake. They are the reason we take chances. Their passing makes us brave and bold and helps us remember to live in the moment. And most of all to love, because without love there is nothing.

This book is for you, Jeff. Thanks for the love you gave to our family.

If you loved The *Little Perfume Shop Off The Champs-Élysées*, then read on for an excerpt from *Secrets at Maple Syrup Farm* …

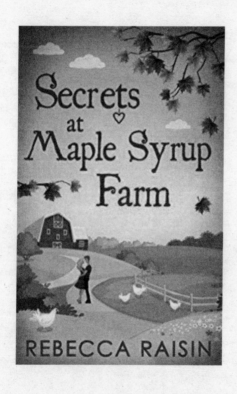

Chapter 1

With the beeps, drips, and drones, it was hard to hear Mom, as she waxed lyrical about my painting. Her voice was weaker today, and her breathing labored, but none of that took away from the incandescence in her deep blue eyes.

Wistfully she said, 'Lucy, you have a real gift, do you know that?' She patted the white knitted hospital blanket. 'Look at that sunset, it's like I'm right there, stepping into the world you've created.'

I sat gently on the edge of the bed, doing my best to avoid the wires that connected my mom to the machine. These days her hair hung lank – the wild riot of her strawberry-blonde curls tamed by so many days indoors, head resting on a pillow. I tucked an escaped tendril back, and made a mental note to help her wash it later.

'You're biased. You have to say that,' I said, keeping my voice light. Beside her, I cast a critical eye over the piece. All I could find was fault. The sun was too big, the sky not quite the right hue, and the birds with their wings spread wide seemed comical, like something a kindergartner would do. When it came to my art, I still had a way to go before I felt confident. Mom was the only person I showed my work to these days.

'Hush,' she said. 'I could stare at this all day. If I close my eyes

I feel the heat from the sun, the wind in my hair …'

That's why I'd painted the picture. She'd been suffering quietly for so many years, in and out of hospitals, unable these days to pack her oversized backpack and follow her heart around the globe. She'd been a wanderer, always looking to the next city, a new host of people, a brand new adventure … but her diagnosis had changed all of that. Even though she never complained, I could read it in her eyes – she still yearned for that freedom.

My mom, a free spirit, looked out of place in the grey-white room. She needed sunshine, laughter, the frisson of excitement as she met other like-minded souls, nomads with big hearts and simple lifestyles. The painting, I hoped, would remind her of what we'd do when she was home again. A short road trip to the beach, where I'd sketch, and she'd gaze at the ocean, watching waves roll in.

'Honey, are you working a double tonight?' she said softly, her gaze still resting on the golden rays of sun.

I had to work as many shifts as I could. Our rent was due, and the bills mounting up, just like always. There were times I had to call in sick, to help Mom. We lived paycheck to paycheck, and I was on thin ice with my boss as it was. He didn't understand what my private life was like, and I wasn't about to tell him! It was no one's business but my own. I kept our struggles hidden, a tightly guarded secret, because I didn't want pity. That kind of thing made me want to lash out so I avoided it. When I had the odd day off, I tried to make up for it by covering any shift I could. We needed the money anyhow. 'No,' I lied. 'Not a double. I'll be back early tomorrow and I'll take you out to the rose garden.'

She gazed at me, searching my face. 'No, Lucy. One of the nurses can take me outside. You stay home and rest.'

I scoffed. 'You know the nurses won't take you all that way. You'll go crazy cooped up in here.'

She tilted her head. 'You think you can fool me? Not a double, huh?' She stared me down, and I squirmed under her scrutiny.

'Don't worry about me. I've got plenty to do here.' She waved at the table. 'Sudoku, knitting, and ...' Laughter burst out of us. The Sudoku and knitting needles were a gift from the lady in the bed over, who'd been discharged earlier that morning. When I'd walked in, Mom's face had been twisted in concentration as she tried to solve the puzzle of numbers. The yarn lay on her lap, knotted, forgotten. She didn't have the patience for that kind of thing, not these days, with her hands, her grip, unreliable at the best of times.

With a wheeze, she said, 'There are not enough hours in the day to waste boggling my brain with knit two, pearl one, or whatever it is.'

I laughed. 'I could use another scarf or two. Who cares if you drop a few stitches?' A million years ago Mom had taken up knitting for a month or so, producing with a flourish a bright pink sweater for me to wear to school. She'd been so damn proud of it, I hadn't had the heart to point out all the holes from dropped stitches. She knew though, and looped a pink ribbon through them, and said, 'Look, it's all fixed with a belt.' I wore that sweater until it fell apart, knowing how much love she had poured into every stitch. It was one of her foibles, taking up a new hobby with gusto, and then dropping it when something else caught her eye. It was a sort of restlessness that plagued her, and she'd skip from one thing to another without a backward glance.

She gave me a playful shove. 'I'm not the crafty one of the family, that's for sure. That's reserved especially for you. Would you put the painting by the window? I'm going to pretend we're at that beach, drinking fruity cocktails, and squinting at the sunshine.'

'We'll be there in no time,' I said, knowing we wouldn't. It was January, rain lashed hard at the window. Detroit in this kind of weather had a gloominess about it; it cast a pall over the city, almost like a cloud of despair. It was different than other places in winter. Sadder.

231

I leaned the painting against the rain-drizzled glass, its colors too bright for the dreary room, but maybe that's what she needed – a bit of vibrancy to counter the grey. The bleak city was not our first choice, but rent was cheap enough for us to afford on one wage. It pained me to think of the places we'd lived when we'd both worked. I'd loved the sun-bleached streets of Florida, and being blown sideways in the woolly weather of Chicago. Those were happier times, when we disappeared for weekend escapades. Home for me had always been where Mom was, as we squished our too-full suitcases closed, and moved from place to place.

Stepping back to the bed, I pulled the blanket up, and settled beside her, checking my watch.

'Before you head to work, I want to talk to you about something.' Her tone grew serious, and her face pinched.

'What, Mom?' I inched closer to her.

She cleared her throat, and gave me a hard stare. 'I want you to make me a promise.' She held up her pinkie finger.

'OK,' I said warily. I'd promise my mom anything, she was the light in my life, but I sensed somehow this was going to be different. I could tell by her expression, the way she pursed her mouth, and set her shoulders. The air grew heavy.

'I mean it. You have to promise me you'll do as I ask, and not question me.' Her lip wobbled ever so slightly.

I took a shaky breath as my mind whirled with worry. 'What, Mom? You're scaring me.' It was bad news. I was sure of it.

She shook her head, and smiled. 'I know you, Lucy, and I know you're going to struggle with this, but it's important to me, and you have to do it, no matter what your heart tells you.'

'I don't like the sound of this.' I stood up, folding my arms, almost to protect myself from what she might say. I stared deeply into her eyes, looking for a sign, hoping against hope it wasn't something that would hurt.

'Trust me.' Her face split into a grin. 'I want you to take *one year* for yourself. To travel ...' She held up a hand when I went to interrupt. 'Hush, hear me out. Tell your boss tonight – you won't be coming back. Then go home and pack a bag, go to the station, and get on the first bus you see. The *very first*, you hear me? Let fate decide. Find a job, any job, save as much money as you can. I thought you might apply for that scholarship you've dreamed about at the Van Gogh Institute. You can stay with Adele in Montmartre. She's excited by the prospect.'

Shock made me gasp. *Take a year for myself?* The Van Gogh Institute? I couldn't think. I couldn't catch my breath.

There was no way. But all I could manage to say was: 'You spoke to Adele about this?' Adele was my art teacher back in high school. We'd kept in touch all these years. She was a mentor to me, and the best painter I knew. I'd left school at just fifteen, and only Adele knew the reasons behind my hasty exit. I hadn't been there long enough to make real friendships. She continued to teach me art on Saturday mornings, cooped up in our tiny apartment. I don't know if she saw something in my work or felt just plain sorry for me.

For years she arrived punctually every weekend, until a friend offered her a spot in her gallery in Paris. Saying goodbye to her had been heart-wrenching, but we kept in contact. She badgered me to share my work, and I sidestepped her gentle nudging by asking her about Paris.

'Adele's all for it,' Mom said. 'And before you go saying no, she agrees you should apply for the scholarship. It's time, Lucy. Your work is good enough. *You* just have to believe in yourself.'

The Van Gogh Institute was a prestigious art school, notorious for being selective about their students, and far too expensive for me to ever have considered. Each year the school was inundated with scholarship requests, and I'd never felt confident enough to try for a place. Besides, I couldn't leave Mom. She needed me more, and whatever ambition I had with my art would have to wait.

'The deadline for entries this year is the last day of April,' Mom continued to urge me. 'So you've got a few months to decide. Maybe you'll paint something even more wonderful on your jaunts. You'll be spoilt for choice about which ones to send for the submission process.' The room grew warm, as so many emotions flashed through me. The thought of sharing my work filled me with fear. I'd tried hard to be confident, but people staring at it, and judging me, made my heart plummet. I shook the idea firmly out of my mind before it took hold. Me leaving for a year? There were about a thousand reasons why it just couldn't happen.

I narrowed my eyes. What Mom was suggesting was just plain crazy.

'Mom, seriously what are you thinking? I can't leave! I don't understand why you'd even suggest it.' I tried to mask the hurt in my voice, but it spilled out regardless. We were a team. Each day, we fought the good fight. It was us against the world, scrambling to pay bills, get medical treatment, live for the moment, those days where she felt good, and we pretended life was perfect.

She took a deep breath, trying to fill her lungs with the air she so desperately needed. 'Honey, you're twenty-eight years old, and all you've seen these last few years is the inside of a hospital room, or the long faces of the patrons in that god-awful diner. That isn't right. You should be out with friends, or traipsing around the world painting as you go – not working yourself to the bone looking after me. I won't have it. Take one year, that's all I ask.' She gave me such a beseeching look I'm sure I heard the twang as my heart tore in two.

'It's impossible.' I summoned a small smile. 'Mom, I get what you're saying, but I'm happy, truly I am. Any talk of leaving is silly.' She must see? Without my work at the diner there'd be no money coming in. Rent, bills, medical treatment, who'd pay for all of it? And worse still, there'd be no one to care for her. How could she survive without me? She couldn't. And I doubted I could either.

'Your Aunt Margot is coming to stay. She's going to help me

out, so you don't need to worry about a thing.'

My eyebrows shot up. 'Aunt Margot? When's the last time you two spoke?' Aunt Margot, Mom's older sister, hadn't struggled like my little family of two had. She'd married a rich banker type, and wiped us like we were dusty all those years ago after she tried unsuccessfully to curb Mom's travel bug. Aunt Margot's view was Mom should've put down roots, and settled down, the whole white picket fence, live in the 'burbs lifestyle.

According to her, Mom traipsing around America with a child in tow, working wherever she could, was irresponsible. There were times we moved so often that Mom homeschooled me, and Aunt Margot couldn't come to terms with it. If only Aunt Margot could see how much life on the road had broadened me. I'd learned so much and grown as a person, despite being reserved when it came to my art. We didn't need the nine-to-five job, and the fancy car. We only needed each other.

A few years ago, Mom tried to reconnect with Aunt Margot, their fight festering too long, but she didn't want anything to do with us nomads. Mom still didn't know I overheard them arguing that frosty winter night. Aunt Margot screeched about Mom breaking a promise, and said she couldn't forgive her. Mom countered with it was her promise to break – I still have no idea what they were talking about, and didn't want to ask, or Mom would know I'd been eavesdropping. But it had always made me wonder what it could have been to make two sisters distance themselves from one another for so many years.

For Mom to reconnect with Aunt Margot now meant she was deadly serious. Somehow, I couldn't imagine Aunt Margot living in our tiny one-bedroom apartment. She wouldn't lower herself. I'd sort of cooled toward my once doting aunt, after hearing her spat with Mom. She'd been judgmental, and narrow-minded, for no good reason.

'We've been talking for a while now. We've really mended the bridges.' Mom tried to rearrange her expression, but it was farcical, her smile too bright to be believable.

I squinted at her. 'Really? Now who's messing with who?'

She threw her head back and laughed. 'Well, we're on speaking terms at least. And she offered to help so you could go away for a bit. So I don't want to hear any more excuses. Got it?'

Stepping back to the bed, I hugged her small frame, resting my head on her shoulder so she wouldn't see the tears pool in my eyes. How could I tell her I didn't want to go? Leaving her would be like leaving my heart behind. Plus, accepting favors from Aunt Margot ... We'd never hear the end of it.

Mom pushed me back and cupped my face. 'I know you're scared. I know you think it's the worst idea ever. But, honey, I'll be OK. Seeing you miss out on living, it's too much. The young nurses here gossip about their weekends and all the fun things they manage to cram into each day, and then there's you, the same age, wasting your life running round after me. Promise me, *one year*, that's all. Can you just imagine what you'll learn there with all those great teachers? Just the thought ... just the thought ...' Her eyes grew hazy as she rewrote my life in her dreams.

I knew to grow as an artist I needed proper training, but that was for people who had lives much more level than mine. My day-to-day life was like a rollercoaster, and we just held on tight for the downs, and celebrated the ups when they came. But Mom's expression was fervent, her eyes ablaze with the thought. I didn't know how to deny her. 'Fine, Mom. I'll start saving.' Maybe she'd forget all this crazy talk after a while.

'I've got some money for you, enough for a bus fare, and a few weeks' accommodation, until you land a job. It's not much, but it will start you off. You can go now, honey. Tomorrow.'

'Where'd you get the money, Mom?'

She rested her head deeper into the pillow, closing her eyes as fatigue got the better of her. 'Never you mind.'

My stomach clenched. She'd really thought of everything. Aunt Margot must have loaned it to her. And I knew that would come at a price for Mom. There'd be so many strings attached to that money, it'd be almost a marionette. There was no one else she could have asked.

When I was in middle school my father had waltzed right out of our lives as soon as things got tough, and since then not a word, not a card, or phone call. Nothing. That coupled with our lack of communication with Aunt Margot, a woman who cared zero about anything other than matching her drapes to her lampshades, made life tough. But we'd survived fine on our own. We didn't take handouts; we had pride. So for Mom to do this, borrow money, albeit a small amount, and have Aunt Margot come and rule her life, I knew it was important to her – more important than anything.

'I just … How can this work, Mom?' I folded my arms, and tried to halt the erratic beat of my heart.

Just then a nurse wandered in, grabbed the chart from the basket at the end of the bed, and penned something on it. 'Everything OK?' she asked Mom, putting the chart back and tucking the blanket back in.

'Fine, everything's fine, Katie. My baby is setting off for an adventure and we're excited.'

Katie was one of our regular nurses – she knew us well. 'That's the best news I've heard in a long time, Crystal!' She turned to me. 'And, Lucy, you make sure you write us, and make us jealous, you hear?'

I forced myself to smile, and nodded, not trusting my voice to speak without breaking.

Katie checked Mom's drip, fussing with the half-empty fluid bag. 'We'll take good care of your mom, don't you worry about a thing.'

'Thanks, Katie. I appreciate that,' I finally said. She gave us a backward wave, and said over her shoulder, 'Buzz me if you need anything.' Mom nodded in thanks.

We waited for the door to click closed.

'What you're asking me to do is pretty huge, Mom.' My chest tightened even as I considering leaving. What if Aunt Margot didn't care for Mom right? What if she upped and left after a squabble? How was Mom going to afford all of this? Did Aunt Margot understand what she was committing to? So many questions tumbled around my mind, each making my posture that little bit more rigid.

'It has to be now, Lucy. You have to do it now; there's no more time.'

My heart seized. 'What? There's no more time!' I said. 'What does that mean? Have the doctors said something?' I wouldn't put it past Mom to keep secrets about her health. She'd try anything to spare me. Maybe the pain was worse than she let on? My hands clammed up. Had the doctors given her some bad news?

'No, no! Nothing like that.' She tried valiantly to relax her features. 'But there'll come a time when I'll be moved into a facility. And I won't have you waste your life sitting in some dreary room with me.'

My face fell. We'd both known that was the eventual prognosis. Mom would need round-the-clock care. But the lucky ones lasted decades before that eventuated, and Mom was going to be one of them. I just knew she was. With enough love and support from me, we'd beat it for as long as we could. Her talk, as though it was sooner rather than later, chilled me to the core. There was no way, while I still had air in my lungs, that I would allow my mother to be moved to a home. I'd die before I ever allowed that to happen. When the time came, and she needed extra help, I'd give up sleep if I had to, to keep her safe with me. In *our* home, under *my* care. Going away would halt any plans of saving for the future, even though most weeks, I was lucky to have a buck spare once all the bills were paid, and a paltry amount of food sat on the table.

'You stop that frowning or you'll get old before your time. I've got things covered,' she said throwing me a winning smile. 'I'll be just fine, and Margot's going to come as soon as I'm out of here. Don't you worry. Go and find the life you want. Paint that beauty you find and I'll be right here when you get back. Please … promise me you'll go?'

I gave her a tiny nod, gripped by the unknown. I always tried to hold myself together for Mom's sake, but the promise had me close to breaking. Dread coursed through me at the thought of leaving Mom, the overwhelming worry something would happen to her while I was gone.

But getting back on the open road, a new start, a new city, just like we used to do, did excite some small part of me. We used to flatten a map and hold it fast against a brick wall. I'd close my eyes and point, the pad of my finger deciding our fate, the place we'd visit next. That kind of buzz, a new beginning, had been addictive, but would it feel the same without my mom?

Want to read on? Order now!

Dear Reader,

Thank you for shutting out the real world and diving into the land of fiction for a while. I hope you journeyed far and wide and had an incredible adventure from the comfort of your own home.

Without you I wouldn't be able to spend my days talking to my invisible friends who become so real to me I name drop in conversation to my family who all think I'm a little batty at the best of times … so thanks again!

My sincerest hope is that you connected with my characters and laughed and cried and cheered them on (even the baddies who I hope redeemed themselves in the end) and that they also became your friends too.

I'd love to connect with you! Find me on Facebook @Rebecca RaisinAuthor or on Twitter @Jaxandwillsmum. I'm a bibliophile from way back so you'll find me chatting about books and romance but I'm also obsessed with travel, wine and food!

Reviews are worth their weight in gold to authors so if the book touched you and left you feeling 'happy ever after' please consider sharing your thoughts and I'll send you cyber hugs in return!

Follow my publisher @HQDigitalUK for book news, giveaways, and lots of FriYAY fun!

Love,

Rebecca x

Dear Reader,

We hope you enjoyed reading this book. If you did, we'd be so appreciative if you left a review. It really helps us and the author to bring more books like this to you.

Here at HQ Digital we are dedicated to publishing fiction that will keep you turning the pages into the early hours. Don't want to miss a thing? To find out more about our books, promotions, discover exclusive content and enter competitions you can keep in touch in the following ways:

JOIN OUR COMMUNITY:

Sign up to our new email newsletter: po.st/HQSignUp

Read our new blog www.hqstories.co.uk

🐦 : https://twitter.com/HQDigitalUK

📘 : www.facebook.com/HQStories

BUDDING WRITER?

We're also looking for authors to join the HQ Digital family!
Please submit your manuscript to:

HQDigital@harpercollins.co.uk

Thanks for reading, from the HQ Digital team

If you enjoyed *The Little Perfume Shop Off The Champs-Élysées*, then why not try another Rebecca Raisin book from HQ Digital?